THE SINS
OF THE FATHER
A MEDIAEVAL MYSTERY

THE SINS

OF THE FATHER

A MEDIAEVAL MYSTERY

C.B. HANLEY

To

K.I.B.

for the fun we used to have.

First published by Quaestor2000 in 2009
This edition first published by The Mystery Press in 2012
Reprinted 2013

The Mystery Press, an imprint of The History Press
The Mill, Brimscombe Port
Stroud, Gloucestershire, GL5 2QG
www.thehistorypress.co.uk

© C.B. Hanley, 2009, 2012

British Library Cataloguing in Publication Data.
A catalogue record for this book is available from the British Library.

ISBN 978 0 7524 8091 6

Typesetting and origination by The History Press
Printed in Great Britain

For I the Lord thy God am a jealous God,
visiting the sins of the fathers upon the children.

Exodus, ch. 20, *v.* 5

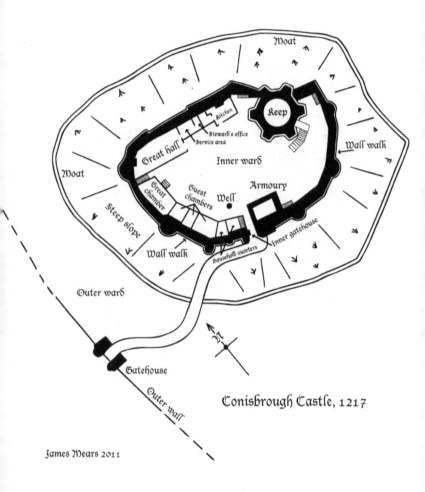

Moat

Keep

Wall walk

Kitchen

Steward's office

Service area

Great hall

Inner ward

Moat

Great chamber

Guest chambers

Well

Armoury

Steep slope

Wall walk

Inner gatehouse

household quarters

Outer ward

N

Gatehouse

Conisbrough Castle, 1217

Outer wall

James Mears 2011

Prologue

Normandy, 1203

The boy was about to be murdered.

He didn't know it yet; he was aware of nothing except his own pain and misery. He could feel the cold against the side of his face and the front of his body, the dampness seeping through his clothing as he lay in the darkness on the filthy floor. The cell stank, but he'd long since ceased to notice it. Something scuttled over his foot, but he didn't move. He kept his eyes closed, knowing that there would be nothing to see if he opened them, nothing except the blackness which had almost sent him mad. For weeks he had lain there, held in place by the weight of the shackles and chains, slowly losing all hope. Nobody would come for him.

When he first heard the sound, he couldn't make out what it was, and thought that his mind must be playing tricks on him. But there it was again: the scraping metallic sound of a key in the lock. As the door to the cell creaked protestingly open, he raised his head. It seemed unnaturally heavy and he flinched as the unaccustomed brightness stabbed at his eyes, attempting to move his hand up to his face; at the same time he welcomed the rush of air into the fetid space. The shadows of three men were dancing in the flickering torchlight, and the boy struggled into a kneeling position to get a better look at them, the weight of his chains dragging him down and rasping the raw flesh around his wrists and ankles. He whimpered at the pain, but it helped to waken him.

He could barely see past the light, but gradually he was able to make out the silent visitors, and cold fear struck anew. The man on the left was extraordinarily tall, stooping, his face masked by a blank expression. He held aloft a burning torch; the other was held by the man on the right, who was looking apprehensive and sick. The light illuminated the face of the figure in the middle, who, in contrast to the others, seemed to be enjoying himself. He smiled, revealing a mouth which lacked two teeth on the left-hand side. The boy forced his bleary eyes to focus on the face and gasped. His voice didn't want to work, but he licked his cracked lips and managed to croak one word.

'You!'

The man's smile widened and he spoke. 'Yes, me. And I've been looking forward to this moment, ever since you were foolish enough to slight me. Revenge is sweet.' His smile gloated as his hand toyed with the dagger at his belt.

So this was it. After the weeks of pain and darkness, hunger and hopelessness, this was the end. The fear was heart-stopping, overwhelming, trying to climb out of his throat, but he must fight it for a while longer. Just a few more moments. Remember who you are. With a huge effort of will the boy drew together the last shreds of dignity and strength and hauled himself upright, despite the protests of his battered body. If this was death, he would meet it on his feet.

The man drew his dagger and stepped forward.

The child was awakened by a battering at the door and the shouts of men. Mama and Papa were roused as well, and the hangings of the big bed were pulled back as they leapt up.

Papa spoke. 'I should have known this would happen. We don't have much time.'

Mama looked frightened. 'Is it him?'

'Yes. But he won't harm you or … ' He stopped at the sound of a scream from downstairs. Mama's hand flew to her mouth and the two of them looked at each other. Papa looked around the room, his head twisting from side to side. 'There's nowhere for you to hide.' His voice sounded strange, rising in pitch as he stalked across the chamber, flinging the bedclothes aside. Mama stopped him, taking his hand, and they gazed into each other's eyes for a long moment. What was the matter? Why were the servants downstairs screaming? Was somebody hurt? Surely Papa would be able to sort out whatever the problem was and then they could all go back to sleep.

Heavy footsteps sounded on the stairs. Quickly, Papa barred the door as someone outside started to pound on it. Suddenly the child was afraid.

'Wait!' Mama ran to the foot of the bed and opened the big kist which held the linen, pulling things out of it and throwing them aside. They had been folded so neatly – if the child had done that, sharp words would have followed. This was difficult to understand.

Papa hurried across the room and bent down, his face very close, his beard tickling the child's face as he whispered.

'Listen. I want you to hide in here and not make a sound. Whatever happens – *whatever* you see or hear – do *not* get out until all these men have gone. You must obey me. Do you understand?' The child nodded wordlessly and was swept up in strong arms and placed in the chest. Papa was twisting the large signet ring with its lion's head off his finger and holding it out. 'Take this and keep it safe. Always remember who you are.' Bemused, for Papa never took off the ring, the child nodded again and clutched at it. A brief kiss from Mama and the lid of the kist was being lowered. Everything went black as the first sounds of splintering came from the door.

It was dark and close in the kist. The child listened as men smashed the door and burst into the room. A clash of swords.

Papa's voice: 'Stay behind me!' The shouts of more men and an unearthly, horrible scream from Mama, ending in a strange gurgling noise. Another cry from Papa, sounding desperate. More clashing of swords and the voice of a different man: 'Disarm him!'. Smashing furniture and the thud of something hitting the floor, then a lull broken by harsh panting. Everything went quiet. Warily, the child pushed the lid of the kist open a crack to see if anyone was looking this way. Nobody was. The child gazed around and gasped in horror: Mama was lying on the floor in the corner, covered in blood and not moving. Her eyes were open, staring at the ceiling. Papa was on his knees in front of her, breathing heavily and being held by two mailed soldiers who were twisting his arms behind him. A richly dressed man stood over him, holding a sword. Papa looked up, his face bleeding.

'I should have known it would come to this. You are the very devil in human form.'

'Please. You must realise that after what you witnessed yesterday, there was no possibility that I could let you live.'

'When our lord hears of this … '

The man snorted. 'Our lord? It was he who ordered me here.'

Papa struggled against the men restraining him. The child had never seen him look so angry. He shouted: 'I did what I did for the good of the kingdom! I didn't want to do it, didn't want to witness it even, but I realised it was the only chance for peace, to stop further bloodshed.' His voice rose. 'I felt sick just being there. But you? You *enjoyed* it!'

The man seemed to think about this for a moment, then spoke again. 'Well yes, maybe I did. The whelp deserved it. This, on the other hand … I'm almost sorry. Almost.'

In one quick movement he brought his sword back and thrust it into Papa's body before ripping it back out again. Unable to believe the sight but powerless to avoid it, the child watched as Papa slowly fell forward out of the grasp of the men, blood spewing from the hole in his body and from his mouth.

As he died, his face turned towards the kist, and for one frozen moment his eyes caught those watching him before the light went out of them and his body slumped to the floor. The child stared, hypnotised, at the blood spreading across the floor and soaking into the discarded bedsheets, but was jolted back to reality by the man's voice.

'Our work here is done.' He smiled, revealing that he lacked two teeth on the left-hand side of his mouth, and turned to walk out of the room. As he left he issued an order to his men.

'Burn it down.'

———

In the grey light of dawn the child wandered, dazed, through the ashes of the building. What had happened? Who was the man? Shut in a private world, the child never noticed the hooves of the horse as they approached, rearing at the last moment to avoid crushing the tiny figure. The child looked up and, for the first time in many hours, saw a kind face. They stared at each other for a long moment before the man spoke, his voice gentle.

'Was this your house?' The child nodded mutely. The man looked at the ashes. 'Your father and mother?' Tears started to run down the child's face as the man registered grim understanding. 'An evil deed. But perhaps some good may come of it.' He leant down from the saddle and the child was encircled in one strong arm and lifted high on to the great horse. It was just like riding with Papa … the tears came again, and as the man and the child rode away from the ruins of the house, one tiny hand was clenched around the ring.

Chapter One

Yorkshire, 1217

Edwin whistled to himself as he crossed the courtyard. He was in a better humour that morning. The Lord knew he had no reason to be, but he'd momentarily escaped the semi-darkness of William the Steward's office, the spring air was fresh, the sun was shining, and he was surrounded by familiar, smiling faces, so his spirits had lifted a little. He sidestepped neatly as one of the masons swept past him without looking, and tossed one of his mother's oatcakes from hand to hand as he continued on his way.

And then, without warning, the fear struck him.

The dread. It had been a constant companion these past weeks, a black demon squatting on his shoulder, and now he stopped in his tracks, the feeling jolting him, overwhelming him, making him feel sick to the pit of his stomach. Every so often he forgot about it, managed to feel happier for just a moment – or even for a longer while – but then it would return. He knew why, of course, but that didn't exactly help. He was dizzy. Quick, find something else to think about. Look at the keep. Think of it; force yourself to concentrate on it and nothing else. Breathe.

He considered the building, the huge whiteness towering over him as it had done since his childhood. He focused his mind. He wondered if there could possibly be a finer or more impressive building in England. Neither round nor square but a strange multi-angular shape, the design had been the idea of the old earl Hamelin, the present earl's father, who'd had it built to replace the old wooden keep which had existed for as long as anyone could remember. Not that Edwin had ever seen the old keep – the stone one had been finished before he was born – but he could well imagine the difference it had made to the appearance of the castle. He tipped his head back to look all the way up to the top: four floors high, plus the wall walk on the roof; how could men construct such a huge edifice? And how many stones had been used in its creation? As usual, the figures arranged themselves neatly in his head, and the dread receded a little, pushed back into the recesses of his mind as he started to calculate how many stones might be in one layer all the way round, plus the buttresses of course, and how many layers made up the building …

So engrossed was he in his reckoning that he was nearly upon the two ladies before he noticed them, and he stepped back hastily with a muttered apology to allow them to pass. The earl's sister, as was her usual custom, swept past without a word, considering him too lowly to notice, but her companion, Mistress Joanna, rolled her eyes at him as she scurried to keep up. Edwin managed a slight smile, forgetting his own troubles long enough to wonder how she managed to maintain such a sunny disposition when she had to spend so much of her day shut up with that old … no, he should stop that line of thought immediately, lest he think something insulting about one of his betters. But still, Mistress Joanna must have to exhibit considerable forbearance to be the companion of the Lady Isabelle de Warenne, and she did it with grace and a ready smile. Perhaps that was one of the things Robert liked about her; Edwin had long suspected that the two of them might be sweethearts.

Robert. Now, there was an idea: maybe he would have some further news about the war; as the earl's senior squire, he had access to information to which other mortals were not privy. Besides, it might help him to keep his own mind off other matters. Where would Robert be?

He had just set off across the bustling inner ward again when a blond head hit him at speed – painfully – in the midriff, knocking him off balance. Momentarily winded, Edwin gasped for air, but steadied himself and put out his arms to stop the boy falling. At one glance he took in the large chunk of bread in one hand, the even larger chunk in the mouth, and the nearby open door to the kitchens, and smiled, properly this time.

'All right, Simon, all right, no harm done, but slow down or you'll choke yourself!' The boy sprayed crumbs everywhere as he tried to offer an apology, but only ended up gagging. Grimacing and wiping the front of his tunic with one hand, Edwin held him steady and then reached out and thumped him hard on the back until he stopped. 'There. Better? Good. Now, if you can stand still for one moment, perhaps you can tell me where Robert is?'

Simon took a deep breath and a swallow. 'Hello Edwin I'm sorry I hurt you he's down at the stables with Martin looking at my lord's new warhorse I wanted to go and see him as well he's a beauty but I had to take a message for my lord!' Another breath. 'Can I go now?' Working his way through the gabbled, pauseless sentence, Edwin translated the answer he needed and released the page, who raced off across the inner ward, narrowly avoiding an incident with one of the serving-men carrying a bucket of water from the well. The encounter had saved him an unnecessary trip all round the castle, at any rate: he changed course and headed out through the gatehouse, waving to the porter as he passed, and down into the outer ward.

There was an open area to one side of the stables where steeds could be exercised, and Edwin's eye was drawn there first, as two of the grooms were putting the finest horse he'd ever seen through its paces. The chestnut stallion was trotting in a circle, a long rein held in the hand of one of the men. Edwin drank in the sight: what would he give to be able to ride a horse like that? He'd ridden before, of course, not like some of the villagers: his father was the bailiff on the earl's Conisbrough estate and often had to travel to some of the outlying holdings on business, and Edwin had accompanied him on a number of occasions as his assistant and scribe. But he'd ridden one of the estate's rounceys, workaday horses which rarely travelled faster than a leisurely amble; the animal in front of him was a destrier, a warhorse destined to carry the earl in battle. It was a magnificent specimen, a perfect blend of strength and grace.

Two other young men were watching the horse. One was more than a head taller than the other, and as Edwin drew near to them he nudged his companion and pointed, and Robert turned to greet him, the smile on his face broadening. Little needed to be said as he moved up to make room, and the three of them stood watching the animal's exercise. After a short while scrutinising the horse's gait, Robert nodded briskly at the grooms, indicating that they could lead it back to its stable. He turned to Martin, having to look up steeply.

'Go and tell our lord that the horse is fine: no ill-effects from the journey. I'll be there shortly.'

Martin nodded and loped up the hill towards the inner ward, seeming to be all elbows and knees as his long-legged strides carried him along the path. Edwin watched him go, wondering when he had last heard the earl's second squire actually speak. Seeing his friend's gaze, Robert remarked, 'I swear if that boy grows any taller we'll be able to use him as a flagpole. I'm already having difficulty in training against his long reach, and once he comes into his full strength there'll be no stopping him. Now come … ' Grabbing Edwin by the shoulder, he steered him towards the path back up to the inner ward. 'You must have a few moments to spare, let's get some air.'

Edwin didn't take much persuading. He'd been helping William Steward with his accounts all the morning, which was not actually his task, but his assistance had saved his uncle several days of puzzling labour. Edwin could never understand how it was that other people couldn't see the neat columns of numbers in their heads, or how they had trouble adding up bushels, or ells, or shillings and pence, but it seemed that they did, so he was happy to help out with something which was no effort to him. But the tiny office which led off the service area behind the great hall was cramped and airless, and he was glad of the opportunity to stretch his legs. He tossed the oatcake he was holding – now somewhat the worse for wear – to Robert and fished another out of the front of his tunic for himself as they entered the gatehouse and climbed the stone steps which led up to the walk around the top of the inner ward's encircling walls. A man-at-arms who was about to come down stood aside and waited while they ascended; Edwin nodded his thanks as they passed, for it was Berold, a local man he'd known since childhood.

It was windy up there, as it usually was, but the air was fresh and free from the normal smells of tightly-packed humanity. Edwin took a deep breath and tried to unwind the knots in his head. They strolled around towards the north side of the castle and then stopped, surveying the bustling ward beneath. The work of rebuilding the castle in stone was continuing: the keep and curtain wall were complete, but most of the buildings inside the inner ward, nestling against the walls, were still wooden. The earl had ordered them replaced, and masons hurried to and fro going about their tasks. Their work was a mystery to Edwin, but each seemed to know his part, and the structures came together like magic under their hands. For many of them it was a lifetime's work; some of them had learnt their trade there from their fathers, who had built the keep itself a generation ago. They were starting with the kitchen, which Edwin supposed was sensible, as that was the part of the castle most susceptible to fire. Then their work would move on to the adjacent great hall, and Edwin thought to himself that it would indeed be a grand place to eat when it was finished. It was no more than the earl merited, though: William de Warenne, Earl of Surrey, was one of the richest and most powerful men in the kingdom, and it was right and fitting that he should have imposing surroundings in which to entertain and impress his guests. Edwin had never met the earl face-to-face, of course, but he'd sometimes seen him at fairly close quarters during the course of his work, and he counted himself fortunate to live under the rule of such a great man. It was the best that someone like him could hope for.

Robert finished his cake and fastidiously picked a few crumbs off the front of his tunic as they continued walking. There was a moment of companionable silence before Edwin asked a question about one of the two things which had been preying on his mind these last days.

'So the earl will join the war against the French invaders?'

Robert sighed. 'Yes, it looks that way.' He fiddled with the thong around his neck which held something he kept under his shirt – Edwin suspected it was a lock of hair or some other keepsake from Mistress Joanna, as he had observed that she had a similar cord around her own neck – and went on. 'Prince Louis holds large parts of the country, so the regent needs to stop him before he gets too powerful. He'll be forced to do something soon, so we'll have to be prepared to march anywhere at his command.'

Edwin was about to press him for more details, but he stopped.

'What's that?'

'What?'

'Over there.' Edwin pointed out along the road that led south from the village, where he could just make out what looked like a moving patch of dust.

Robert screwed his eyes up. 'What is it?'

'I think it's a man on horseback, and it looks like he's in a hurry.'

Robert sounded impressed. 'Your eyes are better than my falcon's. Come on, we'd better go down to meet him – perhaps he's got a message for my lord.'

Edwin could see the man clearly now – as could one of the guards, belatedly calling out – and surely nobody would labour a precious horse that way unless he had a duty of some urgency. They hurried back along the parapet, down the stairs, out of the gatehouse and through the outer ward, just as a man on an exhausted, lathered horse dismounted by the outer gate and demanded that he be taken to see the earl immediately. Robert stepped forward briskly, all business, any signs of relaxation gone. 'I'm Robert Fitzhugh, the earl's squire. I'll take you to him.' As he led the man up the hill, he looked over his shoulder at Edwin and threw him a parting remark. 'I'll try and find you later, to tell you about it.' Edwin nodded, but he doubted that his friend would have much leisure time for the rest of the day, for he had seen the badge that the messenger wore on his tunic: the emblem of William Marshal, Earl of Pembroke and Striguil, and regent of all England.

Earl William de Warenne was a man with a temper. He rarely lost it, but when he did, men trembled at his wrath. His squires, therefore, tried to avoid doing anything which would prompt an outburst, but as Martin stood in the shadows at the edge of the council chamber, he could see that the Lady Isabelle was treading on very dangerous ground.

The earl had been pleased when he'd entered to give the good news about the destrier's condition, but his easy gait and ready smile had turned to tight, controlled movements and short, barked sentences as soon as his sister came in. If Martin had been able to give her any advice, it would have been to avoid the topic upon which he knew she was about to embark, but of course he was in no position to speak to her without being asked, so he kept his mouth shut and watched as she made her situation much, much worse. It wasn't just the subject, which even Martin had heard many times; it was that particularly whining tone of voice which just bored into his head.

The earl's speech became even more brusque and one fist started to clench. Martin cast a glance down at young Simon, to check he wasn't about to do anything which would make him a potential target of the outburst which was now inevitable: he hadn't quite mastered the art of standing perfectly still until summoned, and was therefore apt to bring himself to the attention of his betters at inconvenient times. But he wasn't fidgeting, he was concentrating avidly on the exchange in front of him; of course, the Lady Isabelle had slapped his face only that morning, and in front of a group of smirking guards as well, so he would probably enjoy seeing her brother put her in her place.

The earl was doing remarkably well at keeping his voice level, despite the whining and wailing, but both fists were now balled. Martin set himself to staring straight ahead to avoid looking either of them in the eye, and tried to sink into his own thoughts. His feet hurt: the boots which he'd only been wearing since Christmas were becoming too small, but as they were still in good condition he dared not ask for any more. He would have to make them last, but maybe he could do something with them to make them stretch a bit further? He would have a try later on whenever he got the chance to sit down.

The earl had just taken in a deep breath when there was a sudden knock at the door, and the bellow which had been meant for his sister ended up being directed at whoever was outside. Martin winced when he saw Robert step over the threshold, aware of his spectacularly bad timing, but all was saved by the entrance of a tired-looking, mud-splattered man. He had his back to Martin, but the earl took one look at the badge on the front of the man's tunic and stopped mid-word. He ushered his sister out of the room, virtually shoving her out into the passageway, and slammed the door behind her. The man turned, and Martin could see the emblem of the regent on his chest.

The earl said nothing as he let the envoy speak his message; then, expressionless, he sent Robert off with the man to the kitchen for some refreshment, and Simon to find Sir Geoffrey. As he waited for the arrival of the old castellan he paced up and down the council chamber in silence.

After a few moments a knock sounded at the door, and on the earl's signal Martin opened it to admit Sir Geoffrey, the commander of the Conisbrough garrison, with Simon trailing behind him. Martin might have known that the earl would ask for the knight's advice before coming to a final decision: Sir Geoffrey had been in the service of the Warennes for the whole of his life, as had his father before him, and was the veteran of many a campaign. He nodded wordlessly at the earl and waited for him to speak.

'The regent has decided to act.'

'Lincoln?' Sir Geoffrey didn't believe in wasting words, but despite having listened to the envoy, Martin was still a little hazy on the details. Simon looked at him enquiringly, but he shrugged, hoping that Robert might be able to fill them in later on. He always understood these things better.

The earl continued. 'Yes. He calls "all loyal men" to muster at Newark in four days' time in order to march on Lincoln and relieve the castle. The question is, shall I obey?' Sir Geoffrey said nothing, watching his lord intently. Martin's eyes, too, followed the earl up and down the room as he paced, wrestling with himself. Martin might not have understood all of the message, but what was clear was that the earl's decision might eventually mean life or death for him and many others.

After what seemed like an age, the earl stopped. He turned to Sir Geoffrey. 'Making a truce with him is a far cry from risking the lives of my men fighting for his cause.' He paused, then continued, his voice for a moment sounding a little less sure. 'And yet … the king isn't responsible for the sins of his father, and an English boy king is to be preferred to a French prince.' He folded his arms and spoke with more force. 'We will fight.'

As Edwin walked through the ward a little later, people were running in all directions in a great hurry and there was a buzz of activity and excitement about the place. The news that the earl would shortly be marching off to war had spread around the castle like a moorland fire. He moved quickly aside as a mounted man sped out of the gate, and hailed Martin as the tall squire hurried out of the stables. Martin waved an arm but didn't stop. 'Busy, important news … Robert says … in the hall after the evening meal.' Edwin nodded and Martin loped off.

When Edwin reached the great hall and the service room behind it he found all in an uproar. William Steward was standing amid a throng of serving-men barking orders. He saw Edwin approaching. 'Where have you been? The earl and his men need to leave in three days, and they'll need campaign supplies with them. There's a lot to do and I could use your skill with numbers. Have you time?' Edwin opened his mouth to speak. 'Good, come with me.' Edwin shut his mouth again and followed his uncle.

William led the way into the relative calm of his office and gestured for Edwin to sit. 'I have a list of the supplies which the host will need,' he waved a piece of parchment, 'but I haven't yet worked out the quantities. I want you to find out exactly how many men and horses will be going – I've sent a boy for the muster rolls – work out what each needs per day, and then calculate how much will be needed for forty days. When you've done that for each type of supply, send the boy to me with the details, so I can arrange for the stores to be fetched and packed. Pens and ink are there.' He gestured to the end of the table. 'All right?' Edwin nodded, and William gave him a brief but hearty thump on the shoulder by way of thanks then left, shouting for his wife as he went.

Grimacing and rubbing his shoulder, Edwin pulled the quills towards him and took out his knife to sharpen them. If ever a man had been born to be a steward, William was not he, and as he always did, Edwin wondered how in the Lord's name he had come to be given the exalted position. William had once been a soldier, but had been wounded in the service of the old earl and couldn't continue. He never spoke of the circumstances, but Edwin's guess was that he'd rendered some service to the earl as, instead of being pensioned off or left to find his own way in the world, he'd been made steward, in charge of all the stores and supplies at the Conisbrough estate. He was – in Edwin's opinion anyway – unsuited to the job, having a blunt soldier's outlook on life and no head for figures whatsoever. However, over the years he'd learned his new trade fairly well and was now competent, except when it came to making large calculations. But he deserved a new chance at life: whatever his service to the earl had been, he'd paid a high price for it. He walked with a permanent limp as one leg was twisted; a horrific scar disfigured the entire left side of his face, and part of his left ear was missing. The one advantage of this, if any aspect of such a grave injury could be called an advantage, was that the scar gave his face a terrible, almost demonic look, and all his underlings and the traders who dealt with him were so intimidated that nobody ever tried to cheat him. This belied the fact that he was even-tempered and pleasant, but it was useful nonetheless. He was also married to Edwin's mother's sister, and so deserved not only respect but affection as well, which was why Edwin seemed to spend so much of his time helping him, he supposed. The quills sharpened, Edwin took a deep breath, dipped one in the ink, and started to write. The figures arranged themselves neatly in his head as he became engrossed.

By the time he looked up from his labours the room was almost dark. He smelt the evening meal being prepared and realised he was hungry. Giving the last parchment to a very tired-looking serving-boy, he put the pen down and stretched his arms. He was exhausted, but that was good. Maybe he would be able to sleep tonight. He drifted in something of a daze into the hall, wandered down to one of the lower tables which ran lengthways down the room, and found himself a seat next to Berold. When all were assembled the earl entered, followed by his sister and his squires and page. Everyone stood while Father Ignatius said grace, and then the earl sat, with Lady Isabelle on his right and Sir Geoffrey on his left, which was the signal for all to take their places and begin eating. Edwin nodded his thanks to the serving-man who placed a trencher in front of him, and then began to eat with gusto when it was loaded with a thick pottage and a piece of good maslin bread to dip into it. As it was Monday, meat was permitted, which gave the pottage a hearty flavour, and Edwin applied himself to working his way through it all as quickly as possible. He was so hungry that he ate the trencher as well, feeling a moment's guilt that the soaked bread wouldn't go to the poor, but knowing that there would be plenty of others. As he ate he tried to catch Robert's eye, but his friend was too far away, and was, in any case, busy serving the earl with the different dishes at the high table, pouring his wine, and keeping an eye on Simon to see that he was performing the same services for Lady Isabelle. Martin, who was attending to Sir Geoffrey, was doing so in an exemplary fashion and from what Edwin could see rarely needed a word from his senior.

At the end of the meal the earl rose and retired from the room, indicating to his squires and page that they could now help themselves. He left with Sir Geoffrey; the rest of the people in the hall started to disperse, and Robert, Martin and Simon all took trenchers and piled them high with food before making their way down the hall to where Edwin was. He looked enviously at their meals: it was no feast day, but the food from the high table was still something to be marvelled at. The pottage served to the main hall had been perfectly adequate, but here were some real delicacies such as venison haunch, quails and a tart made with thick, creamy rewain cheese, as well as real white paindemain bread. Edwin felt hungry all over again. Martin and Simon – whose platter was heaped so high he could barely see over it – thumped down on to the bench opposite Edwin, while Robert seated himself next to his friend and indicated that he should help himself to some of the food on the trencher. Edwin dipped a chunk of the light bread into the rich sauce which covered the quails, and savoured it while he waited eagerly to hear all the news.

Robert ate a large mouthful before starting. 'You already know that we're going to join the war?' Edwin nodded. Not only did he know that, but he also knew exactly how many men the earl would be taking, and what supplies would be provided for each of them, but he didn't interrupt. Simon tried to ask a question but choked on the enormous piece of venison which he was busy stuffing into his mouth. Martin thumped him hard on the back and he gave a large swallow before continuing in his piping voice. 'But I don't understand. Why have we changed sides?' Edwin nodded, as he also had to admit to confusion about some of the details. He was glad that Simon had asked, to save him the embarrassment of sounding foolish.

Robert sighed. 'I'd better start from the beginning.' He ate another large spoonful of the cheese tart as he considered his next words. 'All right then. Now, as you know, the old king —,' Simon spluttered again and sprayed breadcrumbs on the table, but Robert seemed to understand, 'Yes, Simon, that's right – he was a bad king.'

Edwin concentrated hard on Robert's words and tried to make sense of it all. King John hadn't respected the rights of his nobles and knights, so they'd rebelled against him. That made sense. The king had had to sign the Great Charter and agree to uphold the nobles' rights, but even then he didn't respect them, so the nobles eventually tired of his empty promises and offered the crown to someone else. Presumptuous, yes, but still making sense. They'd offered it to Prince Louis, the son of the French king. That was a bit of a logical leap – why the French prince and not someone else? He'd have to check up later, but he wasn't going to make himself look stupid by interrupting now. Anyway, Robert was continuing. The earl hadn't been one of these disaffected nobles to start with, but he came round to their way of thinking and joined them later. But then, last autumn, the king died, and he was succeeded by his son, who was only nine years old.

Robert's voice was full of laughter as he looked down. 'Just imagine that, Simon: someone the same age as you being king!'

Simon was busy chewing and didn't answer, but his eyes widened as Robert continued. 'So, clearly this meant that some of the nobles changed their ideas. All of the complaints about John's injustice and misrule could hardly be brought against a young boy.' He paused and took another mouthful. Martin too was eating steadily but hugely, as if he would keep going until the day of judgement, and Edwin hastily helped himself to more bread and sauce before it all disappeared. He listened with care as he savoured the food. Some of the nobles had changed their allegiance back to the young King Henry – and to the regent, who was ruling for him until he was older – and decided to fight against Louis. They didn't really want a Frenchman as king, they just thought that anyone would be better than John. The earl was one of these men, and last month he had made a truce with the regent.

Robert waved his spoon in the air as he concluded. 'And today the regent has summoned all men who are loyal to him to muster and march to the relief of Lincoln.'

Edwin felt that he understood a little more clearly after this explanation. 'So the French forces hold Lincoln?' He had no idea where Lincoln was, but he had heard of it, and it wouldn't do to sound too ignorant. He hoped nobody would ask him any questions.

'They hold the town but not the castle. Look, I'll show you.' Robert enthusiastically started to rearrange cups and dishes in order to illustrate his point, but gave up when he saw the confused faces around him. He sighed. 'All right. Let us speak more simply. From what I could gather from the messenger's words today, Louis holds most of eastern England except the strongholds of Dover, Windsor and Lincoln.' He banged his finger down in three places on the table. 'He himself is currently in London,' – another bang – 'but his army is at Lincoln.' And another. 'The town has surrendered but the castle within it is still resisting, so we will march to relieve them and hopefully destroy much of the French army behind Louis's back.' He thumped his palm down flat, as if to emphasise the finality of it all.

He made it sound so simple. Simon's eyes were shining at the thought, although the earl would presumably make sure that the boy came nowhere near the combat. Still, all three of them would march away with the earl while Edwin would have to remain here at Conisbrough. The darkness, which had been hovering around the edges of his consciousness, threatened to return.

Robert finished his meal and looked across at Martin. 'Come. We'd better get back across in case our lord needs us before he retires.' The four of them rose from their seats and left the hall, Edwin to return to the village and the other three to climb up the stairs and across the bridge to the keep. The earl did have a luxurious great chamber – one of the wooden buildings inside the inner ward which would soon be rebuilt in stone – but Robert had once told Edwin that since his wife had died two years before, the earl had preferred the plain quarters of the keep's bedchamber when he was at Conisbrough, leaving the more opulent apartments to his widowed sister. Edwin supposed that was fair, although he knew little of how the nobility arranged these things. Simon yawned and dragged his feet as they left the building, and Robert gave him an affectionate shove to get him going. 'Let's hope the earl doesn't need *you* for anything else tonight, or you'd probably pour his wine all over him.' He grinned at Edwin. 'Mind you, all three of us are such sound sleepers that our lord practically has to set his dogs on us to rouse us in the mornings!'

They walked across the courtyard, and Edwin turned towards the torchlit gatehouse to the accompaniment of a sleepy goodnight from Simon, a nod from Martin, and a promise from Robert that he would try to visit on the morrow if he could manage it. He nodded to the night porter and walked out through the outer ward, down the road and into the quiet, still street of the village towards his parents' house, where he could see a rushlight still burning in expectation of him. He slowed his pace as he neared the house, the dread returning in waves. He knew what he would have to face when he got there. He couldn't do it. The compulsion to turn and run was so strong that he could almost taste it. He slowed, nearly stopped. But he had to keep going, he must. It was his duty. The demon of fear must be overcome. He clenched his fists, prayed for strength, and forced himself to open the door and step over the threshold.

Chapter Two

Simon awoke just as the dawn light started to filter in through the window of the chamber. Something was poking him in the ribs and he shuffled sleepily to try and get away from it, but it was insistent, digging into his side. He sighed, grumbled and opened one eye to see what it was. It turned out to be the earl's foot, joined onto a body which had already drawn back the curtains of the big bed and risen from it. Horrified at his own negligence, Simon disentangled himself from the earl's two favourite hunting dogs, who were sprawled next to him, and sat up, throwing his blanket aside. He yawned. He hated having to get up in the mornings. Still, at least he was nice and warm, not like he had been in the winter: as the spring wore on even the rooms within the thick walls of the keep lost their chill. He was lucky that he slept next to the fire: this honour should of course belong to the senior squire, but when Simon had first arrived a couple of years ago Robert had let him sleep there to make him feel more at home, and the habit had continued. Simon hoped to himself that nobody would notice and that he would be able to keep the place, so he had never mentioned it, and so far nobody else had either. Robert himself was nearer the door, and the long form of Martin was stretched out, snoring gently, on the other side of the room. Simon kicked them both to wake them, even as he scurried to pour his lord a drink and fetch him water to wash.

Once he'd finished, the earl retired downstairs to his private chapel for a few moments. Simon supposed he should say a morning prayer as well, but it was difficult to concentrate over the groaning noise from his stomach. How long would it be before he could get something to eat? But rules were rules, so he briefly dropped to his knees and asked the Lord's forgiveness for any sins he might have committed since the last time, and added a request that there might be wafers in the kitchen that day. By that time the earl had returned, and Simon followed him down the stairs and out of the keep.

Outside in the inner ward there were plenty of people around doing their jobs, and a lovely smell of warm bread coming from the kitchen. He started to drift in that direction but was brought up short by the earl, who looked up at the cloudless sky, sniffed the fresh air, and announced that they would go for a ride.

Simon looked at him and the earl laughed.

'Never fear – you'll be able to break your fast when we return. But now I need some peace and quiet before all my knights descend on us with their retinues, so off you go and saddle Gringolet for me.'

This was cheering news. Riding out with the earl, on the wide open spaces of his lands, was Simon's second-favourite thing – and, even better than that, it was to be just the two of them, so he would be able to accompany his master like a grown man, and not have to trail along behind Robert and Martin. He skipped down to the stable. Ah. The problem with being his lord's only attendant, of course, was that he now had sole responsibility for preparing his lord's courser, with no Robert or Martin to help or to tell him what to do. He would have to be very careful to do everything properly so that the earl would praise his efforts.

Now, what was it that Robert had shown him? He went over to the end of the stable block where all the tack was kept and took Gringolet's bridle off its hook, slinging it over his shoulder to carry. Next he picked up the saddle: it was really heavy, but he was determined to do everything by himself, so he didn't call a groom to help, although there were several attending to horses in their stalls. Staggering slightly under the weight, he managed to regain his balance and made his way down to the other end of the building. As he went past the stall which held his lord's new warhorse he paused to look for a moment, but scuttled hurriedly past when it snorted and pawed the ground. He was glad he didn't have to saddle such a daunting beast on his own. But seeing it reminded him of the campaign. To think that they would soon be riding off to war! There would be knights, and campfires, and heroic battles … no doubt he would get to play a vital role, and would save his lord's life in battle, to be rewarded with a knighthood and riches. He couldn't wait!

He realised that he was standing still, and that Gringolet, who was in the next stall, was getting excited at the sight of the tack, ready to go out for some exercise. He'd better get on with this. Simon looked around for somewhere to put the saddle down: when Martin was doing this, he just slung it over the top of the stall partition, but there was no way he would be able to reach. Grimacing, he turned it upside down and stood it carefully on its pommel in the straw, leaning against the wall. There would be trouble if the precious saddle were found to be scratched later. He moved to stroke the horse's nose and speak to him, putting the reins over his head and feeding the bit into his mouth. Gringolet was docile, for which Simon was glad, and he had no trouble putting the head-piece behind the ears, pulling the forelock out carefully so no hair would be trapped underneath, which would make the horse uncomfortable. Then he fastened the chinstrap, hardly daring to believe that everything was going so well. The saddle was more of a challenge: Simon flexed his arms before picking it up, but still it took three tries before he could heave it high enough to get over Gringolet's back. Finally it was achieved. Now, what was it Sir Geoffrey had taught him? Always put the saddle a few fingers' width too far forward, and then slide it back, so that the hair underneath was smoothed down in the right direction. Simon was pleased with himself at having remembered.

Finally he bent down and fastened the girth under the courser's belly, doing it up as tightly as he could. Once he got outside he would tighten it again, for he well remembered the time he had failed to do this on his own pony: it had puffed its chest out when he fastened the girth, so that by the time he came to mount it had become loose, and he'd fallen flat on his back as he tried to get on, amid howls of amusement from his elders. He wouldn't be caught out a second time.

Feeling very satisfied with himself, he led the horse outside and left a groom to hold it while he repeated the same exercise with his pony, a task which was accomplished much more quickly. By the time the earl arrived, all was ready, and Simon felt a surge of pride to receive a nod of approval as he held Gringolet's head ready for his lord to mount. Then he too was in the saddle and they were riding out of the gate. What a fine thing it was to be alone with his lord, to be his most important attendant. Now, to remember what he had learned about riding: sit up straight, shoulders back, heels down, and don't pull too hard on the reins. And don't fiddle with your hands, as Sir Geoffrey had always said – another thing he remembered clearly was the stinging flick of the birch on his fingers every time he fidgeted. He was a little disappointed that the earl didn't turn and compliment him on his riding style, but one couldn't have everything. His lord was busy acknowledging the salutes of the villagers with a gracious nod, and Simon watched the movement so he could practise it later.

By the time they returned he was tired: it was difficult to keep up with his lord on his small pony, and he'd had to concentrate hard in order not to fall off. And now he really was very hungry indeed. The earl slid easily from the saddle and Simon managed to dismount uneventfully. His lord was already striding back up to the inner ward, speaking to Sir Geoffrey and Robert who had come out to greet him; everywhere looked busier than usual. Simon just had time to push the stirrups up and pull the leathers through before handing both sets of reins to a waiting groom. He would have to run to catch up. But as he turned to follow the earl, he saw something out of the gate. He stopped for a moment to check that it really was what he thought, and then raced up to his lord, grabbing him excitedly by the arm.

'Look, my lord, another messenger approaches!'

The earl, Sir Geoffrey and Robert all turned to where he was pointing. He felt very proud to be the one who had spotted the envoy first.

One of the guards was accompanying a man in plain clothing who had flung himself from his horse's back and was removing a letter from his belt pouch even as he walked. He handed it over to the earl with a bow and stepped back. The earl looked at the seal on the letter and raised his eyebrows questioningly at the messenger, who said, 'From the earl of Sheffield, my lord.'

Sir Geoffrey gasped. Simon looked at him in surprise. Sir Geoffrey was never shocked at anything. But yet there he was, looking sharply between his lord and the messenger.

The earl broke the seal and ripped the letter open. 'What in the Lord's name can *he* want? I haven't seen him in years.' He scanned the lines written on the parchment. 'He's coming here, with his retinue. Today.' He crumpled the letter. 'Well, of all the … ' he stopped suddenly and looked at the messenger. 'Return to your master and tell him that I shall be *delighted*' – he sounded as though he were speaking through gritted teeth – 'to offer him hospitality until we march for Newark. You may go to the kitchen and seek refreshment before you leave if you so wish.' The man bowed his thanks and left – how come he was getting to eat when Simon wasn't? That was hardly fair – as the earl turned back to Sir Geoffrey. 'He says that as two loyal servants of the king, we should take this opportunity to meet and combine our forces before marching to meet the regent. What can he be up to?' He handed the letter to Sir Geoffrey. 'What do you make of it?'

Sir Geoffrey glanced at the letter and handed it straight back. 'Of the letter, my lord, nothing.' Simon nodded sagely to himself as the earl took the parchment: he knew that Sir Geoffrey couldn't read or write. It didn't seem to stop him being a fine knight, though, so Simon didn't see why he had to learn, either. He would make this point next time he had to have a lesson and nobody would be able to argue. But anyway, Sir Geoffrey was continuing. 'But if you mean what do I make of the earl's motive, I would say he wanted to keep one eye on you. He is probably hoping that you will do something which he can report to the regent in order to curry favour. He does not stand so high under the current regime as he did in the old king's reign.'

The earl nodded. 'Aye, Ralph de Courteville was ever John's lapdog. But he'll find nothing amiss here, of that I am determined.' He paused, then turned to his squires. 'But all this is no excuse for you to neglect your training. Out to the tiltyard, both of you, and practise.' Simon's heart rose – he would slip after them and watch. But the earl had evidently not forgotten him. 'And I believe you have a lesson with Father Ignatius, young man.'

Simon grimaced. He would much prefer to be out in the tiltyard on the flat ground behind the castle, watching Robert and Martin practising their horsemanship. He was about to bring up his foolproof argument about learning to read, but as soon as he opened his mouth, the earl looked at him in that way which brooked no argument, and he shut it again. Orders were orders, so he sighed and slouched morosely towards the gate, kicking his heels as he went.

Joanna sat in the great chamber, a small fire burning in the grate next to her. She was sewing, her head bent over the earl's blue and gold war banner which she held up to the light streaming in through one of the windows; her needle flew in and out as she inserted tiny stitches. It was not a particularly interesting task – all those little squares made tears come to her eyes if she looked at them for too long – but he would need it on his campaign, and the Lady Isabelle wasn't one for stitching. She didn't enjoy it much herself, to be honest, but there was some satisfaction in a job well done. She looked critically at her completed work: the banner would at least not disgrace the earl on his campaign, although it was a shame his sister couldn't bring herself to sew it for him. She tied off the thread and cut the end with a small, sharp knife.

As her concentration moved away from the banner, she sensed someone else in the room and looked up to see that the earl himself was watching her from the doorway, evidently having been there some time. She jumped to her feet, feeling herself redden, but he gestured to her to remain seated.

'You reminded me of my mother for a moment.'

She opened her mouth, but surprise took her voice away.

He moved further into the room. 'I have happy memories of this room. My wife loved it here, furnished it to her own taste,' he waved at the tapestries, wall-hangings and cushioned chairs, 'and said that the light here made her feel happy. And of course we spent long evenings here when I was a small boy; I would lord it over my baby sisters and my mother and father would sit across the fire from one another and talk in low voices. I can still picture my mother in her chair by the fireplace, and for a moment when I saw you sewing it took me back.' He sighed.

Joanna still didn't know what to say. The earl had never spoken to her in this way before, had never mentioned his past. On the one hand, she longed to hear more about the comforting family life, but on the other hand, it was extremely disconcerting.

He shook his head and his tone of voice changed. 'Do you know where my — '

He was cut off by a strident voice issuing from the bedchamber at the end of the room. 'Joanna, this gown is … '

The earl muttered 'Never mind' under his breath, but she wasn't sure whether he was speaking to her or to himself.

Isabelle came through the door carrying one of her dresses, but stopped at the sight of the earl. 'Greetings, brother. And what brings you up to our little domain?' There was not the slightest sign in her voice that she might be pleased to see him, and Joanna readied herself for another confrontation. She was in between them; there looked to be no escape.

He didn't dwell on pleasantries, wasted no greeting. 'Isabelle, I wish to speak to you concerning an important visitor who will be arriving this afternoon.' This looked like a possible opening for Joanna to leave: she curtseyed and started to turn, but the earl forestalled her. 'I would have you stay, for this will concern you also.'

Isabelle swept over to the fire and seated herself in the chair, indicating to Joanna that she should bring another for the earl, which she did before stationing herself behind her mistress. Perhaps if they were to converse about a visitor they might not argue so much. And perhaps the visitor would provide a welcome distraction for all of them.

'This morning I received word from the earl of Sheffield that he will be arriving this very afternoon with his troops.'

'The earl of Sheffield … ' Isabelle was almost purring; Joanna could already see the direction her mistress's mind was taking, and she gave up hope of a peaceful afternoon.

'Yes. Now, he wishes us to combine our forces and then ride to muster with the regent on Friday, but I suspect that he may have another motive.' The earl saw his sister's distraction. 'Isabelle!' Her eyes jerked back to his face. 'This is important! Do you want me to have my estates confiscated?'

That woke her up. 'Why should you have your estates confiscated?'

'Because Ralph de Courteville would happily add my lands to his if he could find the slightest pretext to suggest to the regent that I might not be fully committed to his cause – it's already happened to a number of men. Castles razed, lands laid waste, families turned out … so *that* is why it is vital that we should all be on our guard against careless or frivolous talk. I fully intend to support the new king, but the Lord knows I had no love for my cousin his father, and that might count against me.'

Joanna was taken aback by the vehemence of his tone.

Isabelle also seemed stunned: perhaps the idea of being poor and homeless had bitten deep. 'Of course, brother. We'll be very careful in our speech.' Joanna couldn't remember the last time the two of them had agreed on anything so quickly.

'Good.' The earl spoke with some finality and Joanna expected him to leave, but he didn't rise. Instead he stayed in his chair, drumming his fingers on the armrest. The two women stared at him.

Finally he spoke again, less brusquely. 'I also want you – both – to be additionally careful in the earl's presence. He has something of an … unsavoury reputation.' He looked hard at his sister and then at Joanna. At first she didn't quite grasp what he was saying, but then she realised and her cheeks started to redden. She resolved to try and stay out of the visitor's way as much as possible, not having rank to protect her against any kind of advance. So much for a welcome distraction.

The earl seemed relieved not to have to go into further detail, saying merely, 'Let us hope and pray that we can all get through this visit unscathed.'

Finally he rose to go, but stopped and spoke again, the words coming out in a rush. 'And, of course, as an honoured guest, he will have to be offered these chambers.' He moved quickly towards the door.

Surprisingly, no outburst came. Instead, Isabelle acquiesced in a syrupy voice: 'Of course, brother. I shall be delighted to give up these chambers to the earl and move into other accommodation while he is here.'

That seemed enough for the earl: he reached the door, bade them goodbye, and left.

Joanna watched him go and considered the import of all the things which had just been said. Meanwhile, Isabelle rose from her chair and paced up and down the room. Then she stopped and smiled.

Joanna, knowing what her mistress wanted to talk about, sighed inwardly and started the conversation – better to get it over and done with.

'Perhaps, my lady, the visiting earl will bring his brother with him.'

Isabelle's face took on an expression of fatuous devotion, and she began to extol the virtues of Walter de Courteville. Joanna, who had encountered Walter when he had previously come to pay court to Isabelle and had her own personal opinions about his qualities, said nothing, waiting for the effusive eulogy to end. After Isabelle had exhausted her stock of superlatives, she sat down again and waved a peremptory hand.

'But now we must think of moving out of these chambers before the earl arrives – pack what we'll need into a trunk and summon a servant to carry it. I'll move into one of the guest chambers nearer to the gatehouse. Find the best one and put my things in it.'

Joanna moved obediently into the bedchamber and began to remove Isabelle's toilet articles from the small table and lay out some of her gowns on the bed.

Isabelle followed her in. 'No, you stupid girl, not those ones. I shall want to wear the new crimson gown for tonight's meal, to look my best for the earl.'

Or for the earl's brother, thought Joanna silently as Isabelle flounced out again. She found the new gown and folded it carefully so that it would not crease, or she would be on the receiving end of another verbal barrage. It was always like this, had been since she'd been given to Isabelle as a companion as a young girl, when Isabelle had married into the de Lacy family. After Isabelle had been widowed she had of course returned to her own family, but as nobody had much use for

Joanna, she'd accompanied her mistress. Joanna hadn't wanted to come, but although she bore the de Lacy name she was but a lowly cousin of the head of the family and must go where she was bidden. It wouldn't have been so bad except for the fact that Isabelle seemed to have difficulty in distinguishing between 'companion' and 'servant', and often gave Joanna the most menial of tasks to do, tasks that should have been left to a common maid. Oh well, there were worse situations to be in, she was sure. Life was hard and unpleasant for most women, whatever their rank. At least she didn't suffer starvation or regular beatings, and she could hold fast to the hope that one day her cousin would arrange a marriage for her with some vassal of his, so that she could be wed to some staid man or other and live out her life in obscurity and domestic tranquillity, and wouldn't that be something to look forward to. In the meantime she might dream of handsome princes and noblemen as she packed up her mistress's possessions and went to answer yet another summons as Isabelle petulantly called her name.

Edwin sighed and rubbed his eyes. So much for sleeping well. And this just made it worse: he was contemplating the documents before him, which detailed the exact boundaries of each man's territory within the earl's estates. This was part of his new bailiff's duties which he didn't enjoy: petty disputes over a few yards of land which required hours of research to solve. As he stared at the pages of cramped writing, a peculiar lethargy came over him. This was something which he would have to tackle sometime, but maybe it could be put off until later? Did he have anything else to do which could be considered more important? Or if not more important, then perhaps more interesting? Anything which didn't involve those property deeds would be fine, especially given that he'd spent much of the previous day hunched over the muster rolls. Mentally he made a list of his duties ... ah, there was something. He needed to find the thief who had stolen a knife from the kitchen – Richard Cook was most particular about his equipment, and had counted his knives several times before reporting the theft. Edwin would have to ask him when he had last seen the implement and who might have been in the kitchen at the time, in order to try and find the culprit before the next manor court. The theft of a knife was important, and not just because it had occurred in the earl's kitchen. Who knows why it might have been stolen? He would find out, would enjoy the logic of discovering where it had been taken and why. However, he suspected that just as dinner – the main meal of the day – was being prepared might not be the best time to disturb the cook, who was large, red-faced and in a permanent state of choleric high temper. This was likely to get worse as more and more of the earl's knights arrived at the castle and wanted feeding, so Edwin considered that a prudent course of action would be to make a quick tour of the castle, have something to eat, and then come back to speak to the cook. Good. He felt cheered as he put the documents away again.

Both the inner and the outer wards were busier than usual as he passed through, with new arrivals milling around before being told where to go. There was of course no possibility of housing everyone within the castle walls, only the most important men such as the earl of wherever-it-was would be invited there; the others would have to set up their tents outside. One or two others might be afforded special treatment as well: Edwin could see Sir Geoffrey shaking hands with one of the arrivals, a knight at least as grey and grizzled as himself who was greeting him like an old friend. Edwin suspected that a place to sleep and maybe a cup or two of ale might be forthcoming for knights such as he, although obviously not for all his men: a dozen archers and a small boy were waiting patiently behind him, ready for their orders. Edwin glanced at them and passed on, but his sharp eye moved back abruptly; the men were neat and well-turned out, in their matching livery, but the boy was filthy and barefoot. Inspecting him more closely, Edwin recognised Peter, an orphan from the village who was a beggar and a pilferer and was suspected of being a pickpocket also, although nobody had ever caught him at it. He was watching the men closely, too closely for Edwin's liking, and he made to saunter casually over to warn the lad off whatever action he was contemplating; but as he moved in Peter's direction the boy caught sight of him and darted quickly away, hovering on the edge of the crowd. So he *had* been up to something, thought Edwin; there's plenty of opportunity for crime with all these people around. But it was a shame about the boy: his parents had died several years ago when Peter was very small, but nobody would employ him as they suspected him of being dishonest, which of course meant that he was forced to beg or steal in order to stay alive, which further reduced the possibility of anyone taking him in. But what could be done? That was the way of the world.

As he watched, one of the earl's men noticed the boy and chased him away, adding a cuff to the back of his head for good measure, although there seemed little malice in it. Then Berold – for it was he – turned to Edwin.

'Have you heard? We're going to march to help the king!'

Edwin thought he would have to have had his head stuck in the well not to have heard, but he said nothing, noting the evident enthusiasm in Berold's eyes. Here was one who would be stepping out of the gates and broadening his horizons, unlike Edwin.

Berold was continuing, waxing lyrical about his chance to be a real soldier on a real campaign, not just a guard at the castle, but Edwin paid him little mind. Since his youngest days Berold had had his heart set on joining the earl's garrison, and Edwin had lost count of the number of times he'd been coerced into a game of soldiers when they had both been boys in the village. Not only had he been unenthusiastic for the military life, but Berold's extra two years of age and greater strength had always told, and Edwin inevitably ended up nursing several bruises. But it was difficult to dislike Berold, for his hearty lust for life shone through his every deed. Edwin thought privately that Berold would make a very good footsoldier – strong and not too intelligent. But at least he would have the opportunity to go on the campaign, unlike those who would be stuck behind. Honour and glory and a chance to see the world. Huh.

Perhaps disappointed by the lack of response from his companion, Berold drifted away, barely acknowledged.

Edwin was so caught up in his thoughts that at first he didn't hear the voice calling his name, but eventually Robert got through to him. He and Martin were coming out of the stables, looking hot and dishevelled, presumably having finished some kind of training, an activity which took up much of their time. Martin was rubbing one shoulder, so Edwin enquired after his health, but the tall squire was forestalled by his companion, who noted cheerfully that Martin might have the greater height and reach, but that he still had something to learn in the skills department.

'What Robert is trying to say,' interposed Martin in his deep voice, 'is that he knocked me flat on my back and will therefore be mentioning it at every available opportunity until I gain my revenge.'

There was a slight pause; Edwin was not used to hearing Martin utter so many words at once.

Robert recovered first. 'Would I do that?' His voice was full of insincere incredulity.

'Yes.' Martin and Edwin answered together, and Robert admitted that well, all right then, he probably would.

'But where is our young accomplice? Surely he isn't still with Father Ignatius?' Robert explained to Edwin that Simon had been forced to go to a reading lesson with the priest, and added an impression of the boy's mournful attitude which made the others laugh.

'What are you laughing at?' Simon had appeared beside them.

'Oh, nothing,' said Robert smoothly, 'Edwin and I were just recalling how much we used to enjoy our reading and writing lessons with Father Ignatius when we were younger. Oh look, someone else has just arrived.'

He pointed and Edwin turned, half-expecting that Robert had merely been trying to distract their attention, but as he looked towards the gate he saw that an angel of the Lord had just ridden in.

The young man sat straight-backed in his saddle, riding with an effortless grace. Garbed for war, the light glinted off the shimmering silver of his mail and made his green and gold surcoat glow like the sun. He wore no helmet, revealing a pale, unearthly face which carried a beatific expression and resolute blue eyes; some trick of the light made his wavy golden hair appear as a shining halo around his head. The world around him seemed to recede, and the four of them stood silently and watched as he approached, Simon frozen with his mouth open in wonder at such a vision.

'Roger!' Sir Geoffrey was striding over to greet the new arrival, and the spell was broken. 'Or, I should say, *Sir* Roger. How are you, my boy?'

'Roger?' Robert shook his head, looked again at the vision and then seized Martin's arm. 'Do you see who it is?'

The apparition dismounted and turned to greet Sir Geoffrey, and Edwin saw with shock that it was, indeed, Roger d'Abernon, former squire to the earl, whom he hadn't seen since the latter's knighting ceremony four years before. They hadn't known each other well, the age difference between them meaning that Edwin hadn't been on familiar terms with the erstwhile senior squire like he was with Robert. In fact he'd always been rather in awe of the solemn young man, who approached his service to the earl with the utmost seriousness and was absolutely dedicated to his calling as a knight. It was rumoured that his ambition was to go on crusade to the Holy Land to help free it from the infidel, and Edwin could well imagine him smiting the heathen with the shining light of righteousness in his face.

Solemn he might be, but he was also well mannered and, after he'd finished greeting Sir Geoffrey, he nodded gravely at Edwin before turning to the squires beside him.

'Robert. How are you?'

'I am very well, thank you, Sir Roger.' Robert would never forget the courtesy due to a knight, even one with whom he had shared squirely duties for a number of years.

The knight then turned to Martin, and as he looked up at the young man his face creased into a smile for the first time.

'What on earth have you been eating, boy? The last time I saw you you were no taller than this lad here.' Martin nodded his greeting as Sir Roger crouched so that his face was on a level with Simon's. The boy was still awestruck and stared in wonder at the shining knight, who spoke to him softly. 'And you must be the earl's page.' Simon nodded, still unable to speak as Sir Roger reached out and touched his shoulder. 'Well … ' he looked at Robert who obligingly mouthed the boy's name, 'Well, Simon, I am very pleased to meet you, and I hope you serve the earl well.' Simon nodded again as Sir Roger straightened and addressed Sir Geoffrey. 'I had best go and offer my respects to the earl straight away. Perhaps I may speak with you later?'

Sir Geoffrey assented and the younger knight paced up towards the inner ward. He even walks gracefully, thought Edwin, as they stood to watch him go. Robert could not take his eyes off the retreating figure, and Edwin guessed what he was thinking.

'You'll be a knight one day, just like him.'

Robert watched as Sir Roger disappeared through the gate.

'No,' he said, wistfully, 'I might be a knight, but I'll never be like him.'

It was just as dinner was finishing that the greatest commotion yet started in the outer ward. A guard rushed into the hall and whispered something into the earl's ear and he rose immediately. He turned to those around him, his glance encompassing Sir Geoffrey, Isabelle, Joanna and his squires and page as he bade them all follow him outside. From his place at one of the lower tables Edwin saw them sweep out of the hall, and guessed that the visiting earl must have arrived – Lord William wouldn't interrupt his meal for anyone less. Along with a number of other people he wandered curiously outside to see if he could catch a glimpse of the man who had caused such concern, and found himself next to Sir Roger, now divested of his armour, in the crowd. Edwin craned his neck – oh, to be as tall as Martin – and saw the earl standing ready with the members of his household behind him as a richly dressed man with a retinue of his own was escorted through the inner gate.

Edwin didn't know the earl well, but to his unfamiliar eye he didn't seem composed. But that was ridiculous. He was a nobleman, one of the most powerful in the kingdom, he couldn't possibly be scared of anything, not like a mere mortal. His face was expressionless, although he twitched slightly when he saw the visitor's closest companion, a small weasel-like man who resembled him facially. Some relative? Edwin didn't know. The small man was ignoring the earl and looking directly at the Lady Isabelle, who was staring at him in turn.

The visiting earl, or de Courteville as Edwin had heard him called by some men in the crowd who were better-informed than he, was also accompanied by two squires and a couple of household knights who stood close behind him and looked about them suspiciously, as if ready to defend their master at the slightest provocation. The earl didn't look too pleased by that either, judging by the look of thunder on his face. Edwin overheard mutterings in the crowd behind him about the insult to the earl, and indeed the man did seem to be implying that he needed a bodyguard here inside the very walls of the earl's stronghold.

The earl stepped forward, offered his hand to de Courteville and spoke words of welcome.

'I am very happy to be here, Lord William,' the other replied, 'and it is my hope that together we may form some small part of the king's triumph against his enemies, the French and the English traitors who side with them.' There was a slight emphasis on the word 'traitors' which the earl apparently didn't like much, and neither did some of the men around Edwin, but de Courteville continued before anyone could react. Looking around the inner ward with its untidy mixture of wooden and stone buildings, some of them only half-built, he drawled, 'What an interesting ... *place* you have here, my lord.'

Edwin felt angry on his lord's behalf, but the earl clearly felt that the slight to his home was too petty for him to be drawn. In a tone of exquisite politeness he indicated that the visiting earl would, of course, be offered the best accommodation available. 'The great chamber will be at your disposal for you and such of your ... ' he looked pointedly at the two knights flanking the visitor, '*household* as you deem appropriate.'

De Courteville understood the implication only too clearly, and smiled thinly. 'Why thank you, my lord. I am sure that the accommodation will be more than adequate.' A thought seemed to strike him and he laughed. 'I am sure everything will be just fine.'

Chapter Three

Robert hurried across the inner ward and up the steps to the keep. How many times had he been up and down these today? He didn't know, but too many, at any rate. He was carrying yet another message to the earl, apprising him that one more of his knights had arrived; the earl was ensconced in his council chamber, so that meant one flight of steps up to the wooden drawbridge which led across to the keep's only door, and another which took him from the entrance level – currently crowded with servants ferrying up supplies from the storage area below – up to the room where the earl was surrounded by ever-increasing piles of parchment. Edwin would probably be able to tell him how many steps that was in total, but all Robert knew was that the backs of his legs were starting to ache. So much for the glamour of campaign. He was panting slightly as he knocked on the door.

Within the time it would take to say five paternosters he was hastening back down the stairs and out to the outer ward where he'd left the new arrival. Then he took the knight and his men out of the main gate and around to the north-eastern side of the castle, where the flat area normally used as the tiltyard was covered in a forest of brightly coloured tents, and indicated that they should set up camp there, picketing their horses in a specially fenced-off area further down the hill. The campaign was imminent … it was a good thing he was so busy, or he might have too much time to think. He trudged back round to the main gate and saw that yet another retinue had arrived, but the tall figure of Martin was already speaking deferentially to the knight at the head of the group of men, so he needn't worry about them. Perhaps he might even have a few moments to catch his breath … he felt a tug at his sleeve and looked down to see Simon, but as he braced himself to hear of another task the boy brought his other hand around from behind his back and produced a piece of cheese and a hunk of bread.

'I thought you might be hungry, and there were so many people in the kitchen that Richard Cook never noticed me.' The boy really did have the most infectious smile.

Robert hadn't thought he was hungry, but now that food was in front of him he realised he was ravenous. 'God bless you, Simon, you are the finest attendant a man could have.' He ruffled the boy's hair and crammed the bread into his mouth, remembering from his own youth that braving the wrath of the cook was no mean feat.

Simon darted off again, having plenty of errands of his own to run, and Robert strolled at a more leisurely pace through the ward as he finished the cheese. He'd nearly reached the gatehouse when he all but fell over a small, dirty boy who was whittling a stick with a large knife. The boy took one look at him, dropped both stick and knife, and fled. Robert was looking after him when he heard a voice behind him.

'Do you always have that effect on children?'

Robert turned to see the pale face and blue eyes of Sir Roger looking at him. 'He's never pleased to see anyone,' he replied. 'He always thinks that people will beat him, and he's usually right. Do you remember one of the serfs called Peter?'

Sir Roger's brow furrowed as he tried to recall. 'Did he walk with a limp? Lived on the edge of the village in one of those hovels?'

'Yes. He and his wife were carried off by the coughing sickness a few years ago. Young Peter is their son, and he's been begging a living and working for scraps where he can ever since, although virtually nobody will employ him as he's a thief and a rogue.'

The knight's eyes followed where the boy had fled, and he took on a faraway expression and spoke wistfully. 'Yet the lowliest of God's creatures deserves mercy … ' He bent and picked up the knife.

Robert didn't really have anything to say, as he was sure the knight didn't require an answer from him. A few years ago he might have made a flippant comment, but there was something very different about Roger these days, something which didn't invite intimacy or frivolity. Awkwardly he took his leave and continued on his way.

Having mounted the keep's stairs yet again, he slipped into his accustomed place against the wall of the council chamber to stand in attendance on his lord. His timing was certainly off at the moment – he'd managed to walk in on another tête-à-tête between the earl and his sister, only this time he had no messenger with him to use as an excuse. He tried to vanish into the wall hangings, wishing that, just for once, the lady would choose a different subject.

The earl sighed. 'Isabelle, at this moment I don't have the leisure to speak with you regarding your marriage. I will do so when the time is right.'

'But when will the time be right? I've been widowed for years now. I wish to be married again and bear children before it's too late, but you seem determined to thwart me.'

The earl's voice started to rise. 'As I have told you before, you will marry when I say so and not before, and to a man whom I consider a suitable match.'

'Suitable for you, that is, not me.' She pouted unattractively.

'Of course.'

Robert wondered to himself how she could even think of any other reason to marry. He knew what was coming next, was mouthing the words before they even issued from her mouth, safe in the knowledge that neither of them was looking at him. 'You allowed Maud and Ela to marry again soon after being widowed.'

And the earl's reply was the same as ever. Why did they have to have this conversation over and over again? Why would she not listen? His lord's tone was resigned. 'As I have reminded you before, Maud and Ela are not my heirs. I have no children and no brothers, and you are the eldest of my sisters, and therefore the alliance which you make must be carefully considered. It would be folly to rush into anything too soon.'

Honestly, did she have no family feeling at all? Robert felt only sympathy for the earl. He remembered when the lord himself had married some years ago. He hadn't been the senior squire then, but had been around the earl enough to know that he'd only met his new bride a handful of times before they'd wed. But to marry well had been his duty to his family, so he'd done it. Simple. Although, thinking about it, he'd grown very fond of her during the time they'd spent together, and he'd been devastated when she'd died two years ago. That had been a bad time for all those in the household, as his temper had become shorter than ever and his squires had borne the brunt of it. The earl and his wife had had no children, so until such time as he should marry again the Lady Isabelle was his heir, and so her husband could end up being the next Earl of Surrey. She should just do as she was told and stop goading him, but of course she managed to come up with the worst possible thing to say.

'If only you had allowed me to marry Walter when he asked ...'

Robert winced as the earl stopped in his tracks and started to clench one fist. There was only one thing which irritated his lord more than his sister's 'marriage' tone of voice, and that was the mention of one particular would-be suitor.

His voice rose dangerously. 'Walter de Courteville? That good-for-nothing upstart? Why, the man is cowardly, as slippery as a snake and, moreover, no longer the heir to his brother's earldom now that Ralph has a son. You will marry such a man over my dead body!'

The pacing got faster; the arms started to wave. This was going to be a good one. Still, at least it was the Lady Isabelle on the receiving end, and not him.

'Dear God, the very thought of that weasel becoming the next earl makes my blood run cold,' the earl continued. 'The estates would be ruined within a month, the people starving and dying like flies. Although, at this particular moment, I would happily marry you to Walter or any other worthless nobody who happened to come along, just to be rid of you!'

She opened her mouth to speak again but he finally lost his patience and cut her off with a bellow. 'Out! Return to your chambers, sister – the fate of the realm is in the balance and I have more important things to do than … than dallying here exchanging words with you. Out, I say!'

His voice would have carried across a battlefield and it held the unmistakeable ring of authority. For once the lady knew when to back down. She said nothing but stamped her foot in frustration and turned towards the door. As she flounced out, she muttered something under her breath that sounded like 'you will soon see,' but Robert didn't think his lord had heard.

The earl lashed out with his arm and sent a goblet flying across the room. Robert started to flinch as his lord turned to him, but fortunately he only jerked his head to indicate that he wanted to be left alone, so the squire took the opportunity gratefully, and fled.

He was across the ward and at the foot of the steps which led up to the great chamber when he heard voices from within: one wheedling, one worried, and one in some distress. What in the Lord's name was going on now? He recognised the last voice as Joanna's and bounded up the steps and through the door to see her backed against the wall with one of de Courteville's squires facing her. His hands were on the wall on either side of her, barring her path; the younger squire had one hand on his fellow's arm and was obviously trying to pull him away from the girl. It was all too clear what was happening, and Robert grabbed the older squire's shoulder and swung him round, allowing Joanna to escape out the door.

The squire looked at him and sneered. 'What do you want? I was only having a bit of fun.'

'She didn't look amused.'

'Oh, she was enjoying it as much as me, never fear. Women like to pretend to be scared, but they don't mean it really. Anyway, what is it to you? Is she your sweetheart? Or have you already tried with her and failed?' He leered.

Robert seized a handful of the other's tunic, surprised by the suddenness of his anger. The little ... who did the boy think he was, anyway, coming here where he wasn't wanted and treating Joanna that way? He'd raised his fist, ready to smash it into the smirking face, before he realised that he was being deliberately goaded, and that if he hit the boy the story was bound to get back to de Courteville, suitably twisted, and that wouldn't do the earl any good. Reluctantly he lowered his hand and let go of the tunic, leaving the young man to adjust his clothing, adopt a gloating manner and stalk off.

The younger squire addressed Robert nervously. 'You mustn't mind David, it's just his way. He wouldn't have hurt her.'

Robert rounded on him ferociously. 'And what do you know about it? What do you know about her? Do you think it's funny? Do you?' He stepped forward and raised his fist again. The boy looked frightened, and Robert realised he was taking out his anger on the wrong person: this lad had, after all, been trying to stop his fellow. He only looked about thirteen or fourteen, and was probably intimidated by his bullying superior – in fact he had a nasty-looking bruise on the side of his face. There was no point assuaging his temper by exacting revenge here. The boy was the wrong target. He tried to calm down. 'I'm sorry, I know it wasn't your fault.' He adopted a more conciliatory tone. 'What's your name?'

'Adam.'

'Well, Adam, if I were you I'd be off to see if your lord needs you for anything, instead of wasting your time talking to me.'

The boy nodded and fled outside, leaving Robert alone to contemplate the hours ahead.

Edwin was about to leave the ward when he saw Robert striding past, muttering to himself and pushing his hand through his hair. He hailed his friend, but had to run after him and grasp his arm before he was noticed.

'You look deep in thought.'

Robert stopped and glared at him. Edwin knew that look.

'Do you want to tell me about it?'

Robert pushed his hand through his hair again. 'It's nothing.'

Edwin looked at him.

'Oh, all right! It's everything. I'm angry at the way our new guest and his household seem to have upset everyone already. The earl has enough to worry about without all this trouble in his home. That, and the fact that I have much to do and little time to do it in.'

Edwin was eager to find out more about the campaign, but Robert looked too harassed to ask about it. His own troubles receding, he thought that he should probably try to calm his friend down, then maybe he would get the chance to ask some questions. 'Well, there seems to be a lull in the arrivals at the moment – why don't you come with me for a while and tell me the news? We can go up to the wall walk, so you'll be able to see if anyone else approaches.' He tried not to plead.

Robert looked around him, still seemingly dazed, and acquiesced. They made their way up to their usual place, and he told Edwin of the plans for the earl to join the regent's host to fight off the French invaders. He didn't look too pleased at the prospect, although the telling of it had brightened him slightly, and Edwin was enthralled.

'Just think of all the places you'll get to see, all those fine cities. Lincoln, of course,' – he'd found out that Lincoln was to the south-east and was feeling mightily pleased with his new geographical knowledge – 'but maybe also York or Winchester, or perhaps even London!' Caught up in his thoughts of such amazing places, the reality of his situation hit him again. Robert might see these places, but he, Edwin, would not. His place was here, working for the earl's household, and he would probably never travel further than twenty miles away during the whole of the rest of his life. Unimportant. Insignificant. Even Berold would get to see the places he would not.

Robert spoke. 'What's the matter?'

'Nothing.' He'd brought Robert up here to try and cheer him, but now it was he who needed enlivening. But how could Edwin say he was jealous? Robert had always been his best friend, ever since they were both small boys running around the castle enclosures. So why did the differences seem so important all of a sudden? They never had before. Perhaps it was the thought of war, of glory, of Robert riding off on a fine horse to join the glittering host with its mailed knights and their coloured banners floating in the wind …

'There is something. Tell me.'

'I told you, it's nothing.'

'Tell me, or I'll beat you like Sir Geoffrey did the day we both fell in the river. Do you remember that? I could hardly walk for a week.' Robert grinned.

Of course Edwin remembered. It had been one among many of their childish escapades, albeit one which nearly got both of them killed. But they'd come through it together, just as they'd taken their beatings together. How could he be jealous of Robert? And yet, there was some block between them, as there never had been before.

'It's just … ' He stopped and tried again, groping for the right words. 'I was just thinking about all the things you'll be able to do with the rest of your life. While I'll be stuck here, you'll visit far-off places and see castles and cathedrals, earls and maybe even kings. And meanwhile I'll be here, organising the village's work, catching petty thieves, settling disputes over a few yards of land and adding up William Steward's accounts for him.'

Robert started to say something, and then stopped. He tried again. 'But look, it's not all excitement. At least you'll always have a roof over your head; I might go campaigning with the earl for months in the rain and have to sleep in the mud. Or I might get caught up in a siege and starve, or die of the bloody flux from eating rotten meat. And people do get killed in battles, you know. And maimed or wounded.' Edwin hadn't quite thought of it like that. But would he exchange his safe, dull life for one of danger and excitement? He thought he probably would. Honour and glory and a chance to see the world. What would anyone not give for that?

Robert continued. 'Anyway, I'm not going to be a great man like the earl, am I? I'll just be one of the knights in his service, so I'll be back here often to see you. And if I do ever get a manor of my own, you can come and work for me, if your father can spare you. By the way, how is he today?'

A wave of dizziness came over Edwin. Quickly Robert grabbed his arms and changed the subject.

'But come with me now and we'll go and look at the encampment.'

Edwin tried to breathe normally. The encampment. Yes, they would go and look at that. Breathe in, breathe out. Good, that's better. The spots before his eyes receded. He would take his mind off things by going to look at the tents. But no sooner had they started down the steps than another retinue was sighted in the distance, and Robert had to go and attend to his duties, calling over his shoulder that he would try to speak with him later.

Edwin watched his friend hurry off about his important tasks. The dizziness had gone but he still felt discontented. He needed to find something to do: he didn't want to go to the encampment on his own, but there were plenty of other things he could be getting on with. For a start, he still hadn't looked at that land dispute … but no, the most important task was to stamp down on this black demon and face his fear. He'd waited long enough. He would do it now. He left the castle and walked into the village.

He became if anything even less happy when he surveyed his parents' house from the outside. Care of the garden and livestock was woman's work, and here everything looked well cared-for, thanks to his mother; however, the upkeep of the building was the responsibility of the man of the house, and since ... since *it* had happened Edwin had been spending so much time carrying out the bailiff's duties that he'd had no time to attend to the domestic tasks. The thatch looked thin in a couple of places, and there were one or two crumbling patches of daub, through which the wattle of the inside wall could be seen. Worse, one or two of the precious metal nails which helped to hold the wooden frame of the house in place looked as though they were loose, a fact confirmed when Edwin brushed his shoulder against the doorframe on the way in, and was rewarded with a sharp pain and the sound of his tunic tearing. He sighed. How on earth was he going to find the time or the energy to attend to everything?

The dread hit him like a wall as he stepped inside, stifling him. He felt panic rise within his breast, wanted to scream and run out again, but he forced it down and swallowed it. Look around you calmly, he told himself. This is home; it is where you were born and where you have come back to every day of your life.

There was an appetizing smell in the cottage's main room, and despite himself he sniffed the air appreciatively, the mouth-watering odour telling him that his mother had a savoury vegetable pottage on the fire. The sense of familiarity helped to reassure him.

The inside of the house seemed very dark after the bright afternoon outside, and he stopped to let his eyes adjust as he called a greeting. As he became accustomed to the gloom he saw that his mother's hand was evident here as well: a bright fire, spare kindling and wood neatly stacked, the metal pot over the fire and an earthenware crock of milk standing ready in the coolest place, the corner furthest away from the hearth.

How did she do it? It was as well that she was coping better than he was, or everything would fall apart.

Mother came over to him and put a hand on his arm. 'This will be ready in a few moments; I'll just take a bowl in to your father. How was your day?' She continued speaking as she returned to the fire and ladled out a bowlful of steaming pottage. 'Did you find Robert? Your father will be pleased to see him, old gossip that he is.' Her cheerfulness was brittle.

Edwin stood and took the bowl from her, indicating that he would take it and trying to stop his hand from shaking. 'I did see him but he was called away – he's busy with all the arrivals – perhaps he'll try to come by later, or maybe tomorrow.' He dropped his voice lest the sharp ears in the bedroom hear. 'How has he been today?'

His mother's brave façade dropped for a moment and her eyes filled with tears which she tried to hide, wiping her face with the corner of her apron. 'Not good. He's sinking by the day. Even yesterday he could still feed himself but now he seems hardly able to lift his hands.' Her shoulders shook and Edwin hastily replaced the bowl on the table and moved to comfort her as she crumbled. 'What am I going to do without him?'

Edwin folded her in his arms – had she become a little thinner recently? – and tried to offer reassurance. He was going to have to try harder to take on the role of the man of the house. He didn't know what to say, how best to put his feelings into words. 'I'll keep this roof over your head, mother, never fear. Even if I don't succeed in becoming the permanent bailiff I'll find some work, we won't starve.'

She nodded sadly and patted his cheek. 'I know you will, dear. And I'm proud of you, never doubt it. But … your father and I have been married since I was fourteen, and I don't know what I'll do without him.' She smiled wanly through her tears. 'Losing him will be like losing half of myself, and I don't like the thought of a long life ahead as a widow, but nor will I want to marry again. But I might well live for years yet.'

She was right: many years younger than Edwin's father, she was still a fine-looking, healthy woman. He didn't know what to say, had no words of comfort to offer. But he was saved from trying by a quivering voice issuing from the bedroom.

'Edwin, is that you?' This was followed by a cough.

His mother hastily picked up the bowl of pottage again and gave it to him. 'Here, you'd better take this in before it gets cold.' He nodded and moved towards the bedroom.

And this was it. This was what he was afraid of. He stopped, the fear and the smell of sickness driving him back. It was in his nostrils, in his throat, forcing him back out. But he would, he *would* overcome it. He stepped inside.

His father was lying in the big wooden bed, looking frail against the pillows which supported him, his face drawn with pain. That it should come to this! Edwin had always been aware that his father was old, comparatively speaking, but he'd always been so hale that it had never mattered. But seeing him now, struck down by illness, unable to rise or even to lift his arms, brought it all home to him. His father was as human as everyone else, and he was going to die. He was going to *die*. There was nothing he could do; he was powerless, so afraid, so fearful of the impending death, of having to live his life without the rock which had always supported him, had always been there during his times of happiness and despair. Gently, Edwin sat on the edge of the bed and started to spoon pottage into his father's mouth as though he were a child. How he hated this, and how the once-strong man in the bed must detest having to be coddled like an infant. But he continued, and as he did so, he recounted the news. His father's mind was still as alert as ever, and he enjoyed hearing of the campaign. He took a rasping breath.

'So, the earl will fight? I thought he would. But Lord William will have to march quickly and send all the troops he can muster in order to prove his loyalty, having changed sides so recently. There will be much coming and going in the next few days, though I may not live to see it.'

The fear flickered again in the corners of Edwin's mind. He tried to protest, tried to speak in an encouraging tone about recovering to live for many years yet, but it rang hollow in his ears.

His father attempted a derisive snort, which ended in another long cough. He managed to speak again. 'Do not talk down to me, boy, a man knows when he is dying. I am nearly sixty years old, and that is more than enough for any man. I shall live long enough to set my affairs in order and then I shall pass into God's grace. But I need to know that your mother will be supported.' He looked at his son and his face softened. 'I have faith in you, Edwin. I know you will do well, will be a fine man, a good son and a good husband and father when the time comes. I would have liked to have lived to see my grandchildren, but that is clearly not in the Lord's plan for me.' His voice slowed and became drowsy. 'I am content.'

His head drooped. Edwin looked down at his sleeping father, gently arranged his head more comfortably on the pillows, and moved back into the cottage's main room. He sat down at the table with his mother and the two of them ate in silence for a while before Edwin stood, squeezed her hand, and left to walk back up to the castle.

He told himself over and over again that he wouldn't cry in public.

The door to the great chamber crashed back against the wall as Ralph de Courteville strode into the room, bellowing for his squires. He'd been in a continuous ill temper for weeks. Things were not going entirely well for him at the moment, hadn't been since the death of the old king. Everyone knew that he'd been a particular favourite of John's, and the other nobles were both jealous of his position and wary of his unsavoury reputation. That hadn't bothered him as long as

John had been alive: safe in the knowledge that he would have the king's protection, he could alienate all the other earls, and the rest of his family, and it would matter not the slightest bit. He had far surpassed his weak father, becoming an earl, and he was damned if anyone was going to take that away from him. Moreover, he needed to build from there so his son could rise even higher. But he was at his wits' end. Patronage was everything, but how was he going to get back into royal favour?

If he'd only had some time towards the end of John's reign, he could have formulated some plans, but the king's sudden death had left him unprepared for his next move, and the question of how to wheedle his way into the good graces of the present administration was a thorny one. There was no point in trying to charm the king himself – the boy was only nine and would be unable to rule in his own right for many years to come. No, the person who needed to be won over was the regent. The problem was how to go about it? William Marshal was a legend, the sort of man whose name would echo down the ages. He was over seventy years old, was the most frighteningly loyal and upright man de Courteville had ever known, and he was definitely, absolutely, unquestionably, not stupid. That ruled out de Courteville's two preferred options, which involved either flattery and lies, or offering to perform any little unpleasant jobs which the regent might want done. No, the emphasis would have to be on honesty and loyalty, two rare qualities in these troubled times. The one factor in his favour was that he himself had been loyal to John all the way through his conflict with the barons – well, his position had depended upon it, after all – so he could use that with the regent. The best thing to do would be to uncover some evidence of treachery on the part of one of the other nobles, preferably one who'd already changed sides, so Warenne was a prime candidate. Nothing had been unearthed so far, but he'd only been here a matter of hours

– something would come up. Then he would consult his mental list of those who had slighted him, and have his fill of revenge. The power would swing back his way again, and he could start to build his dynasty.

It was nearly time for the evening meal, so he decided to change out of his travelling clothes into something more suitable, something which would ostentatiously display his wealth and power. Hopefully he could goad Warenne into an indiscretion which could be used against him. He bellowed again for his squires – where on God's earth were they? – and went into the bedchamber. Something caught his eye, and he looked at the bed to see that there was a piece of parchment on it. Frowning, he picked it up and scanned the contents; he had just finished when Adam hurried into the room, panting an apology for his tardiness, followed shortly by David. He turned on them, waving the parchment.

'What's this?'

They looked at each other, unsure of what to say, flinching as he neared them. Adam essayed a tentative reply. 'A letter, my lord?'

De Courteville, his foul mood making him even more impatient than usual, cuffed him hard around the ear. 'I know it's a letter, idiot boy. But who is it from? When was it delivered?' Adam rubbed his ear, and looked at David. 'I don't know, my lord. I didn't see who brought it.'

De Courteville looked at David, who also said he hadn't seen the letter's bearer. Honestly, they were both as useless as each other, the one a milksop and the other forever trying to avoid his duties. He raised his hand, about to pursue the matter further, and saw them both shrink back, but he didn't have the time for this. Abruptly he changed his mind and put the letter into the pouch at his belt, ordering them to find clothes for him.

The great hall was crowded, probably the fullest he'd ever seen it, thought Edwin, as he tried to squeeze into a space at one of the lower tables. Even though most of the ordinary soldiers had been left outside the castle – no Berold this evening – there were still the extra knights and their squires and senior men to fit in; this didn't leave much room for those who normally ate their evening meal in the hall, as Edwin was forcibly reminded by a sharp elbow to the ribs from his left-hand neighbour at the table, a large fellow who was squashed uncomfortably against him. Ignoring the loud military conversations which were going on about him, he looked up at the top table. Well, they had slightly more room there, but not much, and as he scanned the faces, he realised that very few of them looked happy to be there, and that whoever had decided on the order of seating – or perhaps it was all pre-determined by rank, he didn't know, maybe he would ask William about it some time – couldn't have made things much more awkward if he'd tried. The earl, in his usual place at the centre of the table, was chafing in between the two de Courteville brothers, and was speaking to them as little as courtesy allowed, and only in what looked like short, clipped sentences. The visiting earl, on his right, was doing very little to remedy the situation, and seemed to be enjoying the fact that his every remark – what in the Lord's name could he be saying? – seemed to make the earl even more uncomfortable. To the visitor's right was the Lady Isabelle, who was dressed in one of the most splendid gowns Edwin had ever seen, not that he knew much about these things, and he idly wondered why she was wearing it. Despite the fact that she was sitting next to the honoured guest, she was paying very little attention to him and seemed to be trying to catch the eye of the other brother, although that wasn't stopping her from cramming one delicacy after another into her mouth as if she hadn't eaten for a week. To her right were the only two people who seemed happy with their lot: Sir Roger's handsome face was alight with enthusiasm as he spoke fervently on some subject to Mistress Joanna, who was at the very end of the table. She was listening to him avidly – and Robert won't like that, thought Edwin – and graciously accepting his attentions as he politely offered her the choicest cuts from each dish that reached them, and refilled her wine-cup.

To the other side of the table Walter de Courteville sat on the earl's left, although he wasn't taking much part in the conversation as the earl didn't seem to have much to say to him, and Sir Geoffrey, who was on his other side, was pointedly ignoring him. Edwin smiled at the sight: the old campaigner obviously had no time for such a weak-looking, weasel-faced fellow. He was engaged in animated conversation with his other neighbour, the old knight whom Edwin had seen him greet earlier; the latter was identified by his burly table-companion as Sir Hugh Fitzjohn, an old comrade with whom Sir Geoffrey had campaigned in France some years ago. The final figure at the high table was the rather portly form of Father Ignatius, and the tension which abounded seemed to have affected him also, for his usually placid face was creased with a frown, and he kept throwing agitated glances at someone towards the centre of the table, although Edwin couldn't see who. Behind the seated figures scurried the forms of Robert, Martin and Simon, who were performing their usual services, and the visiting earl's squires, who were waiting upon him and his brother.

Too tired to wonder about the various undercurrents of feeling affecting his betters, and ravenous after his hectic day – the cook had been as short-tempered as ever, making such a fuss about his missing knife that anyone would have thought it was made of gold, and several brawls had broken out over the course of the day which had had to be broken up – Edwin turned his attention to the meal in front of him. The food was good: as soon as the cook had heard about his exalted guests he had made every effort to produce as fine a spread as possible, although the short notice and the large number of people may have hampered some of his efforts. Perhaps that was why he'd been even more bad-tempered than usual. Still, the outcome was worth it, and Edwin tucked into a meat and offal pie while allowing the tales of past campaigns and heroic deeds to wash over him. As soon as he could he escaped the noisy, hot, sweaty, crowded hall and headed outside into the cool air. After a few deep breaths he considered returning, but he wasn't really in the mood to listen to the bragging of drunken strangers, so he turned to walk down to the village and return home, sighing at the worry which would await him there also.

———◦◦◦———

Martin's stomach groaned as the earl and his guests finally rose from the table. The stuffed birds and marchpanes looked delicious, and he could hardly wait to try them. He also needed to sit down for a few moments: he was used to being on his feet all day, but all the extra running around had taken its toll, and he still hadn't had the time to do anything about his boots. The guests at the high table started to disperse and Joanna, who had barely looked up from her conversation with Sir Roger throughout the entire meal, moved towards him. At first he thought she was coming to speak to him, and he tried to prepare something gallant to say, but somehow his tongue wouldn't form the words properly. As it turned out, she merely wanted to pass him so she could walk over to the kitchen: he overheard her telling Robert that she would fetch some wine in case the Lady Isabelle wanted some later in her chamber. He watched her go, belatedly realising that the visiting squires were helping themselves to all the choicest parts of the meal. He hastened to load a trencher for himself, and then stopped to help Robert, who was trying to pile up two separate lots of food and was starting to overbalance. Martin caught a wafer neatly and cast him an enquiring glance.

'I've sent Simon to fetch wine for our lord's chamber: Joanna was going to get some for the Lady Isabelle, so he can take some of whatever she chooses, instead of using that terrible swill he found last time.'

Martin nodded. Simon wouldn't enjoy being sent out while there was still food to be had, so he elbowed de Courteville's elder squire away from the marchpanes and took an extra piece to keep for the page. Robert had been caught in conversation by a visiting knight, but Martin couldn't wait and moved away from the visiting squires to sit alone near the door and get some air.

He'd just taken his first huge mouthful of capon when Simon hurtled into the hall, threw himself at him and started to gabble incoherently. Martin caught the jug of wine just before it hit the floor and listened: at first he had no idea what the boy was trying to say, but eventually he caught the words 'Joanna', 'trouble' and 'kitchen', so he cast his meal aside and rose to follow, Simon pulling him urgently by the hand. It was only as he entered the kitchen building and caught sight of two writhing forms in a shadowy corner that he understood.

Joanna was backed against the wall, struggling against the restraining arms of the man who held her. Martin felt fury rush through him and surged forward to intervene, but then recognised the man, and his blood turned to ice as he realised what a dangerous thing he was about to do. Turning to Simon he looked down at the boy and told him to leave: de Courteville hadn't seen him, so there was no point involving him as well. Simon stepped back out of the building, and Martin took a deep breath as he approached the two reeling, thrashing figures, realising that he still had the wine in his hand. Dear Lord, the man was an earl and answered only to the king. What would his punishment be? But he would stop this whatever the consequences. He could feel his heart beating in his throat. He saw with disgust that de Courteville had one hand pressed over Joanna's face to stop her crying out, while the other was thrusting at her skirts. She saw him and her eyes pleaded with him to help, even as she fought and scratched at the man holding her. Rage made Martin bold. He stepped forward and dashed the jug of wine in de Courteville's face.

He was ready with an apology, on the rather thin pretext that he had somehow slipped, but he had no chance to speak. Battle-hardened, the man's reaction was phenomenally fast: in one movement he brought his fist around and crashed it into the side of Martin's face, sending him sprawling to the floor as pain exploded in his head. He might be tall, but he hadn't yet grown to his full strength, while the other was broad and had muscles honed by years of fighting. De Courteville stood over him for a moment and Martin tried to curl up and protect himself from the onslaught which would follow, but the man only looked furiously at the stain spreading over the front of his expensive tunic and stalked off. Crying and wiping tears from her face, Joanna sank to the floor and then turned to help Martin to sit up. He groaned.

'Are you all right?'

Gingerly he touched the side of his face, as if to make sure that it was still there. He felt as though he had been hit by a mason's sledgehammer. But she'd also suffered. 'Yes, I think so. But are you?' He reached out his hand to the tears on her cheeks.

'Yes, I am. Thanks to you.' Gently she put her own hand out to touch his cheek, and tried to wipe away some of the blood which was trickling down from his mouth where the earl's rings had struck him. He felt her touch soft on his bruised face. They looked at each other for a moment, both aware that they'd had a lucky escape.

Martin wiped his face with the sleeve of his tunic and rose a little unsteadily to his feet as Joanna held out her arm to help him. 'Oh, don't thank me, thank Simon. It was he who raised the alarm.'

'Simon? Then I'm grateful to him as well. But it was you that saved me – and you that is hurt.' He towered over her, but she held his arm, making sure he was steady on his feet before she let him go. He wished she would stay like that.

Martin managed some bravado. 'You needn't worry about me, I've had plenty worse from Sir Geoffrey in my time.' He knew that wasn't true – Sir Geoffrey might need to discipline the boys, but he wouldn't attempt to cripple them. But Martin felt the need for some bluster. 'What I'm most concerned about is how I'm going to explain this to the earl in the morning when he sees me!'

They left the kitchen, and Martin walked with Joanna across to the guest chambers. He left her at the entrance and turned, wondering how they would cope when de Courteville, as he surely would, decided to take his revenge.

De Courteville cursed as he threw the soaking tunic on to the bed. That damned squire had ruined what promised to be good entertainment, for the girl was young and attractive, and not coarse like many of the serving-women he'd encountered in his time. He wondered who she was: minor nobility, probably, some offshoot of one of the lesser houses. She couldn't be anyone all that important or she wouldn't be here, waiting on Warenne's widowed sister. Shouting angrily for his squires, he considered trying to find her again – and he certainly wouldn't be stopped this time – but decided against it. He consoled himself with the fact that he would shortly be able to bring the house of Warenne crashing down, and that then he would stand high in the regent's favour. Was all this to be jeopardised for an encounter with a pretty girl? Of course not. He thought of Warenne's head on the executioner's block, of his sister starving and begging in the streets, and felt better.

Adam arrived and de Courteville tossed the tunic to him, ordering him to find someone to wash the wine out of it, saying that he would then have no further need for his services that night, so he could go to bed, as could David when he finally appeared. What was the boy up to?

Why hadn't he come running when he was called? It struck de Courteville with some amusement that the boy was probably about the same sort of business as he himself had been, although perhaps with better luck. Well, he didn't discourage that sort of fun – at least David showed more spirit than the timid Adam – but it shouldn't interfere with his duties. De Courteville thought with satisfaction that a beating was in order, to remind the squire of his place. He would see to it in the morning; in the meantime he settled down to wait. He would be busy later in the evening, and revenge would be sweet.

When he judged it to be near midnight he emerged from the bedchamber, stepping around the sleeping squires, and slipped over to the keep. Warenne didn't keep it barred at night, evidently trusting to the outer and inner castle gates to keep him safe. Little good that would do him when he seemed to have a traitor in his household. De Courteville smiled.

The staircase was dark and narrow. He held both of his arms out to touch the sides as he climbed the first flight, treading carefully to avoid a fall. As he reached the first floor his eyes became accustomed to the darkness, and he was able to concentrate his thoughts on whom his mysterious appointment might be with. The anonymous letter-writer claimed to have evidence that Warenne was about to switch sides again, and said that de Courteville could obtain that proof if he were to go up to the roof of the keep at midnight. De Courteville had considered this unnecessarily over-dramatic, but, after some thought, he'd decided that he would go: if the message was true it would be worth the effort, and if it was false then he would find whoever had tried to fool him and flay him alive.

But who would be close enough to Warenne to have the necessary information? Whoever he was he'd better be able to provide what he promised: the Earl of Sheffield didn't get out of his bed on a cold night and traipse up dozens of stairs on a fool's errand. He passed the chapel without noticing and continued up the next flight and past the door to the earl's bedchamber, treading very carefully lest he wake the earl or his squires, but the sound of snoring from within reassured him. He was breathing more heavily as he climbed the final flight and emerged on to the roof, and stood for a moment at the top of the stairs to catch his breath. He could see no one, but the wall walk curved away round to his right, around the roof. He took a step forward.

After he'd circled the roof several times he lost his patience. He'd forced himself to wait and wait, but it was becoming clear to him that the mysterious letter-writer was not going to appear, and he grew angrier by the moment as he considered the possibility that someone had tricked him. Somebody was going to pay for this, and pay in blood. He decided to take one final turn around the roof, and started walking.

Suddenly there was a movement behind him, but before he could turn he was seized by a terrible pain in his throat. He tried to cry out but had no breath; gasping, he scrabbled ineffectually at his assailant with his fingers, but he couldn't stop the agony, the terrible tearing of the sensitive skin of his neck as something sliced into it. Then an object was held up in front of his face, and words were spoken into his ear. He struggled to focus on the object, but his eyes swam and he couldn't see it. He continued to choke as he listened to the whispering voice, and some of it started to penetrate his consciousness as he understood what it was saying. Of course! If he hadn't been fighting the agony, struggling for his every breath, he might have laughed at the irony of it. Of all the things he'd done in his life, this, *this* was the one he was to die for! The pain in his neck and in his lungs became overwhelming, and he saw bright lights in front of his eyes. In his delirium he thought the red before him was the gate of hell opening to receive him, and he tried desperately to step back from the edge of the abyss. But it grew ever larger, and his mind screamed in horror as he fell forward into the gaping maw of everlasting hellfire.

———

One by one, three people slipped silently out of the keep. None of them was aware that a figure in the darkness had been watching, and had seen them all.

Chapter Four

Adam was dreaming.

He was alone in a strange place, unable to find his way. Where was he supposed to be going? He turned around and around, but he could never seem to face the right direction: everywhere he went, he ended up in the same place. Twisting and thrashing in his sleep, his foot hit a stool and knocked it over, and he awoke suddenly in the darkness. For a moment he couldn't work out where he was, and a tide of panic began to sweep over him. He tried to force it down, as he had done during many a night in his life. For Adam had a guilty secret: he was afraid of the dark. It was an absurd, irrational fear, he knew that, but still he could not conquer it. Of course, he couldn't possibly mention it to anyone, least of all David or his master: his life would be made hell by their taunts. But maybe they would be right to sneer at him: what sort of a squire was afraid of the dark, for goodness' sake? How would he ever become a knight?

The panic threatened to engulf him, as it normally did, but he forced himself to calm his frenetic breathing and his erratic heartbeat and to think rationally. He was in the great chamber at Conisbrough, where he had come with his lord. Good. Now, what was it that had roused him? Had his master called? He rolled over and got to his feet, noticing with relief that David hadn't stirred. He had, as usual, taken the place next to the fire, but the room was neither overly cold nor particularly draughty, so Adam had been quite comfortable himself, wrapped in his blanket. Throwing it aside he padded on bare feet, shivering slightly, to the part of the chamber which contained the bed, and peered around the partition.

A candle was burning, and by the light of it he could see that the bed was empty. Was that what had woken him? Had his lord gone out for a night-time stroll? He wouldn't have needed to go outside to relieve himself, as there was a garderobe in the corner of the room, so there must be some other reason. Tentatively Adam drew nearer to the bed, and felt it with his hand: it was cold. The earl had obviously been gone some time. This was unusual, and for a moment Adam considered whether he should wake David and tell him, but after some thought he decided not to. The older squire was even more irritable than usual when he was woken from sleep, and Adam felt that he had enough bruises to be going on with. Besides, there was always the possibility that he would notice Adam's fear of the night, and that was the last thing he needed. He tiptoed over to one of the windows which overlooked the inner ward and knelt on the seat to peer out, but it was so dark outside that he could see nothing. After his eyes became more accustomed to the very faint glimmer of moonlight in the courtyard, he thought for a moment that he could see the outline of a figure, but it quickly vanished into the shadows and he convinced himself that he had imagined it …

Adam awoke with a start from the light doze he had fallen into and realised that he was still in the window seat, clad only in his shirt and braies. He hadn't thought to wrap himself in his blanket and he was freezing. The reassuring beginnings of a faint pre-dawn light filtered in through the small panes of glass in the window, but it was still very dark. He walked back to the bedchamber: the end of the candle was guttering and throwing grotesque shadows on to the walls, but it produced enough light for him to see that the bed was still empty. This was serious. What if the earl had gone out for a walk and had fallen somewhere? What if he were lying hurt and unable to rise? It was the duty of his squire to find him, surely. A quick glance over at David showed that he was still fast asleep: Adam stood for a moment, unsure as to whether he feared the dark or the wrath of the other squire the more, and then decided that he would have a look around by himself before taking the risk of waking his senior.

Quietly he pulled on his hose, tunic and shoes, and tiptoed past the slumbering form to the door. He opened it slowly, worried that it might creak out loud, but it was silent. Once out into the passageway he went down the stairs and out of the door to the building. Outside the air was fresh, but now that he'd clothed himself and started moving, it didn't feel so cold. It was still almost dark, and he was the only person in the courtyard, although he could hear some faint stirrings coming from the direction of the kitchen. Where would be the best place to look? Perhaps he could climb up to the top of the wall and look from there? Could he get up there in the dark, past all the corners where hidden horrors might lurk? At least up there he wouldn't feel so confined. He had decided on this course of action and was walking over to the steps when he became aware of the huge bulk of the keep looming over him in the darkness. Of course: it was much higher than the walls and would give him a clear view of both of the wards and some of the surrounding countryside, if he waited until the sun was up properly. Was there a way up to the top? He was sure he'd overheard something at the previous evening's meal about there being a wall walk at the top. Well, there was but one way to find out. Using the faint glow of firelight emanating from the kitchen to orient himself, he navigated his way safely across the ward and started up the steps to the keep.

Inside was pitch blackness and oppressive silence. None of the light from the kitchen or from the rising sun could permeate the thick walls, and any residual gleam which might have come in through the doorway was lost as soon as he turned to climb the spiral staircase which was set within the walls. The darkness was closing in on him, constricting him, suffocating him … he panicked and ran outside again. As soon as he stood at the top of the steps he began to relax and cursed himself for his foolishness. Now come on! You have a duty to look for your master, which is more important than anything else. What if he's injured somewhere and he has to lie there all the longer because you are too much of a coward to walk up a staircase with nothing more sinister in it than shadows? Your father did everything he could to get you this squireship – are you going to let him down?

Adam forced himself back inside the door, stood at the bottom of the steps, shaking, and took a deep breath. Wishing he'd brought one of the candles from the great chamber, he started on his way up, suppressing a whimper. The suffocating darkness closed in around him like a blanket and the unfamiliar surroundings made him hesitant, but he slowly made his way up by touching the stone on either side and groping forward with his foot before each step. It wouldn't be pleasant to miss his footing and tumble all the way back down the stairs ... no, don't start thinking of that! He reached the first floor, passing the door to the earl's council chamber and the outline of the chapel entrance. The chapel had a small window, and he could see that it was almost dawn. He wanted nothing more than to stop by that little patch of light, but soon he was past it, so he screwed up his courage and plunged into darkness again as he started slowly up the next flight. The stairwell was eerie in the blackness, and with this added to the worry about his master; he became afraid again and tried to quell the rising sense of dread which clawed at his throat. He rebuked himself once more with the familiar questions: what would his lord say if he knew what Adam was thinking? What sort of a coward was he, to be afraid of shadows? How could he possibly imagine that he would ever be a knight if he couldn't conquer such a simple fear? What would his father think?

He'd reached the next floor. He was now at the limit of his knowledge of the keep: the previous day he'd been as far as the council chamber but no higher. He passed another door, and remembered that the earl slept in the keep: it was his sister who lived in the great chamber, and who had given up her quarters for the duration of their visit. He stood for a moment outside the door, and heard several different sets of snores and breathing, which reassured him that he wasn't, after all, the only human in the building, alone with the shadows. He carried on round the curved passageway and found another set of stairs leading up: this must be the way to the roof. He took a deep breath and set his trembling foot on the first step.

A short while later he arrived on the roof and heaved a sigh of relief as he leant his shaking body against the solid bulk of the wall. The sun was now starting to show itself above the horizon, and golden shafts of light could be seen across the fields: it was going to be another lovely day. He looked outwards and downwards, noting that there was now some activity in the castle grounds and in the village beyond. He started to walk around the top of the roof, keeping his eyes outwards as he scanned for any sign of his master; his gaze had just fallen upon the stable when his foot kicked something soft. A horrible feeling of foreboding came upon him and for a moment he dared not look, but then he set his jaw and forced his gaze downwards, to see that his foot had met the form of his master, lying face downwards. So he *had* fallen! But what was he doing up here in the first place? There couldn't have been much to see in the darkness. Adam stooped and put his hand on his master's shoulder, intending to see if he'd incurred any injury, and heaved to turn him over.

He recoiled in shock and horror, stifling a scream as he backed away. The face was purple and bloated, and a hideous black tongue protruded from the mouth. The body was stiff and cold, and frozen fingers clutched at the neck, where a thin scar ran across the front, encrusted with dark dried blood. But it was the eyes which horrified Adam the most: wide open and bulging, they were staring ahead with an expression of such dread that it seemed that Ralph de Courteville, Earl of Sheffield, had at the moment of his death seen something so terrifying that the memory of it would stay with him until the end of time.

———❦———

Robert was dreaming.

He was a young boy again, locked in a small room. He was banging at the door and shouting for help, but nobody could hear him. He kept thumping his fists uselessly and calling for someone to let him in. No, wait, that wasn't right, somehow. Why should he be shouting that? He wanted to get out, not in … he was half-awake and confused. Gradually he returned to the world of the living, but for some reason the banging noise was still going on … at last, the fact permeated his consciousness that the noise was real and was coming from the passageway outside the room. Who in the Lord's name was causing such a commotion outside the earl's bedchamber? His lord was also rousing himself, and he indicated that Robert should find out who the owner of the increasingly hysterical voice was. Robert opened the door and as it swung open he had to half-catch a boy, face tear-stained and fists still raised, who fell into the room.

At first Robert didn't recognise him, but as he and Martin helped the sobbing figure over to a stool and seated him, he could see that it was one of de Courteville's squires, the one he'd spoken to yesterday. The boy was shivering, and as white as an altar cloth: his eyes looked huge in the pale face, which was marked by several nasty-looking bruises. The lad was trying to say something, was pointing upwards, but he was completely incoherent. The earl motioned to Simon to fetch wine, and he himself took up a blanket and wrapped it around the boy's shoulders. Simon passed the boy a cup, but his hands were shaking so violently that Martin had to hold it for him and force some of the liquid between his chattering teeth. Martin also had a large purple bruise on the side of his face and a cut by his mouth. What in God's name had been going on? There was no time to consider that now – he needed to focus on the task in hand. The earl stooped so that his head was on a level with the boy's, and touched his shoulder before stepping back.

'Now, lad … ' he stopped and turned to Robert. 'What's his name?'

'Adam, my lord, I spoke with him yesterday.' Robert supported the boy on the stool, afraid he would fall if he let go.

The earl spoke clearly. 'Now, Adam, listen to me. Take a deep breath and then tell me, calmly, whatever it is that you are trying to say.'

The boy obeyed and began to stammer. 'My lord … '

'Yes, I'm here. Tell me.'

Adam tried again. 'No, my lord, I meant *my* lord. The earl. Upstairs. On the roof. I found him.' He took another deep breath. 'He's dead.'

The earl stared at him without speaking.

There was a long pause. Everyone was looking at the earl. He shook himself and stood up, reassuming his air of authority.

'Simon, go and fetch Sir Geoffrey.'

Simon was still staring.

'Now!'

Startled out of his private thoughts, Simon scurried out the door. The earl turned to his squires: 'You two, go up to the roof. Check if he really is dead and, if so, bring the body down to the chapel.' Robert nodded and started to pull on his hose and tunic. 'And you … ', he looked at Adam, who was gazing blindly in front of him and still very pale, 'you stay here and finish that wine.' He started to pace around the room as Robert pulled Martin out of the door and up the stairs.

Once they reached the roof the body wasn't difficult to spot. Robert stared down at it in revulsion. He'd seen death before, of course – who hadn't? – but this was … different. The purple contorted face, the tongue, and those awful, staring eyes.

However powerful and feared the man had been in life, there was no dignity in this death. Slowly he bent down and reached out his hand to close the eyes.

Beside him, Martin suddenly retched. Quickly, Robert stood and spun his friend around.

'For Christ's sake, if you're going to be sick, don't do it on the body!' He held Martin's shoulders as the tall squire emptied the contents of his stomach at the side of the path, and then helped him to stand up as he wiped his mouth. 'Better?'

Martin nodded. Still shaken, he looked again at the corpse. 'I suppose we'd better … ' He gestured towards the stairs.

Robert agreed, grimly practical. 'I'll take his head, you take the legs.' He stooped and put his arms around the body under the armpits, clasping his hands at the front of the dead man's chest, as Martin picked up the legs. The body was stiff, which made it easier to carry. Gingerly they made their way down the stairs, carefully avoiding any contact between the corpse and the walls lest they damage it even more. The load became heavier as they continued, and both were panting by the time they had struggled down to the chapel. But what to do with the body? They could hardly put it on the altar. Martin suggested that they lay it on the floor while he went to find a board and some trestles. He left, and Robert was alone with the corpse. He looked down at it, having an uneasy feeling that the eyes were still looking at him through the closed lids. Some dignity … something was needed. He rearranged the dead man's clothing to hide the scar across the neck as best he could, and then looked around him for some sort of covering. Finding an altar cloth – was that blasphemous? He didn't know, but it was the only thing available so it would have to serve – he knelt down and draped it carefully over the body, taking a few moments to adjust everything properly. Then, satisfied with his handiwork, he rose and left the chapel.

Sir Geoffrey was dreaming.

He'd stayed awake long into the night with his old companion Hugh Fitzjohn, drinking and regaling Sir Roger and some of the other knights with tales of their exploits many years before when they'd been young, back in the time when the sun shone more brightly, the air was fresher and knights were bolder. They had reminisced about their campaigns in France fifteen years before, the heroic deeds they'd performed and the acts of chivalry they'd seen. Eventually they'd all drunk too much and fallen into a slumber on the hall floor, but in his sleep Sir Geoffrey dreamt about some of the less gallant aspects of the campaign. War wasn't about knightly heroics, it was blood and mud and screaming, villages burnt to the ground, and the tear-stained faces of women as they wept over their dead husbands and children. He was back there, was surrounded by the maimed and the dead, they were all rising to stand over him in bloody accusation ... in a cold sweat he half-woke to see the ghostly figure of a boy bent over him, and automatically flung his hand up to guard against the attack.

The boy was shaking his arm. 'Wake up, Sir Geoffrey!'

Slowly he came round, mumbling that it wasn't his fault, that he'd only been following orders ...

The figure was still shaking him. God! But his head felt as though a smith was hammering in it. He struggled to focus and gradually the shape materialised into Simon, still urging him to wake.

'All right, all right! Stop shaking me, boy, I'm awake.' He sat up with a groan, and cut short Simon's excited chatter with a wave of his hand. 'Stop, stop! Get me something to drink, then I will listen to you.' The boy obliged, and he took a deep draught of some leftover ale, looking at the slumbering figures all around him. His companions of the night before were still fast asleep, but others around the hall were starting to stir in the dawn light. Stiffly he tried to rise to his feet, but his back and joints protested: he was really getting too old to be sleeping on hall floors, not when he had a proper bed in a chamber of his own. Irritably he waved away Simon's proffered arm – the day he needed someone to help him to his feet would be the day he gave up on life – and stood. Simon was hopping excitedly from foot to foot, obviously bursting to say something.

He growled at the boy. 'All right, what is it? This had better be good.'

Simon started to talk, but then looked around at the others in the hall, and with a burst of what might even have been tact – the boy really was starting to grow up – he beckoned the knight outside before spilling his news.

'My lord sent me for you, Sir Geoffrey. It's the visiting earl – he's *dead*!'

The knight struggled to take this in. His head was still pounding. The boy couldn't possibly have said what he thought he'd heard. 'What?'

Simon tried again, speaking more slowly. 'The visiting earl, Sir Geoffrey. He's dead. On the roof of the keep. His squire came to tell us and my lord sent me to find you.'

'De Courteville? Dead? You mean, *dead*?'

'Yes, Sir Geoffrey.'

'Here, on the roof of the keep, dead?'

'Yes, Sir Geoffrey.'

'De Courteville?'

Simon rolled his eyes. 'Yes, Sir Geoffrey. My lord sent me to fetch you. Perhaps we should hurry.' Sir Geoffrey felt his arm being tugged, and he allowed the page to lead him towards the keep.

By the time they reached the main door he'd regained some of his faculties. Could the news possibly be true? Could there have been a mistake? The earl would surely not have sent Simon with such a message if it were not true. He continued up the stairs, past the door to the council chamber and the chapel. There he stopped: Martin and one of the men-at-arms were inside, standing over a board and some trestles which they'd obviously just erected. Next to them on the floor lay the figure of a man, covered with a cloth. Sir Geoffrey stepped inside and looked down at the shrouded body for a long moment, taking in the shape and what he could see of the clothes. It was true, then. He could feel no sympathy for the man: he'd known too much about him to waste his feelings on such a devil. But the Lord only knew what the implications for the earl could be once the regent found out. This was going to spell trouble for them all.

———

Martin saw Sir Geoffrey and Simon passing, and left Berold to deal with the body while he strode up the stairs behind them. Robert had already got back to the council chamber and was telling his lord that the news was definitely true; he mentioned the wound on the man's neck and said that he'd probably had his throat slit. Martin shivered at the thought of the body he'd seen, and tried to control his heaving stomach.

The earl reacted quickly to the news, sending Robert out immediately to the gate to tell the guards there to let nobody in or out until further notice, and telling the boy Adam, now sufficiently recovered, to wake de Courteville's brother. The earl's lip curled in contempt as he mentioned the name, and Martin wondered whether the man who hadn't been allowed to marry the Lady Isabelle was now an earl in his own right. He took Simon by the shoulder and pulled him over to stand next to him while the earl conferred with Sir Geoffrey. Simon was pale and Martin kept his arm ready in case it should be needed to steady the boy.

As soon as Robert returned, the earl ordered Simon to shut the door and turned to them all. He looked perfectly in control of himself, and Martin wondered how he'd managed to assume such command so quickly. He supposed it probably came naturally to the high nobility.

The earl summarised in a few clipped phrases. 'As we all now know, the earl of Sheffield is dead. He was found early this morning on the roof of the keep. His throat had been cut, so he was almost certainly murdered.' The others all looked at him, and at each other, in complete silence as he spoke again. 'This is, of course, going to cause problems with the campaign.' He took a deep breath and counted off on his fingers. 'Firstly, the regent is not going to be pleased to find out that one of his most important supporters is dead. Secondly, he may blame me for this, as it happened on my estates when the earl should have been under my protection. And thirdly, let us not forget that we have a large number of the earl's men encamped around the castle now under the command of a man who is, at best, unstable.' The earl still seemed in remarkable control, but Sir Geoffrey looked sombre, and Robert and Simon both wore slightly dazed expressions. The earl stopped to pour himself some wine, and slopped it all over his hand.

He stared at it for a moment, and then put the cup and the jug down carefully before continuing, wiping his hand on the side of his tunic. 'As far as I can see, the best thing to do would be to find out as soon as possible who has committed this crime, prove that it has nothing to do with us, and present the culprit to the regent for punishment when we muster at Newark.' It sounded so simple.

The earl looked at them all one by one. 'Now, how best to deploy my troops?' He turned to Sir Geoffrey. 'You will have to take overall control of this matter. I put it in your charge until it is resolved.'

Sir Geoffrey didn't look happy. 'But my lord, surely I should stay at your side? There is a killer on the loose with who knows what motives, and what if he should try to murder you next? You will need someone to watch your back.'

The earl paused for a moment before replying. 'That may be true, but I will stand by my decision. With all the extra people around you will be needed more than ever to keep control of the garrison and the men. I can take care of myself, and besides … ' his gaze swept over Simon and paused briefly on Martin before settling on Robert, 'I will keep Robert by me to act as my bodyguard, should the need arise.' He looked directly at his squire. 'Are you up to the task?'

Robert seemed struck dumb by emotion, but he nodded fervently.

There was silence for a moment before Sir Geoffrey raised another query.

'My lord, surely one of the most important features of presenting the culprit to the regent is that it should be seen to be the right culprit? Is there not some danger here that he will think that you have simply ordered me to place the blame on some wretch, and that he will still suspect you?'

The earl considered. 'There is something in that. But the sheriff is too far away, and by the time he could get here it will be too late. We must leave for Newark as planned. Besides, he will only want to start talking about taxes again, damn him … ' He paused. 'No, it will have to be someone who's already close at hand. Not you then, although you could still remain in *de facto* charge of the operation. We need someone else to investigate, someone to appear impartial, someone of experience … aha!' He and Sir Geoffrey both looked up at each other at the same time, the earl snapping his fingers. 'By law, any crime committed on my estates comes under the jurisdiction of the bailiff, does it not? So he needs to be the one to investigate.' He folded his arms. 'Have Godric Weaver fetched here.' He was turning away when he caught the knight's gesture. 'What is it?'

'Godric Weaver is ailing, my lord, and has not performed his duties as bailiff for several months.'

The earl seemed taken aback. Martin wondered how he could be unaware of the information: Godric Weaver had been the bailiff as long as he could remember, and the absence of the familiar figure bustling around the castle and estates was all too noticeable. His lord sighed. 'I should remind myself of the advice my father once gave me, to pay attention to the running of my estates and the people who run them, lest I arrive back from a campaign or a visit to court to find financial ruin. I'll have to make more of an effort. So, who has been standing in for him?'

'His son Edwin, my lord.'

'Edwin?' The earl screwed up his face. 'The sandy-haired lad? Is he up to the task?'

Sir Geoffrey considered the question before answering, slowly. 'I believe so, my lord. So far he's been an admirable acting bailiff, and … ' he paused, '… and to be honest, my lord, he's easily the cleverest person in Conisbrough. In fact, he's almost certainly the cleverest person I have ever met. In addition, I've known him since he was a child; he's loyal to you, and I have faith in him.' Martin was shocked – he'd never heard such praise issuing from the stern knight. But, thinking about it, it was probably the truth.

The earl took a long look at the captain of his household. But the knight's gaze did not waver, and finally the earl nodded. He spoke again. 'So be it. Summon Edwin Weaver.'

Edwin was dreaming.

It was a pleasant dream, although afterwards he could not remember any of the details, only that it had been peaceful and nice and he had felt calm as he slept. It was the first undisturbed night's sleep he had enjoyed for many a night. It ended when he felt himself being shaken awake by rough hands. Robert was standing over him, whispering urgently as he came around. He struggled to focus, and realised that it was already light – he must have slept for much longer than usual. What was Robert doing here? In the background his mother was hovering, looking worried.

Edwin finally surfaced from the waves of sleep and became aware of the concern on his friend's face. 'Father?'

Robert whispered again. 'No, not your father, Edwin, he's still asleep. I came to get you because the earl wants to see you.'

That woke him up. His heart lurched. 'The earl? Me? Why?'

'Because you're the bailiff, or as good as.' He saw Robert look round at his mother. 'There has been … some trouble up at the keep, and the earl wants to see you. Now.'

Edwin threw off his blanket and scrabbled around for his clothes. The earl wanted to see him. The earl. He put his shirt on the wrong way round. He took it off and put it on again. He'd seen the earl many times in his life before, of course, but only at some distance, as a figure at the high table in the hall or on the back of one of his fine horses. But actually to stand in front of him, to have been especially summoned into his presence, that was something different. He was suddenly acutely aware that his tunic had a rip in the shoulder, and was neither new nor particularly clean, and he brushed ineffectually at his front, looking helplessly at his mother.

Robert was hurrying him. 'Come on! There's no time to find something else, my lord doesn't like to be kept waiting.' He grabbed Edwin's arm and virtually dragged him to the door. 'Mistress Anne, I'm sorry to cause a fuss, I'll explain it to you later, but we have to go!' He shoved Edwin outside and banged the door shut behind them. As they hurried through the village Edwin tried to get some details from his friend, but Robert refused to elaborate, saying that the earl would explain himself. Edwin tried to think – if the earl wanted to see him personally, it must be something very important, more than just a brawl between soldiers. What could possibly be that bad? A few ideas ran through his head, each worse than the last, and looking at Robert's grim face did not help. A tide of panic threatened to engulf him and by the time they reached the keep he was breathless as much from apprehension as from the speed of their approach. Robert took the stairs two at a time, and all too quickly Edwin was standing outside the door of the earl's council chamber. He gulped.

Robert raised his hand to the door but then stopped and turned to him, taking him by the shoulders. 'Now listen. Don't fret, you've done nothing wrong. You're here because the earl needs something doing, and Sir Geoffrey said you were the best man to do it.'

Edwin was stunned. 'Sir Geoffrey said that about me?'

'Yes. In fact he said that you were probably the cleverest person he had ever met.'

'What?'

Robert slapped him on the back. 'If Sir Geoffrey says it, then it must be right. So, hold your head up and look at me.' Edwin complied. 'Now take a deep breath, and let it out slowly. Are you ready?'

Edwin nodded as Robert knocked on the door, opened it, and ushered him in.

He'd never been in the room before. His first impression was of bright furnishings, but he dared not look around; instead he locked his gaze on the man standing before him. He tried to stop himself from trembling, and was almost surprised to find that the earl was a man much like any other. No, not quite like any other … it wasn't just the clothes, although these were of rich cloth, nor the rings on his fingers, although these were of fine gold: these things were just the outward trappings. The man in front of him was of middle height, probably nearer to forty than thirty years of age, dark hair and beard just starting to be flecked with grey. He was compact and solidly muscled, as one might expect from someone who had been training with weapons all his life, but he carried with him an air of authority that was unmistakeable. He was not just the lord of the Conisbrough estates, he was one of the legendary Plantagenets, one of the most powerful men in the kingdom, and the aura of that responsibility was all around him. You could dress him as a beggar, thought Edwin suddenly, and still it would be clear to anyone with eyes in their head that he was the earl … he realised that he was staring and hastily dropped his gaze.

That broke the spell, and the earl looked away, giving a brief glance at Sir Geoffrey before speaking.

'You understand French?'

'Yes, my lord.'

'Good. Now pay attention.'

Edwin straightened up to listen, and was by turns amazed and increasingly horrified as the tale unfolded: the murder of an earl was far, far worse than anything he might have imagined himself. But what had this to do with him?

The earl was continuing. 'As you may imagine, Weaver, this is a matter which is not merely important to me, but also to the lords of the realm, to the regent and even the king. Which is why it must be dealt with satisfactorily.' Edwin felt a jolt go through him at the mention of the word 'Weaver' – that was his father's name, not his. Dear Lord, if the earl thought he could step into his boots just like that … and he still couldn't fathom why he should be standing listening to such a tale. What did it have to do with him, all this talk of earls and kings? So the blow, when it fell, was like a blacksmith's hammer. 'So, are you up to the task?'

Edwin gaped. 'Me, my lord?'

'Yes, you. You are the bailiff, are you not? Any crime committed in my demesne is your concern?'

The room started to spin. He was tumbling into an abyss; he couldn't say a word. Sir Geoffrey stepped in, speaking slowly and clearly. 'Edwin, if your father was able, he would be performing this service for the earl. He is not able. You won't be acting alone, will have help from the earl's household. But we need you to do this.'

Edwin recovered slightly, his mind already at work. Who might have killed the earl? It must have been someone who was within the walls last night, and he supposed it would be easy enough to find out who had been present ... after some thought, the task didn't look so impossible. Given the help of the household and the backing of Sir Geoffrey, he was sure he could work it out. All he needed were his wits and plenty of time. As long as he had the leisure to think, he would be fine. His mind set, he turned to the earl. 'I'm sorry not to have answered straight away, my lord. I am your loyal servant, and of course I will undertake any task you require me to.'

The earl looked at him again for a long moment, and Edwin forced himself to meet that slate-grey stare without wavering. 'Good. You will report directly to Sir Geoffrey, who will give you anything you need, and we will find the culprit.' Edwin essayed a clumsy bow and started to turn, but the earl hadn't finished. 'You have until sundown tomorrow.'

Chapter Five

Edwin tripped over the doorstep as he left the room. Sundown tomorrow? Why, that left him only a day and a half in which to discover everything he needed to know. What would he do? How would he even start?

He looked about him and realised that he'd wandered blindly into the earl's private chapel. It was cool in there, with coloured light filtering in through the window to make strange patterns on the floor. A shrouded form lay on a board, supported by trestles. Edwin stood for a long moment looking down at the figure: this, then, was what all the fuss was about, was why the earl had caused him to be awakened from his pleasant dream. I suppose I should look at the body, he thought to himself, after all, I don't even know how he died, and that's something I'll need to find out before I can discover who killed him. I will look at the body. I must.

He reached out his hand towards the cloth which covered the figure, and then stopped, unsure. How should he go about this? What was he supposed to do? Should he say a prayer over the dead man? Or was that not suitable? He compromised, and, sending up a silent thought to the Almighty, he pulled the cloth away.

After a few moments he opened his eyes.

He supposed he should start some sort of examination of the body, to see what he could discover. He would just have to put his natural revulsion to one side. He took a deep breath. Well, there were no obvious wounds which might have caused the man's death, no crushing blow to the head or gaping stab wounds; the clothes were whole, bore no slash marks. Not a fight or a frenzied attack, then, but something else. The jaw was starting to gape open, revealing that the earl lacked two teeth on the left-hand side of his mouth, but Edwin didn't think that had anything to do with the murder: he'd noticed the same gap when the man had smiled during his welcome by the earl yesterday. No, he needn't concern himself with that.

Edwin's mind was already focused on his task, his distaste dissipating as he bent closer over the body and touched it, looking for any mark. What was that wound on the neck? Here was something …

'What in the name of God are you doing?' The hysterical voice made Edwin jump, and before he could recover himself he was seized painfully by the hair and dragged backwards away from the body. 'You filthy animal! My brother has been foully murdered and yet even his body is not safe from pilferers!' Edwin's eyes were watering, and it felt as though his hair was being pulled out by the roots, the skin being torn from his head. He tried to explain, but couldn't make himself heard over the tirade. 'How dare you do such a thing! I will have you flogged! I will kill you myself!' The man drew a knife. Edwin was paralysed with fear. Oh Lord, he thought, through the pain in his scalp, the first time the earl has ever asked me to do anything and I'm going to get myself killed before I've even started. What will my father say? He closed his eyes and flinched as the knife was raised.

The blow never fell. Realising that he had felt no pain other than that in his head, Edwin risked opening one eye, to see that the man's arm had been caught by Sir Geoffrey, who had entered the chapel silently. With contemptuous ease the knight forced the arm back and twisted the knife away from Edwin's assailant, and it fell with a clatter to the floor.

Sir Geoffrey spoke. 'Let go of him.'

Walter de Courteville, for it was he, seemed momentarily surprised by the strength of the old man, and he sought refuge in bluster. 'How dare you! This ruffian was robbing my brother's body. Is it not enough that he should be murdered within your lord's domain and under his protection, but his body must be desecrated too?' He tried unsuccessfully to free his right arm, still held by Sir Geoffrey, but eventually admitted defeat and released his left hand from Edwin's hair. Edwin fell back and gingerly put his hands to his head to make sure it was still there.

Sir Geoffrey dropped Walter's arm. 'I am very sorry for your brother's death, Sir Walter, as are we all. But this is no cutpurse: he is the earl's bailiff, and was merely viewing the body as part of his search for the truth of what happened.'

Walter looked incredulously at Edwin. 'Bailiff? This boy? Is that the best the earl can come up with? You jest, surely.'

Sir Geoffrey was speaking again. 'It is no jest, I assure you. The earl has complete confidence in his man. Now, if you would like to come with me, my lord will see you now … '

Brusquely he shepherded Walter out of the room, but Edwin barely noticed. He dropped the cloth back over the body and sat dejectedly on the floor, all the skin on his head stinging, as he realised that the man had been right. How was he, Edwin, commoner and erstwhile bailiff's assistant, who had never in his life travelled more than twenty miles from Conisbrough, ever going to solve the riddle of the death of one of the most important men in the kingdom? It was hopeless. He was a joke. The black demons lurked again in the corners of his mind.

He stared into the distance until another voice spoke from the doorway.

'Edwin?'

He looked up to see Martin looming over him as he stepped into the chapel. A large bruise marked one side of his face, but Edwin was too bemused to wonder how he had come by it. Martin was looking from Edwin to the body and back, but misread the reason for his dejection. 'Horrible, isn't it?' His face registered sympathy as he extended a hand and helped Edwin to his feet. 'I have to admit I was sick when I saw it, and then I had to help Robert carry it all the way down here.'

Edwin was still dazed. 'Robert?'

Martin misunderstood again. 'No, he can't be here to help you, the earl wants him to stay with him, so he sent me instead.' He paused, unsure, hesitated, and started again, the words coming out in a rush. 'Look, I know I'm not as clever or useful as Robert, but I'll try to help you as much as I can – I'll do whatever you say.'

Edwin was jerked back into reality. 'What? You, help me? Do what I say? But … '

'Yes, my lord has said that I should help you however I can. I'm excused most of my other duties until you've found the killer.'

Edwin looked up at the younger man, who was gazing at him earnestly. There was something fundamentally wrong in this. 'But I can't give you orders! You're the earl's squire! And I'm just … '

Martin finished the sentence for him. 'You're just the man who's in charge. And I'm used to taking orders. So, what do you want me to do?'

Edwin felt very uncomfortable. How could he issue commands to a member of the nobility? Still, if it was the earl's wish then there was nothing he could do about it. And an extra head and pair of hands might come in very useful, although the thought did cross his mind momentarily that it was a shame it wasn't Robert. 'All right then,' he sounded more decisive than he felt, 'You can start by coming with me to talk to the porter.'

They started down the stairs, with Edwin hoping that he might begin to feel more positive about the whole thing. He wasn't alone. But still, how was he to work his way through this? On top of everything else, the responsibility of finding a murderer on the earl's behalf threatened to crush him. He could feel his shoulders bowing under the weight already, and he hoped they wouldn't break.

Walter de Courteville's mind had been working furiously ever since he had been awakened by Adam, and the possibilities raced through his mind as he made his way across the inner ward to the keep. How should he act? What was the best way to turn the situation to his advantage? Clearly, the most important thing would be to secure the wardship of his young nephew and assume control over the estates: after all, who was the best person to look after the boy but his own uncle? And just four years old; Walter would have control over the lands for many years, and who knows what might happen in that time …

It was at this point that he had pushed past a guard coming down the stairs, reached the chapel and seen the figure leaning over his brother's body. He stood for a moment looking at the corpse, but could feel nothing other than excitement at his own prospects. However, perhaps now was the time to practise the grieving brother act which he would need for the foreseeable future, a mix of sadness coupled with much anger and perhaps a touch of righteous indignation at the insult to his family name. He prepared himself mentally before stepping into the room.

On the whole he felt it had gone quite well, apart from the interference of the old man at the end – and I'll find a way to pay him back for that some day, he thought – the boy had appeared thoroughly intimidated. Walter stood a little straighter, pleased at the thought that someone had been afraid of him. Or had he overdone it slightly? He would have to rethink before he went in to meet with the earl …

But the laughable news that the boy was the bailiff had set other thoughts scuttling through his mind. Supposing nobody ever discovered who had killed Ralph? This was surely a possibility, given the shabby peasant who had been given the task of finding out. If so, might it be possible to intimate to the regent that Warenne had something to do with it? After all, the murder had been committed within the grounds of his castle, so he was certainly to blame for failing to protect his guest, at the very least. But if suspicion should fall on him for the greater crime …

well, surely the regent couldn't allow a man who had murdered a fellow earl to remain in control of such power? Especially one who had not exactly been a pillar of loyalty throughout the past year or so, and whose motives might be open to question? And might there not be an opening there for a clever man, one who might perform some act of service – yet to be determined, but he would think of something – for the crown?

Oh, this just got better and better. A whole plan sprang into his mind. The future was looking rosy, he thought, as he followed Sir Geoffrey towards the earl's quarters. The knight stopped to let him pass into the room and he carefully schooled his face into the correct expression before stepping through the door.

———⊙———

Adam sat in silence, staring at the wall. His fingers clutched at the blanket which was draped around his shoulders, drawing it closer about him as he shivered. So cold … his mind kept going back to the events of the dawn, recounting them over and over. Once more he saw the distorted features, the silent scream, the wound on the neck, which his imagination made ever wider, and those awful, staring eyes … huddled alone in a corner of the great chamber, Adam buried his head in his hands and wept at the horror.

He was disturbed by the sound of the door opening, and looked up to see David entering the room with a purposeful gait. He stopped as he noticed Adam and spoke, his voice as scornful as always.

'What's the matter with you?'

Shaken out of his daze by the very crassness of the question, Adam was roused to defend himself.

'How can you say that?' His voice was squeaking; he needed to control it better. He tried again. 'I found our lord's body this morning, after he'd had his throat cut. What could be worse?'

David shrugged, continuing on his way across the room. 'Probably no more than he deserved,' he said, as he disappeared behind the partition into the bedchamber. 'And people die all the time. What is there to make a fuss about?'

Adam bit back a reply and rose, curious. 'What are you doing?' He pushed past the partition to see the other boy busily pulling items out of a wooden chest, humming to himself as he did so. 'Those belong to our lord!'

David grinned, without pausing in his task. 'Not any more – and we deserve something as a reward for working for him all these years. Here,' he considered a fine tunic and threw it towards Adam, 'I'll even let you have some.'

Adam put his hand out automatically to catch the garment, but then let it fall to the floor as though it had bitten him. 'I won't take it!' He was filled with outrage.

David shrugged once more. 'You're probably right. It wouldn't fit you anyway, you're such a puny, undersized weakling. And anyway,' he turned back to rummage deep in the chest, before pulling out a chinking purse, 'there are much more useful things to find.'

He weighed the purse reflectively and made to stow it safely in his tunic, but Adam knocked it out of his hand. Now David looked surprised. 'What? Oh please, don't tell me you're defending his honour. After what he did to you?' He stretched out his hand to Adam's face and turned it contemptuously so the bruised side was towards him, his voice becoming threatening. 'And believe me, I'll do a lot worse if you don't get out of my way.' He shoved Adam away, roughly.

Adam was in two minds. It was true, he'd hated and feared his master while he was alive, but surely the dead deserved some respect? This disdain before the man was even in his grave was somehow unfitting, and stealing his possessions was obscene. His father would be ashamed if he thought Adam hadn't defended what was right. He took a deep breath and prepared to stand up for himself for the first time.

He was no match for the ruthless David, of course, and he found himself on the floor within moments, the larger boy straddling him, fists hammering into Adam's face as he sought in vain to raise his arms to defend himself. The pain was terrible, the beating going on and on, and the room was disappearing in a red haze before he finally realised that the weight on him was being lifted. He squinted up through half-closed eyes to see David standing over him, threateningly. Adam made to cover his face again, but the other turned swiftly and picked up the discarded purse, before turning back. He took out a coin and flung it down. It bounced off the floorboards before coming to rest next to Adam's prone body.

'Here. I won't let it be said that I didn't give you your share. You'll never find another knight to serve anyway, for who would want a whining child who's afraid of the dark?' He paused, and then administered a vicious kick in the ribs which left Adam gasping, before stalking out of the room.

Adam lay still for a long moment, waiting to see if he would die. When he didn't, he waited again for the pain to subside so he could move. Eventually he managed to raise himself to his hands and knees, and tried to wipe some of the blood out of his eyes, but he only succeeded in smearing it everywhere. Whimpering, he looked around for a cloth, but he didn't dare touch any of his master's clothes which were scattered around the bedchamber. Instead he turned and crawled back to his blanket and rubbed it gingerly over his face until he could see. Tentatively he explored his face with his fingers. Was his nose broken? He thought not – he'd managed to turn his head from side to side to take most of the blows around his cheekbones and eyes. One eye was rapidly swelling and closing, but he still had some sight in the other, enough to see his way as he stood up, staggered, and limped across the room. On the table he found a half-finished cup of wine and drained it, wincing as the liquid burned the split in his lip.

Feeling slightly more alive, he was able to make his way out of the room and the building, before sitting down on the outside flight of steps to consider his position. Whichever way he looked at it, it was bad. A squire whose knight died before he'd finished his training would be very lucky to find another, especially if that squire didn't come from a powerful family. He supposed he could try and find service with his lord's brother … it wasn't ideal, but at least he might be able to retain his ambition of becoming a knight. But what if David decided to do the same thing? He was the senior, was bound to be considered more useful, and was by a long way the stronger and the better of the two in combat and sport. And anyway, did he really want to tie himself to another member of the de Courteville family? Perhaps he could go back to his father's household – as a younger son there would be nothing for him to inherit, but at least he'd have a roof over his head, and he might be able to find work in due course as a retainer of his brother. But it wouldn't be the same as being a knight …

A shadow fell across him and he looked up to see Earl William's squire gazing down at him, the one who had shouted at him yesterday. Adam ducked and tried half-heartedly to hide his face so that the other would not see his injuries, but it was too late. The squire's expression, however, registered only sympathy as he sat down.

'Do you want to tell me about it?' Adam shrugged and said nothing. 'Was it your lord's other squire?'

Adam remained silent and the other squire – was his name Robert? – sighed. 'I see.'

He put one hand under Adam's chin and gently turned his face to the light so he could see the full extent of the damage. 'Honestly, a fair beating, justly administered for a fault, is one thing, but this is another.'

Adam winced at the touch of the other's hand. 'Is it bad?'

'Well, let me see. One of your eyes is completely closed, and the other has blood flowing into it from this cut on your eyebrow. Another cut on one of your cheekbones is pouring blood, as is your nose, and the split lip doesn't look too good, either. Yes, I'd say it was bad.' He looked again. 'Oh, and one ear is red and swollen, but that doesn't look as fresh as your other wounds. And from the way you're sitting and holding your side, there's no doubt some damage there as well.'

Adam listened to the enumeration and wondered if any of the injuries would cause him permanent damage. His eyes were the main thing: any other scars he could live with, but if he couldn't see then he would never get another master.

Robert hauled him to his feet, and he whimpered. 'Come with me.'

'Where are we going?'

'To see someone who can help. Come.'

He supported Adam as they turned to go towards the great hall. Once inside they went through the hall, where preparations for dinner were being made, through the service area and into some kind of office at the end. The man who was there turned to greet them, and Adam shrank back in fear as he saw the disfigured face. The man limped closer and loomed over them. Adam flinched, but Robert spoke briskly.

'Master William, I believe we need your wife's skills.'

The man took one glance at Adam and nodded. 'Aye, you may be right. Stay here and I'll send someone to fetch her.'

He left the room and Robert made Adam sit at the table. After they had sat in silence for a while a woman bustled in. Robert spoke in Adam's ear. 'Have no fear – she's skilled with herbs and poultices, and won't say anything to anyone.'

On seeing Adam the woman exclaimed, and quickly started pulling items out of the scrip she was carrying, keeping up a comforting flow of talk as she did so, to keep his mind off the sting of his injuries.

Adam winced in the anticipation of more pain as she approached him with the rag, but her fingers were gentle as she wiped the blood from his face. She hissed under her breath as she unearthed the damage which had been done, asked Robert sharply what had been going on, but he refused to elaborate, staying back from the table to allow her room to work. She spoke kind-heartedly to Adam, assuring him that he would mend soon enough, as she continued to wipe his face. Adam could not remember the last time somebody had been so tender with him, and he gave himself up gladly to her ministrations, allowing her to finish cleaning and dab a salve onto his wounds to stop the bleeding. It stung, but after what he had been through, it was heaven. When she'd finished, she gently pushed his hair back from his face in a gesture that reminded him of his mother, and he felt calm for the first time since he had woken up in the dark so many hours ago.

Thinking about that made his mind start again on the endless cycle of the events of the morning, and he hastily cast his mind back further to try and cut off the remembrance. How eager he'd been yesterday when he arrived at Conisbrough, as he always was when visiting a new place. He'd been impressed by the sight of the bright white keep, dominating the surrounding landscape. He had unloaded his master's belongings, or such of them as he would need for a couple of days' stay; the rest were for the campaign and had stayed with the remainder of the baggage, down in the encampment outside the castle. Then there had been that incident with David and the girl, but he didn't want to think of that. He'd eaten well at the evening meal, enjoying the meat pasties and marchpane which had been left over at the high table after the lords had finished eating. After dinner he had returned to the great chamber and started to prepare everything ready for his lord to retire for the night. Lord Ralph had come back in, furious, his tunic covered in wine. He had shouted …

'The letter!'

'What?' He had spoken aloud, and he looked round to see everyone staring at him in surprise. He hastened to explain.

'Last evening, after the meal – my lord came back to his chamber and found a letter on his bed. He didn't know who it was from.'

Robert was suddenly all attention, moving towards him to question him keenly. Where had this letter been found? Who had delivered it? What did it say? This might be very important. Where was it now?

Adam didn't know the answers to any of these questions, and he sought to draw the memory from his mind. Where had Lord Ralph put the letter? Where might it be now? He forgot his pain, but remembered to thank the kindly woman for her aid. He hoped he would see her again before he left, and she echoed the sentiment, looking after the boys as they left the office and hurried through the hall and back outside.

The letter was nowhere to be found. Robert and Adam had ransacked the whole of the great chamber and the kists of clothes and belongings in the bedchamber, but the letter remained stubbornly hidden. Adam asked himself over and over again where it might be, but all he could remember was that his lord had read the missive and then put it in the pouch at his belt. The pouch was here – it was among the first things they had found, still attached to the fine belt which he had worn to supper in the hall – but it was empty. Now they sat, surrounded by piles of belongings, at a complete loss.

'I suppose someone has checked my lord's ... checked the body?'

Robert nodded. 'I carried him down from the roof with Martin, and he had no pouch at his belt. He was wearing plain clothes, the sort you might put on for travelling. Not the finery he wore at supper.'

'No, he took that off when he returned to the chamber – the tunic was a new one, but he had spilt wine down the front so he took it off.'

'Oh.'

They sat in silence until Robert rose with some reluctance. 'Well, I'm not doing much good here – I should get back and see if my lord needs me for anything. If I get the chance, I'll tell Edwin about the letter.'

'Who's Edwin?'

'The bailiff. He's under orders from the earl to find out who killed your master. I hope he's having better luck than we are.'

———

Edwin was having no luck. He and Martin had spoken to the day porter, the man whose task it was to look after the gate to the inner ward, but of course he'd been asleep during the previous night, so they'd had to wake the night porter, who wasn't pleased to have been disturbed. He was in an ill temper as he went through the events of the evening. At nightfall he'd closed the huge wooden gates and barred them, and he hadn't opened them until dawn. There was a small postern in one of the gates which would admit a single person, so Edwin was hopeful that someone might have entered that way; the porter, however, was adamant that there had been no visitors. And he would have known, as in order to admit them he would have had to leave the small cosy room in the gatehouse where he'd been warming his hands by the fire and venture out into the dark to unbar the door.

Martin and Edwin left the gatehouse and walked back into the inner ward. Edwin was disconsolate. The first time he'd ever met the earl in the flesh, the first time an important task had been given to him, and he was going to fail in it. How on earth was he supposed to find out who had killed the visiting earl? Or why? There were so many things he didn't know. He walked in grim silence, lengthening his stride to try and keep up with Martin.

As they crossed the ward, they were waylaid by Berold. His face carried an expression of concern which was so unusual that Edwin stopped in his tracks.

'Berold? What is it?'

'I – '

He paused, awkwardly.

'What I mean is … '

'Yes?'

'That is – '

Edwin had never seen him like this. 'Well spit it out then!'

Berold hesitated, looked round him, and finally managed to get some words out. 'You're looking into this murder?'

Edwin nodded. 'Yes.'

'Then there's something I need to tell you.'

Edwin's heart was in his mouth. Was his luck about to change? But the revelation, if there was one, never came. Berold looked over Edwin's shoulder and seemed to spy something behind him. Abruptly he stopped. 'It doesn't matter.' He turned and left at a run.

Martin looked puzzled. 'What was all that about?'

Edwin shook his head. 'I have no idea.' He too was mystified. What had Berold been about to tell him? And more importantly, why had he stopped?

He had no idea how to proceed. This was all going wrong, just because he didn't know what to do. What he needed was more experience, but how was he going to get any if he didn't succeed in this? Then it struck him that, of course, he did have an older, wiser head to make use of, if he could but force himself to go there once more. He would. He must.

He stopped and turned back towards the gate, waving Martin to continue on his way as he made to accompany him.

'You go round and try to find if there's any other way to get into the inner ward. There shouldn't be, obviously, but see if there's the smallest way that anyone else could have got in last night.' He took a deep breath. 'I'm going to go and visit my father.'

Martin had just finished his inspection of the inner ward when he heard Robert shouting to him.

'Our lord has asked me to check and clean his armour. Come, spare a few moments to help me and you can tell me about what you've been doing.'

Martin was unsure whether he should report straight back to Edwin, but he guessed that Edwin might want to spend a little more uninterrupted time with his father. Besides, he could see that Robert was itching to find out what had been discovered, so he agreed. It was unfair, after all, that the senior squire hadn't been entrusted with the task, to say nothing of the fact that he was Edwin's best friend and would clearly like to be helping him in his duty. Martin himself wasn't sure whether he'd be of any real assistance in the investigation: he would probably just mess things up, and prove a hindrance rather than a help. Still, here was a physical task to which he was well accustomed, and perhaps if he spoke to Robert about the murder, he might be able to come up with some useful suggestions. His mood lightened.

The two of them spread all the equipment out around them in the sunshine. The work ahead of them wasn't too arduous – Robert, with his usual efficiency, checked the equipment every so often to make sure it wasn't falling into disrepair – so there would be leisure for talking. As the two of them put all of the mail items into a barrel and rolled them round with vinegar and sand to remove any traces of rust, Martin told of the events of the morning so far, such as they were. Robert listened carefully, and made some choice comments about the behaviour of the dead earl's brother while they laid all the mail out on cloths on the ground. He started meticulously to clean the remaining grains of sand off the hauberk, the great mail shirt which covered the earl's body, his arms and hands, and his legs down to the knees, and to check it minutely for any links which might be missing or damaged. The smallest weakness in the hauberk might result in it tearing when struck by lance or sword, causing serious injury or even death to the earl, so the task was an important one. He agreed with Martin that the lack of information provided by the porter wasn't an auspicious start, but added that he was sure that he and Edwin would soon find out more.

'But what if – ' Martin started and then stopped again, afraid of what the reaction might be if he disclosed his fears. He desperately wanted to be a knight one day, and surely they didn't admit to weakness? He put his head down and busied himself cleaning the chausses – mail leggings which would protect the earl from cuts or thrusts while he was on horseback.

Robert seemed content to wait until he was ready to speak again. There was still plenty to do: around them lay several lances, the heads of which would need sharpening; the earl's great helm, which would be polished until Martin could see his face in it; the shield with its blue and yellow chequered face to be cleaned, and the leather straps on the back to be tested, and then either oiled or replaced; and the earl's sword and dagger in their scabbards on a fine leather belt. They too would be sharpened and polished.

As they worked, Martin decided that he couldn't keep the words inside him any longer. Normally he preferred to keep his own counsel and not go jangling about his thoughts all the time like some people, but now it all came out in a rush: his fears about being able to help Edwin, his worries about the effects on the earl if they failed, and also his apprehension concerning the forthcoming campaign. He spilled it all out and then waited in some trepidation for the response. He couldn't meet Robert's eye.

'Look at me.'

Unwillingly, Martin obeyed, waiting for the censure. But he was surprised to see only sympathy. 'Do you know, you're so much bigger than me that I often forget that you're younger. I'm nervous too, you know, so it must be just as bad for you.' He shrugged. 'There is not much I can say on the subject of the murder, and as for the campaign, well, I've never taken part in one either, or at least not a proper one.'

Martin wasn't fully reassured, but at least he wasn't the only one who was scared.

Robert was continuing, telling him not to belittle his own abilities, but he let most of it wash over him, his relief growing stronger. Then they fell quiet, a companionable silence they had often shared.

They continued with their work. Martin had just finished polishing the earl's helm and Robert was applying a final coat of oil to the sword, when Sir Geoffrey appeared. Robert made as if to rise, but the knight gestured for them both to continue with their task while he looked closely at the rest of the equipment, shooting off some brisk questions.

'The hauberk?'

'I can't find a blemish in it, Sir Geoffrey, nor a loose rivet.' Robert had inspected it in the tiniest detail, but all the links appeared to be intact and in good condition – perhaps not surprising, as the hauberk was such an expensive and valuable item that it was looked after very carefully.

The knight grunted his agreement. 'The shield?'

'The guige is fine, Sir Geoffrey,' Martin gestured at the long strap which would hold the shield around the earl's neck when it wasn't in use, 'but one of the enarmes needs replacing.' He had already removed the largest of the three loops through which the earl would put his arm when holding the shield, and had put the shield aside for the armourer's attention.

'Good.'

Sir Geoffrey himself was now pausing awkwardly, and Martin looked at him in surprise, for it was rare indeed for the knight to be so discomfited. He was wondering how to react when a sudden scream pierced the sunlit morning, making his heart miss a beat. Before he could even think about reacting, Sir Geoffrey had drawn his sword; he jerked his head at the squires even as he turned to run. 'Down in the outer ward. Come!'

The cottage was dark after the brightness of the day, and Edwin had to blink and adjust his eyesight before he continued into the room. His mother came forward, clearly concerned, asking why he had been called away so suddenly by Robert that morning. What could he tell her that wouldn't add to her worries? He decided on a partial truth.

'Don't fret, mother, it was just that Sir Geoffrey wanted to ask me to continue acting for father while he is ill. There are a few things I need to ask him about, though – is he awake?'

Her reply was cut off by a voice from the bedchamber. 'Of course I am awake – and do not speak of me as though I was … ' it was cut off by a fit of coughing. His mother looked worried again, but Edwin touched her arm to indicate that he would see to it, gritted his teeth and went through to the bedchamber.

He was shocked at what he saw: his father was lying in the bed as he expected, but the coughs were racking his wasted body so much that they shook him from his head to his feet, and he was doubled over in pain. Edwin hastened to support him, putting one arm around his shoulders to hold him until the coughs subsided. The old man wiped his mouth with his sleeve, and Edwin was chilled to see smears of red on the cloth. Dear Lord.

'Father … '

His father held up one hand to forestall him, putting a finger to his lips and gasping as he fought for breath in order to speak. After a few moments he managed a hoarse whisper. 'I have been trying to keep this from your mother, so as to lessen her worry, although she is bound to find out soon. But you will not tell her, do you understand?' Edwin nodded as the hand on his arm gripped more tightly. The rasping continued. 'I am not long for this world, but I will give her another few days of peace before she has to become a widow.' The effort of speaking had left him weak again, and he fell back on to his pillow, exhausted, to close his eyes. Edwin did not try to comfort him – or himself – with false platitudes about recovering, for all men knew what it meant to cough blood. Time was running out. Suddenly he did not want to burden the sick man with the cares of the morning, so he sat in silence, helplessly holding his father's hand and looking down at him. The fear became all-consuming again, gnawing, threatening to eat him from the inside out. But what could he do? He must fight to keep it down.

His mother entered the room quietly and spoke to Edwin. 'Can you stay for a while? I have to go to the mill to collect the flour, or we won't have any bread tomorrow.' Edwin looked at her, determined that she shouldn't see his dread and unwilling to speak lest he disturb his father, who was breathing hoarsely. His mother had dark circles under her eyes and looked exhausted, and no wonder; he would like to help her, relieve some of the burden, but how could he explain that to the earl? That he couldn't take on a task given to him by one of the most important men in the kingdom because he wanted to help his mother? It was impossible. Still, he could at least wait here now and let her get some air. He might be in fear, but she must be experiencing even worse. He would be strong.

'Yes, I can stay,' he replied, quietly. 'There's no need to hurry back – why don't you tarry a while out of doors and get some air? I'll stay here until you get back.'

She gave him a wan smile and left, and he turned back to watch his father sleep. However, as soon as she had left the cottage, his father's eyes opened. Amazing how they were still as bright and alert as ever, despite the failing body they served.

'Has she gone?' The voice was still whispered, forced.

'Yes.'

'Good. My dearest Anne. If she had thought me awake, she would not have left, and she needs to get out of the house.'

Edwin almost smiled. Even now, they were both so busy thinking of each other that neither had time to spare for themselves. It had ever been that way.

Father continued, each word a struggle. 'Now, you must tell me of this morning. You may be able to fool your mother with this tale of Sir Geoffrey, but I know that the earl does not send his senior squire out on such a trivial errand. So speak.'

It was a relief to be able to spill all the news of the morning, the strange events, the task laid upon him, the worries and feelings of inadequacy. Edwin hadn't meant to reveal those, but once he started recounting the tale he couldn't stop, and the words tumbled over each other as he explained his actions, and his failure to discover anything thus far.

Eventually he stopped and looked down at his father, who was again lying with his eyes closed. Edwin at first thought that he had fallen into a slumber, and felt guilty for loading him with such cares, but as he made to get up from the side of the bed the old man spoke, and it was clear that he had heard and understood every word.

'How was he killed?'

Edwin was hesitant. 'I – I'm not sure. There's a scar … it looks as though his throat was cut.'

'Have you found the weapon that did it?'

'N-no.' Oh dear, that was probably the first thing he should have looked for. He felt foolish.

The questions went on, punctuated by rasping coughs and harsh breathing. Where was the earl's own knife? Had he been armed himself? What was he doing at the top of the keep anyway? Who else could have gained access to it? Had anyone entered the inner ward after sundown?

Grasping hold of something he knew, Edwin interrupted the flow. 'No, I have asked the porter and he said there were no visitors.' He felt pleased with himself – at least he'd got something right. But it seemed he had failed in this, too, for his sharp-witted father had perceived the error.

'I did not ask you whether there were any visitors – I asked whether anyone had entered the castle. Old Warin might not have mentioned anyone to you if it were someone familiar to him.'

Edwin was ashamed. Why hadn't he thought of that? How was he ever to find the killer if he couldn't even get the simple things right?

His father took his hand. 'Lord, but how young you are. What an age to have something like this thrust upon you, when a seasoned man would be having trouble. Still, you have taken it on, and now you must square your shoulders and carry the burden.'

He coughed again, bringing up more blood, but he seemed determined to continue speaking through the pain. 'All those years ago … I watched your first tottering steps … and now I wish more than anything that I could … that I could be at your side while you take your first … faltering paces into the world of manly responsibility. But it is … not to be.'

This time he could hardly stop the coughing at all. Edwin was concerned that he might try to speak again, but he didn't. He lay there, rasping but seeming to gain no air, struggling like a drowning man. As Edwin watched, his eyes closed and the sleep came over him again, the effort of so much talking clearly having worn him out. But just as Edwin thought about releasing the hand he held, it gripped him all the tighter and the eyes opened again.

'You must act quickly. Make a plan and carry it out.' He gasped again, seeking another breath. 'Do not worry when you have to question somebody – you have the full authority of the earl behind you.' Another breath. And another. 'There is someone here, in the castle or the village, who has killed in cold blood, and that sort will not hesitate to kill again.' This time the exhaustion washed over him more fully, his voice fading. 'Be careful, my son.' One last effort. 'Trust nobody … '

Edwin looked down on his sleeping father, the words striking a chill into his heart. Trust nobody … he stared into space for a long moment, imagining the darkness creeping in from the corners. So vivid was his imagination that a giant shadow really did seem to fall over him, and he gasped and turned.

It was Martin, who had entered so silently that Edwin hadn't heard him. He was about to express relief when he noticed the grim expression on the other's face.

Martin got straight to the point. 'You need to come back to the castle. There's been another murder.'

Chapter Six

Edwin had a mass of questions in his head as he followed Martin up to the castle, but the squire was setting such a pace that he didn't have time to ask any of them. He merely followed, losing his breath, until he was led around to the stable. Outside there was a press of curious grooms and a sobbing maidservant, one of the ones who dealt with the castle laundry.

Martin elucidated. 'She found the body.'

Edwin was confused. 'The maid? But what was she doing in the stable?'

The girl looked at him, blushed furiously, and fled. The smirks of many of the grooms followed her. Edwin didn't know what to say. 'Oh.' He tried to pull himself together and ask something sensible as they stepped inside. 'A body? But how do you know it was murder?'

Martin merely pointed him in the direction of one of the stalls, where Sir Geoffrey and Robert were looking down at a body. It was the knight who answered him. 'Well, unless he managed to stab himself in the back … '

Edwin moved into the entrance to the stall and looked down. A man-at-arms lay face down, a gaping wound in his back, blood everywhere. Oh dear Lord, that form looked familiar … 'Berold?' His voice was shaking.

Sir Geoffrey nodded his assent.

Edwin reeled. He had seen the man only an hour ago, when he'd seemed anxious about something. He'd wanted to tell Edwin something, perhaps something about the visiting earl's death? And now … he looked at all the blood, oozing stickily out over the floor, already attracting the hordes of flies which were ever-present in the stable, and knew that he was about to lose the contents of his stomach.

He continued retching long after there was nothing else to come up, but once the spasms became a little less frequent he was able to stand again.

Sir Geoffrey was still looking at the body, and he spoke to Edwin with a rough sympathy, saying only that one had to get used to such things. He bent to touch the corpse. 'Still soft, still warm. This didn't happen long ago.'

Edwin was aware of that, but he said nothing. What if he'd made Berold stay? What if he'd compelled him to say what was on his mind? Would he still be alive? Was he in part responsible for this death because he hadn't been quick enough to see what was on Berold's mind? He retreated into his own thoughts, hearing Sir Geoffrey talk to Robert, but not taking it in.

'What do you think? Connected to the earl's death? Or just some kind of fight? We must certainly find out who did this, but it must not get in the way of the main investigation.'

In his head, Edwin was sure that the two deaths were connected, but for some reason he was unwilling to say anything until he was more sure. Somehow he felt that the knight would not want to know all the inner workings of his mind; he would merely want to be presented with the right culprit and a brief explanation. What Edwin really needed to do was think. There would be logic in this somewhere, but at the moment he didn't know where. His head hurt and he needed some air.

Sir Geoffrey was continuing to talk to Robert, speaking as though Edwin wasn't there, which in some ways he supposed was true. He tried not to listen, tried to concentrate on the elusive thought which kept slipping out of reach, but the knight wasn't adept at lowering his voice.

'Just look at him: he's a wreck already. I suppose it was only to be expected: he's been dragged in front of the earl, confronted with the body of one of the most important men in the kingdom, and told to find the murderer. And now here's another unexpected corpse, someone he knew – was Berold not a native of Conisbrough, so they might have grown up together? – who's been struck down in his blood.'

Robert murmured something, but Edwin didn't hear what it was. Again, the knight's voice was stronger. 'It's understandable that he should be bewildered, but he's going to have to snap out of it quickly if he's to achieve his goal before the earl needs to march. I hope to the Lord that I didn't give the earl bad advice when I proposed Edwin as the man to take over.'

This time Robert spoke more clearly. 'Perhaps he just needs to get over the shock. He's not used to this kind of thing.'

Sir Geoffrey grunted. 'Doubtless. He just needs some time and space to think, and then he'll work this out.' He took Edwin by the arm and started to steer him out of the building, talking all the while to Robert over his shoulder. 'But this must be stopped before it happens again. Another life gone, probably needlessly. This is not nearly as important as the other death, and it's probable they're not connected, but a culprit still needs to be found. It will no doubt turn out to be one of the villagers or one of the other men-at-arms, but there will need to be a trial and a hanging. In the meantime this death is merely a nuisance.'

He pushed Edwin into the bright afternoon and went back inside.

Joanna wasn't stupid. She'd awoken that morning and helped Isabelle to dress as usual, but her mistress had then wanted to walk all through the inner and outer wards, saying she wanted some exercise. But her barely-concealed excitement and pitiful excuses didn't fool Joanna for a moment. Exercise indeed! When had Isabelle ever shown the slightest inclination to walk anywhere if she didn't have to? Why, she would send a maid – or Joanna herself – to fetch her embroidery if it was at the other end of the room. No, this had something to do with her strange absence in the night.

Joanna had awoken, aware that something wasn't right, but unsure of what it might be. She'd looked blearily around before realising that she was in a small truckle bed in one of the guest chambers. Of course, that must the reason for the sense of unfamiliarity. The furniture was in a different place. No, there had been something else unusual … waking up properly, she'd realised that it was quiet. Too quiet: normally she slept and woke to the accompaniment of Isabelle's snores, but she could hear nothing. Fearful lest something should have happened to her mistress while she slept, Joanna had crept closer to the bed, pulled the curtain aside and looked in. The bed had been empty. Joanna had been afraid; she sat back down, wrapped a blanket around her shoulders, and waited.

When she finally heard her mistress return, she had feigned sleep so as not to be discovered. She had listened as the other got back into bed and lay awake for some time. Then Isabelle had finally dropped off to sleep and Joanna had followed suit, until the rays of dawn streaming into the chamber had awoken her and she had risen to start the preparations for her mistress's day. But what had been going on?

It was not until mid-morning that she'd heard the news regarding the visiting earl's death, for by then the gossip was around most of the castle. It was shocking – not that she was exactly sorry, for the memory of his rough hands on her made her shudder, even in the bright light of day. The thought had stayed in her mind as she followed Isabelle back out of the keep and into the inner ward for yet another tour around it. Ahead of her she could see Martin, or at least his back, as he strode off in the company of Edwin, the bailiff's son, dwarfing the shorter man as they walked deep in conversation. She wondered what they were talking about. It was sure to be the murder, for there could be no other topic of conversation that morning. The event was so shocking, so unexpected, that it overrode everything else.

Shortly the news would spread throughout the kingdom, for the death of an earl would have echoes far beyond the confines of Conisbrough. She was suddenly jealous of the men, and their ability to speak of these things, to hear the news and have the right to be told the facts. The Lord knew she would rather be discussing such weighty matters than traipsing around after Isabelle as she made another turn about the castle wards.

By the time they sat down to dinner, she was convinced that Isabelle's distraction had something to do with Walter de Courteville. She was staring at him, leaning towards him, pining after him, trying to catch his attention. But he was studiously ignoring her, speaking to the older knight, the friend of Sir Geoffrey's whom she had seen yesterday evening. A thought struck Joanna, one so scandalous that she immediately sought to quell it. But it wouldn't go away. The absence of Isabelle during the night. The insistence on walking around the castle this morning, probably looking for Walter. The fawning looks she was giving him. His disregard of her. Surely, surely, she hadn't spent the night in his bed? It was appalling. Unthinkable. But possible?

She was shaken out of her reverie by her neighbour, Sir Geoffrey, who noticed that her cup was empty, and gestured to Martin to fill it. The squire had been in his usual position behind the knight, but Joanna hadn't noticed. As he bent over to reach her cup, she saw the purple swollen bruise on the side of his face, and her heart went out to him instantly. How he'd suffered in her defence! He'd braved the wrath of an earl for her, and she would be forever in his debt. Just as well the man was dead, or he would doubtless have found some way to exact revenge on a defenceless squire. She smiled at him as he filled her cup with wine, and he looked into her eyes in silent understanding.

And now the meal was over. As the men departed she rose to leave, until she noticed that Isabelle hadn't moved. Walter had risen and hurried away so early that it was bordering on discourtesy, without so much as a gesture towards her. Now she sat, alone at the high table, looking forlornly at his empty seat as the servants collected up the gravy-soaked trenchers to distribute later to the poor.

She looked so broken-hearted that Joanna felt a rush of sympathy towards her, despite her normal dislike of her mistress. All women were destined to suffer at the hands of men – they should support each other in a sisterly fashion in such an hour of need. Gently she persuaded Isabelle to rise, and accompanied her back to her room in the guest quarters.

———————

It was calm up on the wall. Edwin was not actually sure how he'd got there, but in his oblivion he had taken himself to one of his favourite peaceful spots. He needed some peace and quiet in order to take everything in and put together a plan of what he was going to do. He sat in one of the battlement embrasures at the top of the wall, arms around his knees, looking out over the village and the surrounding countryside, and letting the sun and the breeze play on his face. It was quiet: other than those detained at the stable, everybody who was entitled to a meal at the earl's expense would be eating dinner in the great hall, and the masons working on the kitchen had also stopped for food. There were one or two people walking amongst the houses in the village, some coming out of the church, and further away he could see small figures labouring in the fields. One of them would be Berold's father.

Thoughts cascaded through his head. Now, the visiting earl was certainly alive at suppertime, as he has seen him in the hall. And he was dead by dawn this morning, as that's when his squire found the body. So what happened to him in between? Did anyone else see him? What was he doing? Why was he on the roof of the keep? And why would anyone want to kill him? All right, stop there. Going down the path of 'why' created too many questions to which Edwin didn't yet have the answers.

Think of practical things instead. What time was he killed? He needed to narrow that down, so he would have to find anyone who saw de Courteville after supper. The gates were shut at nightfall, as usual, so if it was after that then the killer could only be someone who was inside the gates – although that still left a large number of people, surely. What about all the masons? Edwin didn't know them very well. No, they all stop work at nightfall and then go to lodgings outside the gates, so it wouldn't have been one of them, although he supposed he should check that they all left as usual. Plus there was always the chance, as his father said, that someone who was known to the porter might have come in, and he hadn't paid them much mind. Oh dear, he would have to go and talk to him again, and he hadn't done that very well the last time. He was not doing anything very well at the moment – what was he going to do if he couldn't find the killer by tomorrow? How would he tell the earl that he'd failed? And father would feel so ashamed of him … stop! Get back to the facts. What about Berold? His death must be connected. The deaths are different – he was stabbed in the back, with all that blood … no, stop that as well. What did he want to tell me? Was he on duty in the inner ward last night? Perhaps he saw someone, witnessed the earl's murder, and that put his life in danger. But how did the killer find out that he'd been seen? That was something Edwin didn't know, but it was reasonable to assume that was what had happened. So, someone gets into the keep and kills the earl in the night. Berold sees him, and the killer needs to murder him too so that he's not discovered. So he need look for only one person. The task is no more difficult than it was before, it's just that the murderer has one more death on his hands. Just? There's nothing 'just' about it. A second victim, this time someone who'd done nothing wrong, a simple village man who spent his boyhood wishing to be a soldier, only to be struck down in his blood in a stable in his home village before he could ever go to war.

But thinking of the tragedy will not help. What did he need to do now? Make a plan, that's what father would say. So, find out if anyone else entered the castle gates. Find a weapon. Find out what time the earl was killed, or at least narrow it down further than 'sometime between supper and dawn'. Think about who could have gone up to the keep at the same time – what was everyone else doing last night? Try to discover who might have wanted him dead – for who in Conisbrough had known the man, apart from the earl and Sir Geoffrey? Or had anyone known him before? He'd heard that de Courteville did much evil in his life – perhaps someone wanted revenge. People don't just go around killing anyone they fancy, certainly not peers of the realm, or at least Edwin hoped not, for it would make his task all the harder. No, people normally kill for a reason, although the reason doesn't always make sense to others. He'd known his father bring justice to a number of wrongdoers in the past, and he always looked for a cause, not just the facts of who was where, and when. But who here could have had a reason to kill the visiting earl, a man of such importance? He needed to do some more thinking.

'You should be careful there, you know. Someone might decide to push you over the edge.'

Edwin hadn't heard the sound of footsteps, but he surfaced at the familiar voice, and moved up in the embrasure to make room for Robert. He'd spoken in English, as he always did when they were alone, claiming that he needed the practice. French was, of course, the language of the nobles, and they and their Norman-descended men spoke it to each other; but the old English tongue was still the language of the people, used amongst themselves. Edwin had grown up speaking English at home and in the village, but as he grew older and needed to help his father, and as he came into contact with more of the earl's immediate retinue, he had perforce to learn French and was now as fluent as anyone. Robert's grasp of English was more tenuous, as he had less cause to use it, but he tried hard and was popular among the villagers as a result. He always said that one never knew when a second language would come in useful – Edwin had always pictured him being able to give commands to his men when he was a knight – so he should continue to attempt it whenever he could. He never had any trouble communicating with Edwin, as his friend was always ready to help him with any difficulty, and besides, as Robert had once jokingly pointed out, if things really got difficult they could always speak to one another in Latin, for both had been sent to learn the language of the Church and the law at the knee of the local priest. Edwin was profoundly glad that he was fluent in French, for it had saved him embarrassment when speaking with the earl earlier that day, but he was happy now to speak and think in his own tongue. Hopefully things might become less complicated.

Robert continued. 'Why did you not come in for dinner?'

Edwin sighed. 'I needed to think. It seems that the earl has given me an impossible task.'

'Nothing is impossible. Tell me about what you were thinking.'

Edwin forbore to correct his friend's grammar, and instead filled him in on his findings so far, few as they were, and on the thoughts he'd been having and the plan he'd made. As he mentioned his idea of finding the time of the earl's death, Robert brightened.

'I might be able to help you there.' Quickly he told Edwin of his morning, how he'd come across Adam and heard about the letter, and how neither of them had been able to find it despite searching the chamber so carefully. 'So you see, although we couldn't find it, we know that he was alive after dark, for Adam saw him entering his chamber to change his tunic.'

Edwin pondered a moment. This would be a great help, for now he knew that the murder had taken place after the gates had closed. Then something struck him. 'Why did he need to change?'

Another voice piped up from behind them, and Simon's head appeared around the corner. 'I can tell you that!'

Robert smiled at him and ruffled his hair. 'So what do you

know that we don't, whelp?' He looked down good-naturedly, but his face turned grim as he heard Simon's tale of the events in the kitchen the previous night. By the time the page had finished, his fists were clenched. 'How dare he? God's blood, if he were not dead already I would kill him myself.'

Edwin agreed with his friend's sentiments, but nodded as more things came together in his mind. 'So that's why Martin had a bruise on his face this morning – the visiting earl must have hit him when he came to Mistress Joanna's rescue. And it's also why the earl was in such a foul temper when he returned to his chamber, as your friend Adam said.'

'He is not my friend – I pitied him, that's all. But yes, you're right. So what are we going to do now?'

Simon spoke hurriedly. 'That's why I came. My lord wants you to attend him, as he wants to ride out on his new destrier. He sent me to find you.'

Robert jumped to his feet immediately, but then turned to Edwin with a disappointed look. 'Sorry I can't help you more, but I must go to my lord. Tell me later what you've found out.' Receiving a nod in reply, Robert hurried down the stairs and across the inner ward.

Edwin sighed as he watched his friend's departing back. How much more reassuring it would have been to have Robert at his side while he explored the tangled web of murder which confronted him! But it was not to be. He looked down at Simon, who was fidgeting, his eyes pleading, ready to be given a task, sent on an errand, anything that would help. His features lit up eagerly as Edwin's gaze fell upon him.

'Come on then – you can help me question the porter again.'

'Really? What will we ask him? What will he know? Can I ask him questions myself? Will he … '

Chattering excitedly, Simon allowed himself to be ushered down the stairs.

'I told you before, boy, there were no visitors to the castle last night. Now get out of my way and let me get back to my bed.'

This was not going exactly as Edwin had hoped. He'd felt businesslike and efficient as he'd approached the gate, but the terseness of the night porter, awakened once again, had put him off, and now the man had brushed him aside and was about to walk away. A lifetime of obeying orders ensured Edwin's compliance, and with a heavy heart he was about to step aside and let the man pass when he saw that Simon was looking at him with a disappointed face. Seeing the boy so crestfallen and looking to him – him! Edwin, son of a commoner! – for a lead, Edwin's confidence suddenly grew and he stepped in front of the porter and stretched out an arm to prevent him leaving, much to the man's surprise. After all, who would be more intimidating? The porter, or the earl, when Edwin had to tell him he'd failed? He certainly didn't relish the thought of that, and the apprehension made him bolder.

'Master Warin, may I remind you that in my father's absence I am acting as bailiff, and that the earl himself has given me the task of finding the killer. So you *will* stay here and answer my questions.'

The tone of his own voice surprised him, and he'd clearly taken the porter aback as well, for Warin stopped, speechless. A useful lesson in authority, then: borrowed authority at the moment, to be sure, but a firm hand and steady voice would work wonders. He felt as though the day had been worth something at last. Now, what was he going to say? He needed to sound calm and in control. Speak steadily, he thought to himself.

'Now, master porter, you weren't listening to me. I didn't ask you if there had been any visitors, I asked if anyone had entered the gate.'

The tone had worked quite well, but perhaps the wording had been wrong. The man was looking at him as though he was either mad or stupid. The porter sighed dramatically and spoke with heavy sarcasm. 'And as I have already told you, *Master* bailiff, nobody entered.'

Edwin felt let down. All this for nothing, then. He was about to turn away when Warin added an afterthought.

'Oh, well, nobody apart from the priest, that is.'

Finally! A piece of information! Simon was gazing in admiration at him following his masterly display, which was quite the most pleasant happening of the day so far. So much so that he never even noticed when he confidently issued a command to a member of the nobility, instructing Simon quite naturally to run to the church and find Father Ignatius. The boy scampered happily away, and Edwin turned back towards the keep.

At the head of the stairs, he hesitated. His feelings of self-assurance had sustained him all the way into the keep, where he had entered without any feelings of uneasiness. But now he was about to go back into the chapel to inspect the body once more, and some of his awkwardness came upon him again. It was only a body. He'd seen the dead before. There was nothing to be afraid of. But his stomach was still quivering after his recent experience in the stable, and he had to force himself to step into the room.

He was immediately taken aback to see a figure kneeling beside the body. The man turned as Edwin entered, and he found himself looking into the pale features of Sir Roger. The knight wore his customary serene countenance, but there was something else there, some degree of hardness, some steel behind the eyes. Edwin found himself staring.

Sir Roger, surprised, recovered himself first. 'Edwin. What brings you up here?'

Edwin stammered, words suddenly falling over themselves as he sought to explain the task the earl had laid upon him. Facing down the porter was one thing, but this was a knight. Luckily, Sir Roger seemed understanding.

'A formidable task, even for one experienced in these matters.' He gave Edwin a shrewd look. 'And yet, you have the look of a man who will succeed.'

Edwin said nothing, but felt his heart swell.

Sir Roger continued, his calm face breaking into a half smile. 'Well, I suppose you'll want to know why I'm here?'

Edwin tried not to fall over his words again, and failed.

'Don't be anxious. In such a situation, all must be questioned, no matter how innocent they seem. Remember that.'

Edwin finally managed to speak. 'Yes.'

'Good. I was here praying for the dead man's soul.' The smile vanished and the look of determination returned. 'He was an evil-doer, a sinner who is surely burning in hellfire, but every Christian' – he spoke the word as though it were fouled by the dead man's presence – 'deserves some measure of God's mercy at the last.'

The pronouncement had the ring of the last judgement about it, but before Edwin could ask Sir Roger what he meant by his statement, the knight had left the room.

He turned to the body, hesitating with his hand over it for a moment before respectfully removing the covering. It was stiff and cold, and he had some trouble as he tried gently to manipulate the limbs to see if they held any answers. There were none: the body bore no mark except the one on the neck, and Edwin bent over to have a closer look. He was in exactly the same position as he had been that morning when he had been so violently interrupted when another step sounded behind him. He flinched automatically, remembering the pain as his hair had been all but torn out, but it was only Martin, who entered and crouched down next to him, joining in the inspection.

Edwin tried to sound confident. 'It must have been this wound which killed him.' He looked at it again – a slim, neat cut which extended around the front of the neck from ear to ear, but which was deepest at the front. Surely it was too neat to have been the work of a sword or dagger?

Martin had the same thought. 'If he'd been involved in a struggle, wouldn't the wound be … messier?'

'You're right. And where is all the blood? It looks completely different from … you know.' He couldn't bring himself to say it, didn't want to remember.

'Perhaps someone cleaned it up?' Martin sounded doubtful.

'Hardly likely – and anyway, there'd be some trace of it somewhere.' He thought for a moment. 'He wouldn't bleed if he was already dead – maybe someone smothered him and then cut his throat afterwards?'

'Why would anyone want to do that?'

'No, you're right. That's a stupid idea. So how did he die? It must've been a really small, sharp knife, not a proper dagger.' Something else struck him. 'In fact, surely this was a different weapon altogether from the one which killed –' The name stuck in his throat but he forced it out '– Berold? The wounds are completely different.'

Martin didn't reply. He was staring at the body, frowning.

'What is it?'

'I'm not sure, exactly. I only saw the body for a moment this morning before I had to turn away to retch my guts up. But there's something … different about it.' Edwin made as if to reply, but Martin forestalled him, raising his hand. 'And don't ask me what it is, because I can't put my finger on it.' He shook his head. 'I'm sure it will come back to me later, and as like as not it won't be anything important.' He sat back. 'Now, what have you been doing since this morning? I didn't see you at dinner. What do we need to do now?'

Edwin started to tell him about the last couple of hours, but remembered that he himself had set Martin a task that morning.

'Did you find any other way for someone to get into the inner ward?'

'Not really. There's one tiny hole in the wall behind the kitchen where the masons have had to remove a stone to put some scaffolding up, but it's hardly big enough for a rat to get through. Nobody could have entered that way.'

'Oh. That leaves us back where we started, then.'

'Well, at least we now know that the killer must have come in through the gate. So tell me what you've been doing.'

Edwin continued from where he'd left off, from his conversation with his father up to sending Simon to find the priest. 'So', he concluded, 'I believe that the key to this may rest with him. Let us see what we can discover from the good Father.'

Chapter Seven

Simon was hungry. As he rushed out of the gate to follow Edwin's order, he was conscious of an empty feeling in his middle. How long had it been since dinner? Ages, surely. Not that he ever got the chance to fill his belly properly, mind – he was so busy serving that he couldn't sit down to eat all the courses, he just had to fill a platter with what was left afterwards. No wonder he had to keep visiting the kitchen in between to filch what extras he could. Although he suspected that some of the kitchen workers didn't mind quite as much as they pretended to, or he'd never get away with quite so many delicacies. But what could he do now? Must he *starve* until the evening meal was prepared? He sighed as he skipped down into the village at the bottom of the hill.

Conisbrough was familiar to him, of course. It was not overly large, but had three main streets arranged around the green, and was important enough to hold a market each month, when farmers and traders from the surrounding countryside would come to sell their wares. There were always delicious pies to be bought, if one had managed to save a few coins. Behind the neat houses on the three main streets were some meaner dwellings, some seemingly no more than piles of brushwood badly stacked together. The ones scattered just outside the main part of the village were the worst: home to the poorest labourers, they were squat, dank hovels whose inhabitants hacked and coughed and died off in droves each winter. He was glad he had no cause to go there.

He admired the church as he drew near to the village, for it was built in stone like the keep of the castle, although it was actually by far the older of the two structures. Edwin's father, who was the oldest person he knew, had once said that when he was small, he remembered his own grandfather telling him that the church had been of stone even as far as *he* could remember, so that was as far back in the distant reaches of time as anyone was likely to reckon. Although it was so old, it was kept in regular repair by the men in the village, and the new thatch on the roof shone brightly. There would not be many places which could boast such a fine church.

The village also had its fair share of fine houses, for among the single-room dwellings which were home to the labourers and their families there were some which were larger and had separate rooms inside for living and sleeping. One of these belonged to Godric Weaver and his wife Anne, Edwin's parents, and Simon slowed as he passed it, looking at the garden with its neat rows of vegetables and herbs. Nothing that grew under Edwin's mother's jurisdiction would dare grow out of line. He stopped to look over the fence which separated the garden from the enclosure where she kept her livestock, in case there might be a couple of eggs there. Not that he would think of taking them, of course, but if he took them in to her she might reward him with one of her oatcakes. His mouth watered at the thought. However, she'd obviously completed her chores there already: there were no eggs to be seen, but the four hens scratched around contentedly, the two young pigs which would provide next winter's meat were happily rooting through a trough of swill, and even the cow looked as though she'd already been milked. He sighed, and half thought of entering the cottage anyway; Mistress Anne was always very friendly. But then he remembered that Edwin's father, the bailiff, was very ill, so he decided better of it and carried on along the street.

As he continued towards the church, he smelled the delicious aroma of new bread and slowed, sniffing the air. The scent was issuing from one of the neat cottages around the green, and as he watched, a shutter opened and the goodwife placed some flat loaves to cool on the sill. As she saw him gaping she smiled and spoke. 'It's young master Simon, isn't it? The earl's page?' Simon took a moment to adjust to the English language, and then agreed that he was, and she smiled. 'I expect you're hungry?' He nodded. 'Ah, I know boys, and boys are always hungry. You have much growing to do, I am sure. Here.' She took one of the loaves and tore the end from it, handing the warm hunk to him. 'You take that and be on your way.' She patted his cheek as he thanked her and turned away. The bread smelled delicious and it made his mouth water as he tore it in half. He would have some now and save the rest for after he found Father Ignatius. He stowed one piece safely in his tunic and crammed the rest into his mouth.

His stomach satisfied for the moment, he remembered his quest. Why was it he was trying to find the priest? Oh yes, Edwin had asked him to do it so they could find out why Father Ignatius had been into the inner ward after dark. There was also another thought which Simon tried to catch, something about people getting in and out of the keep during the night, but he couldn't remember what it was. Still, Edwin would probably work it out – he was very clever. It was fun working with him for a change, very different from being with Robert and Martin of course, but not in a bad way. But Edwin wouldn't be going with them on the campaign, so he'd better sort out all his answers before they went – that was what his lord had said.

The thought of going on the campaign and seeing real battles made him so excited that he became hungry again. Perhaps just a little more of that bread? It wouldn't be greedy if he didn't eat all of it. He pulled it out from his tunic and tore off another small corner, virtuously putting the rest back. He chewed reflectively as he arrived at the church. As he entered the cool stone interior, he smoothed the crumbs from his tunic and took off his hat, turning it round and round in his hand as he blinked to accustom his eyes to the gloom. The church was empty. Or at least, it was empty of the living.

In the centre of the space a shrouded figure lay on a board. The face was covered, but Simon knew it was the man-at-arms who had died in the stable earlier that day. He took a step forward, but didn't want to go too close: a sticky pool of blood had oozed out from underneath the body, and flies were buzzing all around it. Simon stood for a moment, wondering what really did happen to you after you died, and how you could go to heaven and live there nicely forever when your body looked like the stinking corpse before him. The man would be buried on the morrow, put in a pit in the ground like many others before him, and spadefuls of earth shovelled over what had once been his living body.

He shivered suddenly and wished to be away from the place, the body, the scent of death. He edged around the church, giving the putrid object in the middle as wide a berth as possible, and made his way to the door to the sacristy before knocking hesitantly. 'Father?' He poked his head around the door, but the sacristy, too, was empty. Strange. He went back outside and walked around the churchyard, weaving in and out of the hummocks of grass and the wooden crosses, calling the priest's name, until he reached the timber-framed cottage behind the church. Here he knocked again, and was pleased when the door opened to reveal Agnes, Father Ignatius's housekeeper. Before Simon could speak she forestalled him.

'Have you seen the good Father?'

'What?'

'Have you seen him? Is he up at the castle? If he'd been up there this morning he would normally have returned by now, for he doesn't often stay to dinner.'

'But I've come to look for him here!'

They looked blankly at each other for a moment, before voicing the same thought. 'So where is he?'

This was not good. This was definitely not good. How was he going to explain to Edwin that he'd failed to find the priest? And where was he anyway? He should be here, in

Conisbrough, at his church. He poked his head back inside the church on the way back to the castle, in case Father Ignatius had been in there all the time, but eventually realised that he would have to go back and tell Edwin that he'd failed. He kicked a stone crossly along the street.

As Simon sulked back through the village, he heard a commotion coming from one of the cottages. It was the one he'd stopped by earlier, where the woman had given him some of the freshly baked bread. He stopped just around the corner to watch. The woman was coming out of her house, holding a small boy painfully by one ear and screeching at the top of her voice. 'You filthy, thieving little animal! How dare you steal from me! I don't bake good bread to waste it on rogues like you! I should have you up before the court for robbery and see you flogged!' With each exclamation she shook him, still holding on to his ear, almost lifting him from the ground, and Simon winced in sympathy. She ended her tirade by giving the boy a stinging slap in the face and pushing him away, hard, so that he fell in a ragged snivelling heap. She stepped forward and raised her hand again, but as he cowered away she merely tutted in disgust and withdrew into the cottage.

Simon stepped out of his hiding place and offered his hand to the boy to help him rise. Obviously fearing that he was about to be struck again, the boy initially tried to scrabble away backwards, but then he overcame his fear and took the proffered hand. As he stood, Simon surveyed him. It was difficult to tell his age, for he was so dirty that his face could hardly be seen. About Simon's own age, perhaps, or possibly younger. Certainly much smaller and thinner, and all bent and twisted, as though he was old before his time. Simon had always thought himself to be small, surrounded as he was daily by grown men, but now he was conscious of his size, feeling unusually large and well-built next to the scrawny boy. He looked uncomfortably at the other's pinched unhappy face, ragged clothes and bare feet, aware of his own fine garb and sturdy boots. He essayed his English again.

'Why was she shouting at you?'

The boy looked at his feet, unsure of how to respond. He mumbled.

'What?'

'I was hungry, sir.'

Nobody had ever called Simon 'sir' in his life, and to his surprise he found that it felt slightly uncomfortable. 'Why? When did you last eat?'

'Yesterday. A man gave me some old bread.'

Simon couldn't believe his ears. Yesterday? Why, the boy must be ravenous! How had this happened?

'Where are your family? Why have you not eaten? Where do you live?' He was filled with indignation that the boy's mother had not seen fit to feed him – had he performed some misdeed for which he was being punished? Simon could sympathise there, of course, but he would take a beating any day rather than being deprived of food.

'They're dead. I don't live anywhere – just … round here.' He gestured half-heartedly, his arm encompassing the whole village.

This was terrible. That this should happen in Conisbrough! He would tell the earl straight away, and he would see that the boy was clothed and fed. In the meantime … 'Here.' He held out the other piece of bread which he had saved, the injustice of the situation striking him. The woman had given him some bread freely, as she thought he was hungry. And so he was, but he'd already eaten a hearty meal that day at dinner, to say nothing of the wafers he'd charmed from one of the kitchen servants earlier. But here was a boy who was really starving, and she had turned him away with threats and blows. It wasn't fair. Was this because he was noble and the other wasn't? He'd always taken his position for granted, but now it was beginning to dawn upon him that he was more privileged than most.

The boy was looking at him as though he were an angel, unable to believe his luck. Then he snatched the bread and crammed it into his mouth as fast as he could, nearly choking on it, before his saviour could change his mind. Simon watched him, all his own appetite gone, thinking to himself that he would never consider himself hungry again. As soon as the boy had finished, he backed away a couple of steps and then turned and fled, before Simon could ask him his name.

———

'What do you mean, gone?'

'I mean he isn't there.'

Edwin and Martin had waited for Simon in William Steward's small office behind the great hall. The boy had looked very thoughtful as he arrived, and, crucially, he wasn't accompanied by Father Ignatius. Now he confessed to his failure in the task. Edwin noticed how downcast the little figure was, and searched around for something to cheer him. Simon normally liked it whenever he came in here, for it smelled of the spices which were kept locked away in great kists around the walls. Edwin's eye fell on something which hadn't yet been put away. 'Look, William has just had some new cones of sugar delivered. He might let you break the tip off one if you ask.'

'I don't want any.'

Martin gaped. Edwin thought he must have heard wrongly. 'Did you just say ... '

'I told you, I don't want any.' The piping voice was firm. 'I'm not hungry.'

Edwin blinked, and thought to himself that the boy's failure to find the priest must have affected him more than he'd thought. He tried to offer some comfort. 'Never mind. Father Ignatius has probably gone out to see some parishioner in need – a sick man, perhaps, or a poor family. We'll find him later.' Simon looked marginally brighter. Edwin sighed. He might have succeeded in cheering Simon up, but the task loomed ever more impossible. A rising tide of panic threatened to engulf him, but he fought it back, determined to tackle the problem logically. Somebody had crept up the stairs of the keep, onto the roof, and murdered a man in cold blood. The same person had then stabbed an innocent man in the back, in the middle of the day in a crowded outer ward.

He thought again of Berold's death, as he had again and again since he'd been summoned to the body. The weight of the guilt threatened to crush him, added to the other worries and cares already piled on his sagging shoulders. Could he have stopped it, would he have prevented it if he'd only made Berold stay and tell him what was on his mind? Perhaps if Berold had unburdened himself, made public what he knew, he wouldn't be dead. But this just circled around to the same question again – who had killed him? And who had killed the visiting earl? The same person, surely, but it could be anyone.

Actually, that wasn't the case: it had to be someone who was within the wider castle that day, but it was also someone who had been within the inner walls after the gates were closed. Well, that was a start. 'We'll make a list of everyone who was in the inner ward after nightfall.' He went to a kist in the corner and took out parchment, pen and ink, and returned to sit at the table. He sighed. 'Come on then.'

It was some while later when Edwin sat back to look at the ink-stained parchment in front of him. The list was long indeed, including all the extra guests who had stayed in the hall the night before. 'This is hopeless.'

Martin and Simon said nothing. Simon stiffened suddenly, looking towards the door as someone approached. It was Mistress Joanna. She hesitated by the entrance and cleared her throat. 'I … was just wondering if there was anything I could do to help.' There was silence for a moment, then she confessed in a rush. 'I've been walking up and down outside, wondering if I dare disturb you, but I couldn't stand the thought of another long afternoon at my embroidery while there were so many other things going on. I know it's not usual, but … '

Edwin thought to himself that it was not exactly usual for someone like him to be in charge of anything, so to involve a lady as well probably wouldn't make that much difference. Any new thoughts would be welcome, the way he felt at the moment. But on the other hand, he was unsure of how to address her, or on what terms she had joined them. 'Mistress, er … '

Martin saw his confusion and explained to Joanna that they'd been making a list of everyone who might have been in the castle, as only these could have accessed the keep.

She nodded. 'May I see it?'

Edwin passed over the sheet, ashamed of his scrawl, for she would be used to looking at writing which was much more carefully done, in a psalter or a decorated book of poetry. She made no comment, however, other than being able to add one or two names which they'd missed.

So, what do we do now?' she asked, as she looked around at Martin and Simon. They both looked at Edwin, waiting for him to speak; she blinked and, after the barest pause, turned to face him.

Edwin wanted to work through the problem in a logical manner. 'Well, now we know who was here, we will need to work out who had the chance to get to the top of the keep. Do you know of anyone who might have been moving around the castle after nightfall?' Martin and Simon shook their heads. Edwin looked directly at Joanna for the first time. 'Mistress Joanna?'

She paused for a moment before answering. 'No. No, I don't know of anyone who may have been abroad last night.'

The destrier was a magnificent beast, thought Robert, as he cantered across the countryside behind the earl. It felt very decadent to be out here riding, what with everything else going on, but the earl couldn't possibly go on campaign and risk riding into battle on a horse which he wasn't familiar with, so time had to be found.

Once they reached open land he stopped to watch as the earl put the horse through its paces, starting and stopping, wheeling and turning, trotting and cantering, trying out different manoeuvres which might be needed on a battlefield. It had, of course, already been trained by the dealer who'd bred it, but when a man would be entrusting his life to an animal in battle, he needed to be at one with it, to feel its every movement beneath him. The earl was a superb horseman, having been placed in his first saddle before he could even walk and spent much of his life there ever since. But even he would need some time to become more familiar with such a highly-strung animal as a new destrier, and as Robert watched, he could see the movements of man and horse becoming finer and smoother as each got used to the other. After an hour he was mesmerised by the movement, could have sworn that the earl and his warhorse were one as they weaved and swept in front of him.

Eventually the earl brought the stallion to a snorting halt in front of his squire. 'A fine animal, eh?'

'Very fine, my lord. Although he has a slight tendency to lower his head as you wheel to the left, which may be dangerous in the field.'

The earl nodded. 'Well done. I'd noticed the same thing myself.' He smiled proudly. 'Well, shall we see what he does when we give him his head?' He spoke in a matter-of-fact voice, but Robert could sense a certain amount of boyish enthusiasm, and his own spirits lifted. The fresh air, the space, the superb animal, the presence of the man who had been like a father to him for nigh on fifteen years. Robert looked back at him eagerly, scanning the countryside around for some landmark. 'Shall we say the tree on that ridge, my lord?' He pointed.

The earl nodded his agreement, and instantly the two of them were off, spurring their mounts into an exhilarating gallop. Robert whooped as he felt the wind in his hair and the movement of the horse under him, the elation of travelling at such a speed. He was the fastest thing in the world, flying, soaring above the ground as his horse's hooves pounded into the earth. This was true freedom. He held a lead over the earl to start with, a lighter man on a lighter horse, but slowly his master caught him and then edged past, bending low over the destrier's neck. His own horse was a courser, a fine enough animal in its way, but no match for the prize warhorse, and the earl started to draw away. The courser did, however, have the advantage of freshness, so Robert was no more than a length behind the earl as they thundered past the finishing mark and drew up, laughing, to catch their breath, each praising his own animal for the effort it had expended.

After some while they turned back towards Conisbrough, walking the horses now. As each step passed, drawing them back towards the village, they grew more sombre. The earl looked as though he wanted to say something, but Robert didn't press him, waiting instead for his master to speak first. When he did, it wasn't what the squire expected to hear.

'Something is troubling you.'

Robert started. Had his face betrayed him? He wondered how to reply. 'My lord, I … ' what could he say? He supposed he may as well be honest, even if his master didn't like it. 'My lord, I must tell you that I can summon no sadness at the Earl of Sheffield's death.' There, he'd said it. 'Yes, it is a shame that any man should die before his time, but although his life has been taken so violently, I feel no particular sorrow. All I feel is that it will cause you a great deal of trouble.'

The earl said nothing for a moment, seeming to weigh his words. But his reply was encouraging. 'I'm glad to find you so honest, Robert. And I must also admit that I had little personal feeling for the man.' He sighed. 'Perhaps we should say a quiet prayer for his soul when next we have the chance, for the Lord knows he will have need of it, and it may help to banish our uncharitable thoughts.' Robert nodded, and there was a brief silence between them before the earl continued. 'But you're right that it will cause me trouble. I fear that there is some deeper purpose at work here, that his death is also meant to harm me in some way. If we can't prove otherwise, how am I going to explain to the regent that the man was murdered on my land – even in my home – and that I couldn't protect him? At the very least, I'm guilty of failing to ensure his safety, but there will be those among my political opponents who will seek to prove that I had him killed for my own purposes. If our new bailiff doesn't provide me with something to tell the regent, I will be at a sorry pass indeed.' Almost as an afterthought he added, 'And of course, this latest death, this soldier – what was his name? – won't make things simpler. There will be unease among the people. But that can wait: the main thing is to find the murderer of the earl, so that I can try and save some face with the regent.'

Robert did not know what to say. Eventually, he asked the obvious question. 'But what will it mean for you, my lord? If the killer isn't found, what will happen to you?'

The earl sighed. 'I honestly don't know. The regent will never trust me again, for certain, and I will lose any influence I may have had at court. But it could be much worse: I could lose some or all of my lands, even my life. The regent is known for wanting justice for all men and if he finds me guilty of murder, my earldom will not save me.'

The seriousness of the words bit into Robert and he felt a deep sense of panic at the thought of life without the earl, the man who had guided him throughout his boyhood and youth. It was so unfair that he should suffer for the deeds of another. He felt resolve swelling inside him. 'My lord, you must know that everyone at Conisbrough is your loyal servant. We all look up to you, not just as our liege lord, but as an example to follow. There are many men here who would happily die for you, should it come down to it.' He paused, not wanting to sound over-dramatic, but now was a time for plain speaking. 'My lord, I am one of them, and I swear I will die before I see you lose your lands and position.'

The fervour in his voice seemed to impress the earl, so he didn't seek to make a flippant reply or dismiss Robert's vehemence, as he might sometimes have done. Instead he replied, grimly, 'Let's hope it doesn't come to that, then. I would rather have you live for me than die for me.'

They rode the rest of the way in silence.

Chapter Eight

Edwin sat alone in the steward's office, trying to think. Martin had been called away by the earl; Simon had been summoned by Sir Geoffrey for some sort of lesson, and Joanna had left to tend to her mistress. Initially he welcomed the silence, but now it seemed overwhelming: thoughts ran and jumped through his head as he tried to order them, but he could not. Strangely, he now found himself drawn to the task he'd been trying to avoid for the past few days: looking through the estate's documents in order to settle the land dispute which was due to come up at the next manor court. It wasn't as though he had the time to deal with it, what with everything else, but perhaps … perhaps if he concentrated on that for a while, and pushed the other thoughts out of his head, things might become clearer. Or at least he could stop panicking for a while.

Yes, that was the thing to do. If he was going to be the bailiff, he'd better get used to this sort of thing anyway, as it was one of the duties, normally the one that he relished least. Organising the work of the men of the village was simple enough: they were used to it and had the reeve to oversee them. No, it was the legal part of the job which took up much of his time, for everything had to be correct in the last detail, and the estate's records were invariably written in a tiny, cramped hand which was difficult to make out, not to mention the fact that some of the scribes seemed to have used a system of obscure abbreviations which he found difficult to decipher. But now the distraction would be welcome. He opened one of the great chests which lined one wall and rummaged inside until he found the documents he was after: two large grants of land which, in minuscule writing, described the exact boundaries of the lands of the two men who were in dispute. He sat down at one corner of the table in order to make best use of the light slanting in through the one small window, and started reading.

After all the procrastination, it was easier than he'd anticipated. The grants of land were clearer than he'd hoped: the area in question definitely belonged to Aelfrith, one of the disputants. The fact that Aelfrith's father had let his neighbour use the land while he was alive was neither here nor there; his son had every right to do with it as he willed now that it was his. Satisfied, he rolled up the grants to put them away. All he needed to do now was write down his findings so he could use them at the manor court; he was reaching for pen and ink when Sir Geoffrey strode into the room, with Simon trailing mournfully at his heels. Seeing Edwin he apologised for disturbing him at his labours, but pointed out that there was nowhere else suitable for them to work, given that the earl needed his council chamber to greet his remaining knights as they arrived, and that they couldn't use the hall lest any food or drink be spilled on the rolled-up parchments which he carried under his arm. Edwin said nothing: Sir Geoffrey was the castellan and could go wherever he liked without needing to ask Edwin's permission. He moved up closer to the corner to allow the knight more room.

Sir Geoffrey unfurled the parchments and motioned to Simon to weight down the corners so that they would lie flat. Edwin stole a surreptitious glance at the uppermost document and only just suppressed a gasp at the beauty of it. The page was covered in rows and rows of shields, painstakingly drawn and beautifully coloured, showing what were clearly the arms of various families. He looked down at his own rather scratchy penmanship and wondered how anyone could produce such a marvellous work of art. Oh well, there was no sense in dwelling on that. He had his own work to attend to, even if what Sir Geoffrey was saying sounded far more interesting ...

'Now, Simon, it's very important to be able to recognise these arms straight away.'

'Why?' The boy was staring at the intricate designs.

'Well, what if your lord should ask you to take a message to the Earl of Chester while you're all encamped around Lincoln. Do you know what he looks like?'

'No, Sir Geoffrey.'

'Well then. But you don't need to know the man: if you know what his arms look like you'll be able to find his part of the encampment, and you will be able to identify his men. And what if you were in a battle? The helmets which everyone wears now cover the whole of a man's face, but if you can see the arms on his shield you'll know who he is, will you not?'

'Yes, Sir Geoffrey.' Simon sat up straighter and looked with more enthusiasm at the parchment as Sir Geoffrey jabbed at the shield at the top, which Edwin could see was red with three golden lions on it.

'Now, this is the most important one – who do you think it is?'

'The king?'

'Aye, the king. Any castle where he is in residence must fly his arms as well as the owner's, so important strongholds keep a banner with this design on it.'

'Have we got one?'

'We certainly have. In fact the old king visited here once, oh, must have been fifteen or sixteen years ago now, in the old earl's time. You wouldn't have been born then.'

'And even Martin would have been a baby,' said Simon, amazed at such ancient history. He screwed up his face as he struggled with the arithmetic, 'and Robert would have been … '

Four, thought Edwin, he's the same age as me, and that's how old I was when the king came to stay. He remembered seeing the king from a distance as his father held him on his shoulders so that he could catch a glimpse. But that was before Robert came, even the nobility don't send their sons away *that* early in their lives. He came later, was that before or after the old earl died? He couldn't remember, but it was round about then. And Mistress Joanna arrived not long after, when the Lady Isabelle was widowed – he remembered finding her crying once when Lady Isabelle had been nasty to her, poor little thing. But that was when the earl's wife was still alive: what a beautiful lady she was, and always smiling …

Sir Geoffrey was continuing, and with a start Edwin realised the ink had dried up in his pen. Hastily he dipped it again and bent his head over his work, pretending that he wasn't glancing over at the beautiful parchment as Sir Geoffrey pointed at more shields.

'Now, after the king come the earls. First, the two easy ones. Who is this?' He indicated a blue and yellow chequered shield which even Edwin recognised.

'My lord!' Simon looked proudly at the small coloured patch sewn on his own tunic, showing that he was part of the earl's personal retinue.

'Yes, our lord, the Earl of Surrey. Good. And this?' Edwin followed the knight's finger as he pointed at a yellow shield with three red chevrons on it.

Simon squeaked excitedly. 'My father!'

'Right again: the arms of de Clare, the Earl of Hertford.'

'But these arms won't be mine when I'm grown up and a knight, will they? They'll go to my brother Gilbert, won't they?'

'That's right. He's the heir, so at the moment he will have a label over the arms, and when he inherits from your father he will have them like this, undifferenced. In fact, one day he'll also become the Earl of Gloucester in right of your lady mother, who is an heiress, so he'll be an earl twice over, and will also have the right to another set of arms, if he so chooses.' He pointed to another shield. 'But anyway, back to our lesson. How many older brothers do you have?'

'Four.' Simon sounded mournful, but Edwin thought how much fun it must be to have brothers.

'As the fifth son you will have an annulet, a ring, on your arms.' Sir Geoffrey seemed to be enjoying his explanations, a side of him Edwin had never seen. To him the knight had always been the figure of ultimate authority at the castle – the earl wasn't there all the time, had other estates elsewhere, and besides, he was far too important a personage for Edwin to think of in any capacity other than as a semi-mythical figure – and it was something of a shock to discover that the intimidating knight could smile and enjoy something as simple as explaining the rules of heraldry to a young boy.

Sir Geoffrey was pointing at other shields. 'The Earl of Pembroke – that's the regent – the Earl of Chester; the Earl of Derby; the Earl of Arundel; the Earl of … ' Edwin tried to concentrate on his writing, but was thwarted once more as he caught the change of tone and the words '… the Earl of Sheffield.' He looked up to see that the knight was no longer smiling.

Simon seemed to understand the undertone. 'The man who's dead. Did you know him, Sir Geoffrey?'

'I met him once or twice when I was campaigning in France with the old earl some years ago, and I knew *of* him.' His tone was serious. 'He was a personal favourite of the old king, and some say that he carried out many of the dark deeds which John wanted done.' He shook his head.

Simon seemed on the verge of asking a question, but the knight forestalled him, turning to the second page of the document, which held many more shields. 'Now, after the earls, some of the lesser barons and knights. Sir Hugh de Lacy – that's Mistress Joanna's cousin – Sir Reginald de Braose … ' Edwin made another attempt to return to the task he was supposed to be performing. Now, the piece of land in question is south of the village of …

'Whose are these?' Simon was pointing to the very bottom of the page, where two coloured shields were pictured upside down with thick black lines through them.

Sir Geoffrey cleared his throat. 'Ah, well, that was a bad business … '

Rolling his eyes at his own inability to concentrate, Edwin gave up on any pretence at working, put his pen down and turned to listen to what was sure to be an interesting story.

Sir Geoffrey didn't seem to mind the extra audience. 'As I say, it was an unpleasant business. These arms belong to two knights, Sir Hugh d'Eyncourt' – he stabbed his finger at the left-hand shield, which was green with a snarling gold lion's head emblazoned on it – 'and Sir Stephen Fitzwalter.' He pointed at the other shield, which was blue and depicted a silver eagle. 'Nobody knows exactly what happened, but they both died in separate accidents within a day of each other. Fitzwalter drowned in a river, and d'Eyncourt and his wife and child were killed in a fire. At the time it just seemed unfortunate, but shortly afterwards King John had their estates confiscated and their arms struck dishonourably from the roll, so they'd obviously done something which displeased him greatly.'

Simon gazed, fascinated, at the shields. So did Edwin: what dark deeds could these men have perpetrated? His mind span with ideas of murder, treason, betrayal …

Sir Geoffrey was rolling up the parchment and tucking it under his arm as he prepared to leave the room. 'That's all for today. We'll look at this again soon, Simon, and I'll ask you about the bearers of all these arms, to see how many you can remember. But now I believe you have another reading lesson.' He shook his head. 'In my day it was enough that a knight should be able to ride a horse, use a sword and lance, and speak the truth; but today it seems that you must all be learned men as well. Nevertheless, it's by the earl's order, so off you go.'

Simon made a face as he followed the knight out of the room, and Edwin smiled. Then he looked down at the parchment on which he had been writing. His penmanship, never the neatest at the best of times, had suffered from all the interruptions, and the page was so covered in mistakes and blots of ink that it was almost illegible. Sighing, he put it to one side to be scraped clean later, and drew a fresh sheet in front of him to start again.

———

Joanna was trying to think of some way in which she might be able to raise Isabelle's spirits. Her mistress had sat mournfully through the evening meal, hardly noticing the fine food, and had left as soon as it was polite to do so. But what could she do? It struck her that even after all these years she didn't really know Isabelle all that well, and the thought distressed her. Clearly she hadn't been a good enough companion. So occupied was she with these thoughts that as she entered the guest quarters she almost collided with Walter de Courteville, who was rounding the corner on his way out. She started back, afraid for a moment that he would repeat his brother's action of the night before, but he merely stalked past. Joanna wondered if he'd even noticed her presence.

She opened the door to Isabelle's chamber and stopped, taken aback. Her mistress was lying on the floor, curled into a ball, weeping as though her heart would break.

She had to admit that there was a small moment when she was tempted to shut the door and creep quietly away, hoping that she hadn't been noticed, but the thought was banished almost as soon as it sprang into her mind. Instead she shut the door behind her to guard Isabelle's privacy, and stooped to lift the sobbing woman from the ground.

'There now, my lady, there now. Hush.' She didn't know what to say but soothing words found their way to her lips, and she stroked Isabelle's hair as she tried to lift the shaking body, racked with sobs. Finally the heaving of the shoulders gave way to quivers, and Isabelle took some deep shuddering breaths.

'Hush, my lady. I'm here, there is nothing to be afraid of.' She wasn't sure whether she should ask what was the matter, or whether it would simply be better to keep her counsel. But as Isabelle's crying abated, she seemed to want to talk.

'How could he say such things? How could he? He can't have meant them.'

Her face puffy and swollen, she looked up at Joanna. 'Oh, I'm worthless! I've always known it, for what use are women to a noble family? We are nothing, chattels to be passed on to the nearest ally. But to think that I wanted him. Oh, the … the humiliation!' This last was accompanied by another huge sob, and again it was a few moments before she was in a fit state to speak. Joanna thought she had better say nothing and let Isabelle release as many words and feelings as she needed to. Clearly her suspicions about her mistress and Walter de Courteville had been correct.

'I was so stupid! So blind! All these years I've preened myself – I, the daughter of an earl! No man would be good enough for me, except one of the highest birth … fine ideals, until I fell in love, or so I believed.' The voice rose to a wail. 'Yet here I am, lying on the floor of a guest chamber, humbled and debased by a … a nobody. And his words will haunt me for-forever!' The weeping overtook her again, and Joanna held her mistress in her arms and rocked her like a child.

Finally Isabelle raised her head again and looked straight at Joanna. 'But do you know what the worst thing is? There is not one man in the world who cares for me, not one whom I can trust.'

Joanna looked steadily at her. A thought grew in her mind. She was about to say something which might well send Isabelle into hysterics again, this time directed at her. But she had to speak. 'My lady, I think you're wrong.'

Isabelle stared at her for a long moment, but no words passed her lips. Joanna decided to plough on. 'My lady, I believe there is one man in whom you could confide, one person to whom you could relate the matter, one person in whom you should have trusted all along.'

Good Lord, Isabelle was actually listening to her. 'And above all, my lady, one person who might be able to help you gain revenge.'

Slowly, Isabelle stood. She wiped her face and straightened her wimple. There was no mirror in here, so Joanna wordlessly tucked the stray hairs back inside it and made her look respectable. Isabelle smoothed down the front of her gown, took a deep breath, and opened the door.

Sir Geoffrey peered into the fading light as he surveyed the rows of tents and equipment. Having put the precious scrolls away carefully, he was now down in the tilting yard, making sure that all was well with the encampment before night fell. He would have no disorderliness here. He spoke sharply to one man, telling him to pick his gear up from where it was scattered on the floor and stow it somewhere safely. He turned to Adam, who had been silently shadowing him, either hoping to be of help or through lack of anything else to do, and gave a short lecture on the importance of looking after one's equipment while on campaign, concluding by pointing out that if a man's life depended on his armour in a battle, it would do him no good suddenly to find a broken strap or a hole where the mail had been weakened by rust. Adam nodded – he was a good boy, it was a shame he had no master now, for he was eager and quick to learn. Sir Geoffrey had initially been bothered by his presence, as someone unknown, but he'd found a keen pair of ears, a sensible mind and a willingness to help out with any task which might be forthcoming; Adam had also asked one or two pertinent questions which betrayed an intelligence and interest which was sadly lacking in much of today's youth. His prospects were bleak, though: Sir Geoffrey had no need for a squire – and besides, he was too old to be training one at his time of life – and the earl didn't really require more than three. The loathsome Walter would probably not take him, but that was doubtless just as well for Adam. Still, something might be done – he resolved to himself to ask around and see if there were any knights in the earl's retinue who might take the boy on. Certainly he would try to find someone who wouldn't beat the lad to a pulp – he'd been having some trouble recently, judging by the sight of his battered face.

They took one last turn around the encampment, watching as men made themselves comfortable around small fires. The homely smell of wood smoke drifted through the air, accompanied by the scent of the simmering pottage which was being cooked in many places. Some men were stirring the loaded pans; others warded off the boredom by oiling weapons, playing dice or simply chatting to each other. One man started to play on a small wooden flute, but the tune was too mournful for his companions, who urged him to find something more lively. He responded, and Sir Geoffrey and Adam left the encampment with the pungent aroma of the smoke in their nostrils and the sound of merry singing in their ears. If Sir Geoffrey knew that much of the cheerfulness was forced, an attempt to ward off the fear at the thought of the campaign ahead, he didn't burden the boy with the knowledge. There would be time enough for him to learn. The sun was setting and as they walked through the darkened gatehouse the lad instinctively shrank nearer to him. Sir Geoffrey laid a companionable hand on his shoulder, and they strode up to the inner ward in silence. Once they were inside, Sir Geoffrey made his way to the keep to make his last report of the evening to the earl, Adam still trailing at his heels.

The stairs in the keep seemed to get steeper every day, and Sir Geoffrey felt his knees complaining as he reached the first floor. He was glad to find the earl in his council chamber, for if he'd retired to his private quarters it would have meant another flight. Unusually, he was alone, with no squires or servants in attendance. Briefly Sir Geoffrey reported that all was well in the camp, although there was an inevitable uneasiness among de Courteville's men. It hadn't yet spilled over into anything more serious, but he had men watching who would let him know as soon as there was any trouble.

The earl was commending him on his forethought when there was another knock at the door. Looking surprised, he noted that he wasn't expecting any other visitors; he opened the door himself, to be greeted by the sight of his sister looking distraught. Sir Geoffrey didn't have the energy to listen to another round of their bickering, but he wasn't dismissed, so he settled back against the wall, trying to engage his mind anywhere except the chamber in front of him.

Edwin had spent a fruitless hour looking for the orphan Peter. He'd just finished his rewritten deposition for the manor court when a message from Robert had reached him, saying that the boy had been seen with a large knife which might have been the missing one; since then he'd been searching everywhere. Amid the hustle and bustle of the castle, particularly given the frantic preparations for departure which were going on, one small boy could easily conceal himself. Edwin had been through the inner ward – not that Peter was likely to be there, unless he'd managed to slip past the guard – and down to the outer ward. Here of course it was even more crowded, a mass of humans and animals all spilling out of the booths and workshops which lined the outer wall, busy working, running, shouting or just milling around. Here was the business which kept the castle and its household running: here were the mews for the earl's hawks and the doghouse where his hounds were kept; here were the carpenter, the cooper, the fletcher and the potter; here was where goods and livestock were delivered from the surrounding areas, and here was where the confined world of the castle met the wider world outside. Here also was the stench of man and beast, and Edwin wrinkled his nose as he passed a particularly noisome handcart, being pulled out of the doghouse by one of the boys who had the unenviable task of clearing up after the hounds. The boy didn't have far to travel with his burden, though; as Edwin watched, he hauled the cart over to the edge of the moat and tipped its contents into the ditch, which stank so much anyway that the extra waste would make very little difference.

The odours of all the various activities assailed Edwin's nostrils as he walked through the ward, eyes sweeping every nook and cranny: the grease used on the creaking wheels of a cart, which was loaded with barrels of what smelled like salted herring; the more pleasant scent of wood, as the carpenter turned his lathe to work and the cooper shaved a barrel stave; and the sharp tang of hot metal as he neared the smithy – one of the only places where the stink of human sweat and waste was overpowered. Despite the pressing nature of his search, he stopped for a few moments, as he had done since he was a child, to watch Crispin the smith working his magic on a red-hot piece of metal, and received a nod in greeting. But the boy, the boy was nowhere. After he'd finished searching the ward, Edwin went out of the gate and tried the encampment, the village and the church. One woman said that she'd caught him trying to steal bread earlier that day, but nobody had set eyes on him since. Now it was getting dark. Frustrated, Edwin turned to go back up to the castle. As he neared the gate he had to move to the side of the road as a cart loaded with barrels was passing through the other way. Provisions for the campaign, no doubt, being prepared in advance. Not that it was much in advance, for the earl was to leave on the day after the morrow. This reminded him again how little time he had to complete his task, and how little he still knew.

Watching as the cart moved slowly past, he was struck by an idea. If I were a hungry boy, he thought to himself, where would I be? Annoyed that he hadn't thought of it earlier, he walked in through the gate and around to the open space where other carts were being loaded with food. The earl's marshal, the man in charge of the household's travel arrangements, was fussing and flustered as he consulted lists and pointed the carriers in the right direction, and there seemed to be much confusion. Edwin looked around carefully: sure enough, a small figure lurked in the narrow space between two of the buildings set against the outer wall, watching avidly. No doubt he was hoping that something would fall, which might mean it would be discarded or overlooked. Aware of the boy's speed despite his frail-looking frame, Edwin moved surreptitiously along the side of the building. He had no desire to lose his quarry again.

'Got you!' He jumped in front of the narrow opening, spreading his arms wide to prevent any escape. Peter tried his best, but there was no way out behind him; he lunged forward, but Edwin caught him and lifted him bodily off the floor. He weighed virtually nothing, but struggled as best he could, and shouted.

Edwin looked around him, embarrassed at the noise. However, after a quick glance the men who were working turned away. Nobody had any interest in a ragged boy who had been apprehended by a respectable-looking man. Clearly he'd been caught doing something he shouldn't and was about to get his punishment; he was poor, unimportant, and invisible.

Edwin held Peter until his struggles subsided, trying to make plain that he only wanted to talk and didn't intend any violence. He started to carry his prize back down the alleyway, but the confined space held the Lord knew what, and it stank. Instead, he stepped out into the twilight and wondered where would be a good place to go. He headed for the stables.

He was just inside the door when he remembered why he'd been in the stables earlier, and he nearly turned and left again. But there was nowhere else where he could have a quiet word with the boy, so he made his way in. He realised with some irony that similar thoughts might have been going through the head of the murderer earlier, and decided to store up that theory for later. In the meantime he needed some more information.

Inside it was relatively peaceful: sounds came from one or two of the stalls, indicating that a couple of grooms were checking hooves and currying steeds, but otherwise it was quiet. Edwin considered the hayloft above, realised that he was unlikely to make it up the ladder without either letting Peter go or causing both of them some injury, and instead moved into an empty stall and thankfully sat down on a pile of straw. He loosened his grip on his captive slightly, keeping hold of a fistful of the ragged tunic, and inspected the boy before him.

Lord, but he was dirty. Edwin was not fastidious himself, but never in all his life had he been as filthy as that. The boy stank to high heaven and Edwin's hand felt soiled and greasy just from the contact with his clothing. Underneath the matted hair and the layers of dirt a small face peered out, thin and sharp. The cheeks were pinched and the eyes hollow and streaming with tears. The boy wiped his sleeve across his face – it was difficult to see what might be served by the gesture, for each was as grimy as the other – and sniffed. The tears continued and his small shoulders shook.

Edwin was at a loss as to how to begin. He looked at the abject creature in front of him and felt nothing but pity, but he had his duty.

'Peter.'

No effect. He tried again.

'Peter, I need to talk to you about the knife you had yesterday. Where did you get it from?'

Silence.

'Did you steal it from the kitchen?'

The sobs continued unabated. Edwin didn't know what to do, but the pressure of his situation was starting to tell on him. He must get some sort of information here. Hating himself, he took the boy by both shoulders and shook him hard.

'Listen to me! You must talk to me or you will be in more trouble. Did you steal the knife from the kitchen?'

If anything, the sobs only increased, and Peter sank further into his misery. Edwin raised his hand to strike the child, but then thought about what he was doing, and loathed himself. Here was the lowest of the low, the most unfortunate creature he'd ever come across; orphaned, friendless, starving, petrified. And he had been about to hit him in order to make him speak. Was this how his life as bailiff was going to be? Bullying the weak? He relented and lowered his hand. But he still needed some answers. He had one more idea.

'Peter, listen to me – if you speak to me and tell me what I want to know, I'll see that you get something to eat.' A pause in the shivering and crying. 'And maybe even a new tunic, something warm to wear.'

How in the Lord's name was he going to do that? The food, maybe, for he could rely upon his mother if needs be. But the clothing? He himself had only one spare tunic, and it would swamp the boy for certain. But maybe he could use some of the money he'd saved to buy something off one of the women in the village, one whose son had outgrown something. Maybe somebody would be glad of a coin in place of an old tunic which was too small.

His new approach was working. The sobs stopped and an incredulous face looked at him through the tears. 'Really?'

Edwin had always been told that he had a soft heart, but looking at the hope on the face in front of him, he knew he would do whatever it took. 'Yes, really. But first, speak. Did you steal the knife?'

'Nobody was using it.'

That was a start. 'So you did have it?'

'Yes.'

'Did you get it from the kitchen?'

A nod.

'What did you do with it?'

'I wanted to sell it. But nobody would buy it. Then I wanted to use it to kill something to eat, but I couldn't catch nothing. Then the squire and the knight saw me with it, and I ran. I dropped it, and now it's gone.'

Such a long speech, but still no joy for Edwin. If this knife was the murder weapon, then Peter certainly wasn't the murderer, nor would he be able to shed any light on who was. A thought struck him.

'Which squire? Which knight?'

Peter didn't know their names, the great ones who moved at the edge of his world, far above him. But for the promise of food and clothes, he would try. 'The earl's squire. Not the tall one, the other one. And the knight with the shining face.'

Well, the squire had to be Robert, surely, which fitted with his message, but the knight ... 'What do you mean, shining face?'

Peter didn't have the words to express the picture in his mind. 'Just ... shining. Like a light.' Edwin still looked bemused, and Peter could see his meal slipping away. He tried again, and was rewarded with a flash of inspiration. 'He used to be here. Another squire.'

There could only be one knight who fitted that description, but how might he be involved with this? Edwin recalled that he had seen Sir Roger praying over the body. But what possible connection could he have to all this? He could never have set eyes on the dead earl before this week, so what cause would he have to kill him? Still, this was new information. Edwin ordered his thoughts. He must first find Robert, to see what he might have discovered since this morning, and then he would have to talk with Sir Roger again.

Peter was staring at him in hope. No, before all the other tasks, he must keep his promise here. First, the food. He rose, with the boy looking at him expectantly. 'Stay here, Peter, and I'll bring you some food.' Peter's face fell – clearly he had no expectation that anything would be forthcoming. As Edwin started to move away, the boy desperately tried one last gamble, perhaps thinking that more information might mean more chance of food. He clutched at Edwin's sleeve, his small hand gripping tightly.

'I saw them.'

Edwin stopped. 'Saw who?'

'By the keep. In the night. When the man was killed.'

Edwin sat down again, thumping to the floor, unable to believe his luck. He looked closely at the boy. 'Are you lying to me? I can assure you, if you are, you will get nothing.'

Peter was eager now, sensing that he had power. He shook his head. 'Not lying.'

'All right then, answer my questions. What were you doing in the inner ward, up by the keep?'

The boy looked uncomfortable. 'Looking for somewhere to sleep. There aren't many places here, because people see me and tell me to go away. So I went to see if there was a place up there. There was a little hole in the wall. I climbed in.'

'Did the guards not see you?'

'No. I hid. I saw one soldier but he didn't see me.'

'Do you know which soldier? His name?'

A shake of the head. But surely it had been Berold?

'Where were you hiding?'

'Under the steps to the keep. Out of the wind.'

Edwin grew more excited. If this was true, Peter could have seen who went into the keep. But wait, what had he said? Not 'he', but 'them'.

'How many people did you see? I mean, after everyone had gone to bed.'

Peter looked thoughtful for a moment and then, with concentration, he held up four fingers.

'Four? You saw four people going into the keep?'

Peter nodded.

'Were they all together? Who were they?'

The boy shook his head. 'Not together. None of them. They went in, but they didn't all come out. All except the dead man.'

Edwin was having some difficulty with the way in which Peter was expressing himself. Why could he not articulate clearly? With sudden insight, he realised that it was probably because nobody ever spoke to him, or at least didn't speak to him properly, so he never had cause to practise his speech. His heart went out again to the waif, and he kept his patience as he tried to question him again.

'So, four people went in,' he held up four fingers, and then folded one back down, 'and three came out?'

Peter nodded. 'They came out ... not together. Apart, but not very far apart.'

Edwin grew more excited. 'Who were they?'

The words were halting, but the meaning sent a shiver through him.

'The other visitor – the little man – the earl's sister, and the priest.'

Edwin sat back in shock. This wasn't what he had been expecting. What on earth had the three of them been doing in the keep during the night? Had they gone together, or separately? He needed to find out more about Walter, and it was now more imperative than ever that he find Father Ignatius. He rose and turned to leave, but was stopped by the small grubby hand still holding his sleeve. He looked down into the hollow eyes. First things first.

'Stay here and I'll bring you some food.'

Disbelief. The hand gripped harder.

Edwin hastened to reassure the boy. 'Honestly, Peter, I'm not fooling you. You stay here while I go to see the steward's wife: she is my aunt and will give me something if I ask for it, but if she knows it's for you then it might be more difficult. I'll come back as soon as I can.' He slipped out of the stall, back towards the stable door, passing the two stalls where men were working, still concentrating on their horses. He had much to think about – those who had entered the keep, for a start, to say nothing of the missing knife, which was assuming an ever greater importance in his mind. Nobody would use their own knife to kill a man if they could use somebody else's, surely – but had someone taken it and crept into the keep under cover of darkness? Was it one of the people Peter had seen, or could it have been someone else? And what had Berold seen? He hardly noticed where his feet were taking him as he walked up towards the inner gatehouse.

Peter looked miserably after him. He was hungry, he was cold, and he was frightened. So much had happened since the death of his mother and father, and none of it had been pleasant. He remembered their faces only vaguely. They hadn't been the most loving of parents – his father had been wont to beat him when the mood took him, and his mother was always so tired – but they had been his, the only family he had since his little brother and sister had gone to heaven a number of years before. Since the day when his parents were buried in the frosty, hard ground, his life had been one of cold and misery. He stole to eat, for what else could he do? But worse than the hunger was the absolute sense of being alone. He had no one to speak to, no one to share anything with, no one to comfort him in his pain. His sole dealings with people involved a rough and impersonal kindness at best, a gruff word and a few scraps, or a curse and a blow at worst. He had no friends; he was utterly alone in the world. The previous night he had crept up, alone, into the inner ward, squeezing in through a tiny hole in the wall, and had found a lonely corner in which to hide, dark and unwelcoming, but at least out of the cold wind which swept the night. There he'd curled up until the first pre-dawn sounds came from the kitchen, and he'd crept away again, unnoticed, to begin another solitary and hungry day.

The tears welled up again and he cried, huge harsh sobs which racked his whole body. He'd hoped that Edwin's kind face had heralded some food at least, but it looked as though he would sleep hungry again. Thinking of sleep, he looked at his surroundings. Here in the stall it was warm and dry, with straw to cover him. He'd seen a horse being taken out for some exercise earlier, so it would probably come back at some point, but until then, nobody knew he was here. If he stayed very quiet, perhaps he could hide under the straw and remain unnoticed even when the horse came back, and then he could share its warmth throughout the night. He lay down and burrowed into the straw.

Over in another stall, the groom who had been checking the hooves of the earl's destrier stood up. The task was finished and he was away to his evening meal – his sweetheart would have saved him a few tasty scraps, knowing that he was too busy to come up to the hall. Before leaving he leaned over the barrier to the next stall, where he had heard someone else working, and was halfway through a friendly greeting when he realised who it was; he'd worked in the earl's service for some time and recognised his household past and present. He stopped, aware that he might have sounded too familiar or given offence. 'Beg pardon, my lord, I didn't know it was you.' He received a smile and a wave of forgiveness in return and left the stable, whistling.

Sir Roger straightened up from his horse, looked around the deserted stable, and moved quietly towards the stall in the corner.

When Edwin returned a short while later with bread and cheese, he was surprised to find Peter gone.

Chapter Nine

As the evening drew in, Robert and Martin were crossing the inner ward. Robert was eager to ask what had been discovered so far, but just as he opened his mouth, Simon suddenly pushed past him and ran at full pelt across the courtyard, seizing Father Ignatius by the arm. Startled at being thus assailed, the priest turned in fright to shake off his attacker, before realising who it was.

'Yes, my son, what is it?'

Robert rushed forward and pulled Simon back, unclenching his fist from Father Ignatius's sleeve, shocked that he should lay hands on a man of the cloth in such a manner. He gave the boy a clip round the ear, but half-heartedly, for he was more interested in the priest, who looked careworn and nervous, and was already trying to slip away. Martin whispered urgently in Robert's ear that he should delay Father Ignatius while he fetched Edwin, and immediately Robert turned on what he hoped was his best charm, asking the priest to step inside with them for a few moments. Father Ignatius looked about him, fearfully, trying to demur, but Robert steered him slowly across the darkened yard towards the steward's office. Once inside it was easy to make much of him, offering wine while Simon fetched a chair. Still, they couldn't keep this up forever, so Robert hoped his friend would arrive soon. This might be his best chance to find out what Edwin had discovered so far.

Soon enough Edwin arrived – strangely, he was carrying some bread and cheese, which Simon eyed hungrily as soon as it was put down on the table – and greeted the priest.

'Father, you must know that we've been searching for you all day, to ask you about what happened last night.'

Father Ignatius looked ill at ease. He was about to say something when Edwin forestalled him.

'And please, Father, don't tell me that you were abed the whole night and saw nothing, because you were seen entering the inner ward after darkness had fallen.'

Robert looked in surprise at his friend, taken aback by the new-found authority in his voice. He seemed to have become stronger in such a short space of time. But he didn't dwell on the thought, for the priest was speaking.

'I had not thought to lie to you, my son,' he admonished, 'for I was abroad that night. But I am not at liberty to speak of the events which befell me, or at least not until I have spoken with our lord the earl.'

He settled back, trying to look dignified, but Edwin's reply was immediate. 'You needn't worry, Father, for I have already spoken with our lord. He knew I was looking for you and bade me say to you that you may tell me all, for the murder of the visiting earl will have serious consequences for all of us.'

Robert was impressed. He knew for a fact that Edwin hadn't spoken with the earl since their brief conference at dawn that day, and the ease with which Edwin was lying – Edwin, who was never able to dissemble about anything! – was almost frightening. Only someone who knew him as well as Robert might recognise the significance of the restless hands, picking away at his fingernails, behind his back. Father Ignatius had no idea, and looked relieved.

'Truly?'

Edwin nodded, and Robert took the hint and weighed into the conversation, agreeing with his friend.

Father Ignatius looked as though a great weight had been lifted off him. He took a sip of his wine and began to speak.

'In truth, I am glad to own it, for I have been wandering afar all this day, seeking the Lord's forgiveness. What I did last night put my immortal soul in grave danger.'

Shocked, the four others in the room leaned forward to listen to the priest's tale.

———⟆⊙⟅———

Adam tried to make himself invisible as he stood against the wall. After his return from the campsite he hadn't really had anywhere else to go, so he'd followed the kindly knight back up into the keep, hoping he might be able to be of service to him in some small fashion. He didn't appear to have a squire, so there was some hope there. From what he could see, David had been trailing round after their lord's brother all day, so there seemed little chance that Adam would gain anything by following suit. Besides, the old knight was nicer to him.

But the knight had headed straight for the earl's council chamber, and Adam felt somewhat embarrassed to be there. Trying to find a new lord was one thing, but disturbing such an important man was another. He had thought they might withdraw once the lady entered, but Sir Geoffrey had only looked enquiringly at the earl, who had not explicitly dismissed him. And so he stayed, and Adam couldn't quite find the right moment to draw attention to himself by leaving, so he stayed too. He hoped he wouldn't get in too much trouble. But so far his presence had not been remarked upon, and he hadn't been thrown out; fortunately, as he already knew, squires weren't really noticed by their betters until they were needed for something, at which time they were expected to be present and ready. But anyway, with any luck he could stay invisible until he could find a convenient opportunity to slip away without incurring the wrath of the earl.

However, he suspected that he would end up in real trouble once they realised how much he'd seen and heard.

The lady, whom he recognised as the earl's sister, paced up and down the room. Eventually she stopped, burst into tears and flung herself into the earl's arms.

'Oh William!' she wailed, 'I don't even know how to begin! There's something I have to tell you … ' she dissolved into sobs.

Adam was surprised at how gently the earl cradled her in his arms, stroking her head and letting her weep herself out. He couldn't imagine his lord ever doing anything remotely similar.

As her shaking subsided, the earl spoke.

'Isabelle, my darling sister, it will be all right. There's nothing to worry about.'

She raised her tear-stained face to him. 'But William … '

He shushed her gently. 'I said it would be all right. I think I know what you're going to say.'

The lady Isabelle looked at him in surprise. 'Please, William, let me speak. I can't rest until I've told you everything.'

The earl nodded without speaking, and led her to a chair before pouring her some wine. She took a gulp and then began to speak.

'You know that I've been … eager to marry again since I was widowed. You know, also, that I admire – or did admire – Walter de Courteville.' She didn't look at him, seemed afraid to meet his eye, and Adam wondered why. 'Well, I – we – became impatient, and Walter devised a plan which he said would make everything end well. He sent a message to the parish priest, saying that you had decided that we should marry, but that under the circumstances – the impending campaign, the danger – you wished it to happen in secret. Then we would be in no danger while you were away, but if anything should happen to you, I would have a protector who would rule in your stead. I was not sure that Father Ignatius would agree – he must have thought it odd, for sure – but Walter persuaded him, and he was to meet us in the chapel in the keep at midnight. We thought that it would be less noticeable for him to come into the ward than for us to go out, to get to the church. That's why it was easier to be in the guest chambers.' She stopped and took another gulp from the goblet, her fingers clenched around the stem.

Adam hadn't known his lord's brother very well, but he knew enough to be unsurprised at such deviousness. If Lord Ralph had found out about this, there would have been a huge row, no doubt with cups flying and smashing everywhere. Adam shuddered simply thinking about it.

The lady was continuing. ' … in the chapel … but Walter and the priest arrived soon after. And there we were m- m-married.' She stopped and looked as though she was about to cry, but she took a great breath and carried on in a level tone. 'Father Ignatius left us, and we went our separate ways back to our quarters. Walter said … ' she almost broke down again, but managed to continue, her voice shaking a little, 'Walter said we shouldn't consummate our union yet, that we should wait until a more opportune time. But since then, he's refused to speak to me, and when I came upon him alone earlier he said that it had all been a mistake, that he never loved me at all. And now I don't know what to do!'

Her composure finally cracked and the words spewed out in torrents. 'I called him into my room, told him how much I loved him, but he only urged me to secrecy.' Adam listened as she told her tale, and imagined the scene which had taken place between the two of them.

'Isabelle,' said Walter, 'Isabelle, my sweet, this is madness! I must leave – we must wait a little longer before we tell the world of our marriage … it wouldn't be safe.'

'I care nothing for safety,' Isabelle responded, 'I just want our marriage to be acknowledged before the world.'

Walter turned on her. 'You foolish woman,' he said heatedly. 'Did you honestly believe that it was all real? Let me explain. I am a man of talent, of ambition. You are a ridiculous old maid suffering from the delusion that you are somehow attractive to men. The only attractive thing about you is that you are your brother's heir. Well, now I am the heir to an earldom myself, and I don't need you. Thank God for the mercy that we didn't lie together, so it isn't valid. As far as I am concerned, it never happened, and I'll think of it as a nightmare to be forgotten in the light of morning.'

Isabelle's voice rose to a squeak as she came to the end of her tale. 'And the worst thing was, I could tell that he *enjoyed* saying it!' She could stave the tears off no longer and they coursed freely down her cheeks as she sobbed into her brother's shoulder.

Adam sensed the waves of anger emanating from the knight beside him, and could barely contain his own outrage. That anyone should treat a noble lady so! It was scarcely credible. Walter de Courteville deserved to be called to account for such barbarous behaviour. And there was one thing which he now knew for certain: he would rather starve than be squire to such a man.

The lady forced more words out between great shuddering breaths. 'I can't bear him, but under God's law we are man and wife! Oh, what shall I do? William, what shall I do!' She fell on her knees, burying her face in her hands.

There was a deep silence and Adam was almost too frightened to breathe. He couldn't possibly imagine how the earl might react to such a confession. After a few moments the lady lifted her face to look at her brother, and Adam too risked a glance in his direction. To his immense surprise, his countenance held only compassion.

'My dear sister, how you must have suffered. Don't worry, I'm not angry with you, only with him. To take advantage of you in such a way! To prey upon your womanly feelings! He's a disgrace.'

'But William, what can we do?' She sounded desperate.

He put his hands to her head, cupping her face. 'Never fear, Isabelle. Your situation is not as desperate as it may seem. You have told me your tale, but there is also something I must tell to you.'

Edwin looked at Father Ignatius, aghast. 'You did *what?*' Behind him, Robert whistled in disbelief.

The priest looked at them uncomfortably. 'I did it on the orders of the earl, I tell you.'

Robert spoke in a more sceptical tone than Edwin would have dared. 'But surely, Father, you take your orders from the bishop?'

Father Ignatius had the grace to look ashamed. 'Yes, of course I do, but we must all obey our secular lords as well as our spiritual ones, and anyway, he has the right to rule over his family. Walter came to me, explained that the earl wanted his sister to marry him, and that he wanted it done in secret – a quiet ceremony during this time of upheaval, he didn't want the marriage to be announced until after the forthcoming campaign – and it seemed relatively straightforward. And such a generous donation to the church funds! I will be able to have the roof mended, and provide food for the poor for many days to come. And there might even have been be enough left over for a new pair of candlesticks for the altar … ' he trailed away and stopped uncomfortably, looking at the surrounding faces. He cleared his throat. 'Anyway, having already received word from the earl himself, the knowledge of what I was about to do made me hesitate for a while, but eventually I made my way from my cottage up into the keep. It was no great trouble to explain to the night porter that I needed to go to the chapel – he's used to me coming and going for the various services of the day. As I came through the gate into the inner ward, I saw somebody cross the courtyard and enter the keep, but I realised that it must be the groom, so I followed behind and went up the steps. The great door of the keep was open as usual – as you know, it's only ever shut in times of trouble – so I passed through and turned into the staircase. The Lady Isabelle and Walter were waiting for me in the chapel.'

There was silence in the room for a moment. Edwin tried to think. Three people, all in the keep on the night de Courteville was murdered. They might all have had the opportunity to go up the stairs to the roof; they might also have had different reasons for wanting to do away with the earl. He was about to stand and take his leave, the better to consider matters, when his arm was seized by Father Ignatius.

'But you don't understand, my son. There is more.'

'More?' What more could there possibly be?

'Oh, believe me, it's much worse. My soul shall do penance in purgatory for many agonising years for what I have done.'

Edwin leaned forward once more.

'I have no taste for what I'm about to say, but now I've started I may as well confess all.' He shifted uncomfortably. 'For you see, before the message from Walter de Courteville arrived, I'd also had a communication from our lord the earl. In it he said that he suspected that de Courteville would try something of the kind, and that if he did, I was to go along with it and pretend to marry them. But in fact I should miss out a crucial part of the service, or otherwise dissemble, to ensure that although they thought they were husband and wife, in reality they weren't.' His face white, he crossed himself. 'May the Lord forgive me for abusing the holy sacrament so.' He fell silent.

Robert whistled again. 'So, since yesterday, Walter de Courteville and Lady Isabelle have been going about thinking that they were legally wed?'

Father Ignatius nodded. 'I informed the earl of what had passed, and he bade me stay away from the castle and village today, until he had considered how best to proceed. He didn't want me to tell anyone. But of course, if he's said to you that I should tell all, then that's different.'

Edwin blushed at the thought of his deception, but fortunately nobody noticed in the torchlit semi-darkness. But how else was he supposed to proceed? He needed to find out as much as possible before sundown on the morrow

– less than one full day – and he needed people to give him information. He refused to feel guilty. But even so, lying to a priest … he hastily changed the subject.

'So what will the earl do now?'

Father Ignatius looked at him wearily. 'I don't know. Luckily for me, that's for him to decide. Now, if you will excuse me,' he rose to leave, 'I have prayers to say, for the good of my soul as well as that of Berold, who lies in his shroud in my church, and for his family.'

As he was leaving the room, Edwin was suddenly struck by another thought and called him back. 'Forgive me for detaining you further, Father, but I have one more question. If you were performing a wedding ceremony, or at least pretending to' – the priest winced – 'where in the chapel would you have been standing?'

Father Ignatius looked surprised. 'Why, in front of the altar, of course, with the two participants kneeling facing me.'

This is what Edwin had guessed. 'So, you would have been facing the door?' The priest nodded his assent. 'And during the time that you were facing the door, did you see anyone going past in the passageway? Anyone who might have been on their way up to the roof of the keep?'

The others were unnaturally still, perhaps realising the significance of the question. Father Ignatius considered it carefully before shaking his head. 'No. Even though I was involved in the rite, and indeed struggling with my own conscience, I would have noticed had anyone passed, for fear that they would see us. But in all the time I was there, nobody passed the door.' He nodded a farewell and left the room.

Adam couldn't quite take in the significance of what the earl was saying. By the look on her face, the Lady Isabelle couldn't either. 'William, what are you saying?'

He smiled. 'I am saying, my dear, that you are not married to that good-for-nothing, that nobody can say that you are, and that we will have some suitable revenge on him for his duplicity.' He sat back, almost smirking.

Comprehension slowly began to show on her face. She ventured a tearful smile, and then a small laugh. 'Lord, I do believe he will have a surprise in store for him.' Adam worked his way through the consequences, and found that the prospect was appealing to him as well. The lady continued. 'What will you say?'

'I don't know yet. I'll consider it, and decide how best to act.'

She agreed immediately. 'Of course, brother. You will know what best to do.' There was a slightly awkward pause during which Adam thought he might be noticed if he so much as breathed, before she spoke again. 'Oh, if only I'd listened to your counsel in the first place! I might have spared myself all this.'

He looked serious. 'Indeed. Perhaps now you'll realise that I have all of our best interests at heart. Can you imagine the disaster which would follow with the estates in the hands of that toad?' She looked contrite and on the verge of tears again. He spoke more gently. 'But only now do I understand how much this matter of your marriage means to you. I've delayed too long, and as soon as I return from this campaign, I'll give the question my full attention.' She nodded, still looking subdued. He patted her shoulder. 'And … ' the words came out in a rush, 'And I give you my word that, although I shall seek a match for you which is in the best interests of our family and our lands, I shall never ask you to wed any man absolutely against your will.'

Adam had never heard of such a privilege, and he wondered at the earl's generosity. He thought fleetingly of his own little sister, who had been toddling around last time he saw her, but who would be much bigger than that now. Would he look after her as well as the earl cared for his sister? He thought he probably would.

The earl helped his sister rise from the floor, brushing a few stray rushes off her skirts. 'Come now, Isabelle. Tidy yourself, for you are a great lady and must have pride in your appearance.' She straightened and assumed more dignity. 'Better. Now, return to your chamber and ensure that you have a good night's sleep.' She nodded and withdrew.

The earl paced the room, but stopped mid-stride and snapped his fingers. He raised his voice and called. 'Robert!'

As there was no reply, the earl looked around the room and seemed genuinely surprised that his squire was not in attendance. 'Martin?' He peered into the darkened corner where Adam and the knight were standing. 'Geoffrey? Of course, I'd forgotten you were there. Where are those cursed boys when I want them?'

'I am afraid I don't know, my lord – I can only guess that they are about some business with young Edwin.'

'Well, that's as maybe, but I don't want all of them away at once. Who's that there with you – de Courteville's squire?'

Adam trembled. The moment of judgement had come. How was he to be punished? But the earl merely spoke brusquely. 'Good. At least someone thinks of my needs. Find Robert for me and fetch him here, there's a good lad.'

Adam nodded, and was already moving before the earl could speak his next words.

'Tell him to find de Courteville, wherever he's hiding, and bring him … no, wait.' Adam stopped at the threshold. The earl spoke in a different tone. 'He's probably the sort of man who prefers to lie abed in the mornings,' – his voice dripped with contempt – 'so tell Robert to go and find de Courteville at daybreak, or just before, and bring him to me. There are a few things I wish to say to him.' He smiled unpleasantly.

Looking forward to being the agent of Walter's discomfort, and fervently glad that he'd escaped the chamber unscathed, Adam almost skipped out of the room.

Edwin and the others were still considering the import of what they had heard when Adam appeared in the room, making them all jump. They leapt to their feet as he looked around.

'Excuse me. I … I was told that you would all be here.' He looked around, nervously. 'I've been sent by the lord earl, to ask Robert to attend him.'

Robert gasped, and Edwin suddenly became aware of the fact that it was full dark. Robert looked stricken. 'Our lord has been unattended all this time? How could I … ' He swept the room with a quick glance and spoke to Edwin. 'I must go – let me know later what you talk about.' He strode out of the room, Adam at his heels speaking of some task which he needed to perform.

After he'd left, the others looked at each other. Or rather, Edwin and Martin looked at each other, and Simon looked at the bread and cheese, which Edwin had completely forgotten about until now. He rolled his eyes. 'Go on then.' Simon seemed to hesitate for the barest moment, but then tucked in eagerly, leaving Edwin to wonder once again where the intended recipient of the food had got to. But he now had other matters on his mind. He looked at Martin, not sure how to start discussing the priest's revelations. There had been so many shocks. For a while they spoke of their astonishment, of the sheer unbelievable nature of what they'd heard. A secret wedding which was no wedding at all, high-ranking nobles deceived, a priest celebrating a false marriage in the full knowledge of what he was doing – it was simply outside of anything they'd ever encountered before.

But enough of the gossip – Edwin must think of the facts.

'So-o,' he considered, carefully, 'if Father Ignatius didn't see anyone go up the stairs, it must mean that the earl was killed either before the wedding ceremony started, or after they'd finished.'

'Agreed.'

Simon said something unintelligible through a mouthful of food; Edwin regarded him for a moment, in case he was going to repeat it, then shrugged and turned back to Martin.

'It also means that any one of the three of them could have gone up the stairs afterwards, if they left separately, and then killed the earl. Nobody else would know anything about it.'

'Also agreed. But why?'

'That is what we need to find out.' Edwin thought for a few moments before continuing. 'But surely we can discount Father Ignatius. He's a priest – he couldn't kill anyone. And what purpose would it serve? Why would he want to murder the earl? It doesn't make any sense.'

'You're right. But by that token, we must also discount the Lady Isabelle. Why would she want to kill him? And how could she do it? He was a strong man, and she's only a woman.'

'Ye-es,' said Edwin, 'but if she believed herself wed to the earl's brother, then maybe she thought she would be a step closer to being the countess if he were dead? For then she would be married to the heir. De Courteville had but one son, is that right? She wouldn't be far away from her ambition with only a child in her path.' My God, he thought, is this what I've come to? Suspecting the Lady Isabelle, the earl's own sister, of murdering a guest under his roof? How can the world have turned upside down so quickly? How can we be talking about this?

Martin shook his head. 'But in that case, surely it's much more likely that Walter would have killed his brother? He would be the one with all the power, after all, if he were to inherit. And who knows – he might have held some secret grudge against his brother, for that often happens in families. I think we need to find out more about him.'

Edwin thought the same: surely Walter was the most obvious suspect? He could have killed his brother and then stabbed Berold after he'd found out that he had been observed. Edwin also admitted to a feeling that it would be nice if the culprit turned out to be a stranger, and not someone from the castle or village, someone he knew. It would be easier that way. He needed to – but no, it was getting very late to do anything else today.

'Well, it will have to wait – we can hardly drag the man from his bed to question him.' Lord, but he was tired. How long had he been awake? The morning seemed like a lifetime away. Had it only been yesterday that he had been living his normal life? To be concerned with local matters on one day, and to be overtaken by events of national importance on the next – it was scarcely credible. He was half-convinced that he would wake up and find that it had all been a dream, such was the air of unreality.

It had gone very quiet over in the corner where Simon was sitting. Edwin turned to look at him, half expecting him to be asleep, but he was sitting upright on a stool, staring into the distance with a thoughtful expression.

'Simon?'

He'd broken the spell. The boy turned round to look at him, weariness showing in his eyes. 'I was just thinking.'

'What about?'

'What you were saying earlier about the time when the earl must have been murdered.' He didn't elaborate, making Edwin irritable.

'Well, what about it?'

'I don't know.' Edwin sighed in exasperation, but Simon continued. 'There's something – but it can't be.' He looked around at both of the others. 'No, it can't be. Just forget about it.' He sighed, suddenly looking even younger. 'I'm tired.'

Martin walked over to him and hauled him up off the stool. 'Go to bed then. Our lord will need you tomorrow, and you'll be no use if you're so tired that you can't stand up. Go on, off with you. Don't wake the earl on your way into the bedchamber.' He shoved Simon gently towards the door, and the boy staggered out into the dark room beyond.

Martin came back into the room to face Edwin, who spoke. 'You should go as well.'

'But we have much to discuss yet. We need to work out what we're going to do tomorrow. We've only got one day left – we shouldn't waste the night in sleep.'

But Edwin was shaking his head. 'No. You'll have a busy day tomorrow too, and you'll need your wits about you. Go now, and leave me to think.' He was too tired to notice that he'd become more used to issuing orders to members of the nobility.

'What will you do?'

'I'll stay here. It's too late to go back down to the village. There are others asleep in the hall here – perhaps I'll join them.'

Martin hesitated. Edwin could see that he was exhausted. 'Well, if you think it best … '

'Yes, I do. Go.'

Edwin watched the tall figure leave the room, stooping as he walked under the lintel of the door. Wearily, he forced himself to stand. He followed out through the service room and into the hall, where shrouded figures lay in various attitudes on the floor. He groped around until he found a spare blanket, but then took it back into the office. He wouldn't be able to think out in the hall. He moved a stool back against the wall, and sat back on it, wrapping the blanket around him. He schooled himself into calmness, staring in front of him and inhaling the scent of spices. He needed to order his thoughts and here, in the peace of the room, would be the best place.

He realised that he hadn't thought about his father for several hours, the first time this had happened in weeks. Was he coming to terms with the impending loss, or was it merely that he had so much else on his mind that the demons had been pushed back out of his thoughts? He certainly had much else to occupy his mind. He tried to say a prayer for Berold, but couldn't think straight for long enough to offer it properly to the Lord. The death provoked stronger feelings in him than the other, partly as Berold seemed more of an innocent, but also because nobody else seemed much bothered by it, intent as they were on the death of a man of higher rank. Was Berold not equal before the Lord to any man? He didn't really know whether that was the case, but it was certain that here on earth he counted for much less than the dead nobleman. Hadn't Sir Geoffrey himself said that the soldier's death shouldn't distract him from his main task? Well, he would avenge Berold, would give him some peace in his grave by finding out who had killed him. He would spend the night deep in thought until the pieces of the puzzle became clearer.

He blew out the tallow candle and settled back.

Outside in the courtyard, Martin stumbled for a moment on an uneven stone, and stopped to regain his balance, waiting until his eyes had become accustomed to the blackness. In truth, it wasn't full dark, for the moon hadn't yet waned, but it was still darker than the office with its flickering candle. He moved slowly through the yard, thinking how eerie the castle was during the night. Only a day before, a man had made almost this same journey, and had met his death. Martin shivered and looked warily at the shadows around him, becoming afraid. He tried to pull himself together. He was being foolish, thinking that anyone might harm him – after all, whoever killed the earl no doubt had a good reason to do so.

He thought of the visiting earl again. Surely there must have been many people with a reason to wish him ill. He was hardly the most pleasant of men. As Martin passed the kitchen, he recalled the events which had taken place there last night. He dreaded to think what might have happened to Joanna if he hadn't been there. Joanna ... for a moment he was lost in a pleasant reverie, but he was jolted back to awareness by a thought. He stopped still in the darkness of the yard, considering the import of it. Joanna had come to speak to them earlier, to discuss what had happened. He himself had welcomed her. But she was Lady Isabelle's companion, in her presence day and night. Lady Isabelle had been abroad for much of the night before, walking between the guest quarters and the keep, and up to the chapel for her false wedding ceremony. And yet, when they'd asked Joanna, she had asserted that she knew of nobody who might have been awake and moving about the castle at the time.

Martin felt cold. Why had she said that?

Chapter Ten

Edwin awoke in a panic as someone started to strike him. He fell off his stool and shouted for the onslaught to stop, trying to avoid the blows. He risked looking up to see that his assailant was William Steward.

'Lord, boy, what are you trying to do to me, sitting there in the dark against the wall? Don't you know you should never take a soldier by surprise like that? A few years ago in a different place and I might have killed you.' He grabbed a handful of Edwin's tunic and hauled him off the floor.

Edwin apologised. He felt dizzy. He'd sat in the darkness for much of the night, thinking his way through things, but had eventually dozed off, still in his sitting position. Now he was so stiff he could hardly move, and his muscles ached.

'What are you doing here, anyway?'

'I was talking in here last night, and it was too late to go back home, so I thought I'd stay here and try to get some things straight in my mind.'

William grunted. 'Aye, well, it's a hard enough task you've been given.' He found another stool and sat down. 'What have you discovered so far?'

'Not much.' Edwin summarised what he knew. He was right, there was little enough of it, but explaining helped him to fit different pieces of information together.

William sat in silence while he listened, apart from expelling a long breath at the mention of the priest's story. Once Edwin had finished, he spoke. 'It seems as though you know more than you think.'

Edwin sighed. 'Yes, but I still have no idea about the most important answer I need. Who killed the earl, and why?'

William clouted him gently on the shoulder. 'You'll find out. I don't know either, but I can tell you one thing – he was a wicked man.'

Edwin was interested. 'What do you know of him?'

William shrugged. 'Nothing from my own experience. But while we were on campaign in Normandy all those years ago, I heard tales of evil deeds. Those taken prisoner by him or his men weren't safe, even if they were knights. It was the custom, of course, for knights to be ransomed, even if common men like me were slaughtered because they weren't worth anything. But de Courteville seemed to care nothing for the money. Oh, he got rich enough, but if there were any he'd taken against, any who might have slighted him, he would rather have his revenge than their gold.'

Edwin felt chilled. But here was the opportunity to ask William about that long-ago campaign, to try and glean some information while he could. He couldn't help thinking that the key to this mystery might lie in the past rather than the present, so the more he knew about it, the better. He asked the question.

William expelled another long breath. 'I swore once never to speak of that campaign, but if you think it'll help you, I'll try.' He settled himself more comfortably on the stool.

'War is an evil thing. You may have heard tales of chivalry and high deeds, but it's not like that. Pray God that you never have to go near a field of battle. The commanders may have some kind of view of how things are going overall, but for the common soldier it's all about what you can see in front of you. Who will come running at you, trying to kill or maim you? How will you defend yourself? What will you do if someone comes at you from the side or from behind while you're already engaged with someone else? There's nothing you can do except take each moment as it comes.'

His eyes took on a far-away look, as though he was seeing not the room around him, but shades from long ago. 'The bloodlust in another man's eyes, or the fear in them. The sound it makes when you run the steel of your weapon into his body, the noise of his screams, the struggle to wrench the bloodied thing out of him so you can use it on someone else. The feeling of your comrades around you, some standing shoulder to shoulder with you, others falling in agony. Their cries, and the knowledge that you can do nothing to help them, even if it's someone you've known since childhood. And this goes on and on, hour after hour, until you're so exhausted you can hardly stand, but you know that if you drop your guard for a moment, you'll be one of the ones writhing on the floor, screaming for the mercy of a blade to put you out of your agony. Until finally it stops. Your enemies are fleeing – or you are – and there's no one left to fight. You step over mutilated bodies, over severed limbs, over spilled guts, wading in the blood, looking for the faces of your friends, or at least those that still have faces that you can recognise. You finish off any enemies in cold blood, while trying to save those of your own who might have a chance of recovery. The birds start to circle and the flies hover, ready to feast on the dead, and you leave knowing that you'll never get the smell of blood out of your nostrils, and that you'll never wash it off your hands.'

He paused for a moment, looking blindly down at his hands. Edwin felt sick, but he was mesmerised: he'd never heard William talk like this before. But there was more to come.

'Oh, but there's worse than the battlefield. The true battlefield comes along but seldom. All the time in between you're seeking to destroy your enemies' lands and resources, either to gain supplies for yourself, or simply to ensure that he shall not have them. A *chevauchee*,' – he struggled with the French term – 'the nobles call it, a fine, grand word. But what it involves is seeking out villages, the places where people have made their homes and their livelihoods, just like here, and stealing everything and burning their homes to the ground. Do you have any idea what that's like? The screaming, the flames, the women, the children … God forgive me. I've never killed a child, but I've seen it happen, and there is no sight more guaranteed to stay in a man's mind until the hour of his death.' He bowed his head and crossed himself.

Edwin sat in silence, the nightmare images playing in his mind. How could men do that to one another? He asked William.

'Well, common men do it because they're ordered to. Knights do it because they think it's their purpose in life. And nobles do it because they seek more power and more lands, so they're powerful enough to keep doing it to other people and to ensure that nobody can do it to them. And anyone caught in the middle is there because they're unlucky. The only hope that we can have in life is to serve a lord who's strong enough to protect us, so that we may live our lives in peace. God knows there are thousands who haven't been so lucky.' He pointed to the scar which disfigured his face. 'Have you never wondered how I got this?'

Edwin had wondered often, almost every day, but he dared not speak lest the spell break. He nodded.

'It was on that campaign in Normandy, fifteen years ago. The one where we were fighting to decide who would sit upon the throne of England. It was a nasty campaign, even by normal standards – I'd never been on one like it. Villages of no importance and no worth burnt to the ground simply for enjoyment or revenge. Nobles with personal grudges against each other – a sure way to make sure that everyone suffers. We'd gone to forage for supplies and had come upon a village. Our earl was with us – unusual, for he normally stayed with the other nobles and left us in the charge of his knights while we went looking for supplies. He was a kind-hearted man, the earl, and he gave orders that we should take the supplies and the livestock, but that the people were to be spared if they offered no resistance. Soft-hearted. But not all were as merciful as him. Some of the knights began attacking the villagers, and they tried to fight back. It was pathetic – they had sickles and pitchforks, against fully armed knights and men-at-arms. There was a massacre, not just the men but some women and children as well. As the village burned I could see bodies everywhere. I was wounded – one of the village men came upon me while I was carrying off flour, and I didn't see him until it was too late. He had an axe in his hands, and brought it down on my leg, crippling me such that I still suffer from it today. One of my comrades killed him, and I tried to drag myself back to the edge of the village where our wounded were being gathered. I saw the earl, looking in horror at the bodies around him. Suddenly a woman came at him from behind, with a knife. She was crazed by grief – I suppose some of the children must have been hers, or one of the dead men her husband – and the earl didn't see her. I called, but wounded as I was, I couldn't get there fast enough to stop her striking entirely. All that happened was that I got myself in between her and him, and received this for my pains.' He ran his finger down the massive scar and the tortured mess it had made of his face. 'When we left the village the earl swore that he would repay me for the service. It was clear that I would never soldier again, but he would see that I didn't starve. So here I am.'

His tale concluded, he sat back. 'I have spoken of it only very rarely, for it's not a scar to be proud of. Only my wife and a few others know of it.'

'What happened to her?'

'Who? My wife?'

'The woman who wounded you.'

'Oh. I don't know, but we didn't kill her. Even after what she'd done, the earl couldn't kill a woman in cold blood, so we left her there. She was no further danger. We left her and the other survivors weeping in the ashes of their homes with the bodies of their loved ones around them. As many have wept over the years.'

Edwin didn't know what to say, except to offer up a silent and fervent prayer that such violence should never come near him or his family and friends. But he had more questions about the campaign.

'What did you mean when you said that it was to decide who sat on the throne of England? Surely the old king inherited the crown from his brother?'

'Aye, he did, but there was another claimant, another brother, who was by that time dead, but he left a son. This son was only a boy when King Richard died, but there were some nobles who sided with him. Whether they honestly thought that he was the rightful king, or whether they just saw an opportunity for gain, I don't know. Sir Geoffrey will know more about that sort of thing, for he was there as well. What I do know is that after three years of campaigning the boy was captured, and after that nobody saw or heard of him again.'

Edwin was aghast. 'You mean, the king had him murdered? His own nephew?'

William shrugged. 'It's the only explanation. These nobles are different from you and me, Edwin. Once they set their hearts on the crown, nothing will stop them, even if they have to murder their families. No war is nastier than that between kin.'

'But yet … ' Edwin was still shocked.

'Ah, but King John was an evil man all round, or so I hear. He did many dark deeds during his life. There was one time when he captured some enemies – a noble and his mother – and he had them starved to death in one of his dungeons.'

Now *that* Edwin was not prepared to believe. 'Starved? A nobleman? And his *mother*? A lady? That can't be true.' But a small part of him believed, and was revolted.

'I told you, that particular war was more vicious than any I've known. And the king's cruelty rubbed off on those who followed him, de Courteville among them. Sir Geoffrey will tell you.' William looked up at the small window. 'But I've talked too long. Look, the sun has risen and I've done nothing except remember things which are best forgotten. I have work to do, and so do you.'

Edwin stretched and rose. 'Yes. I'm still on the track of the knife which might have been used to kill the earl, for it's the only one I know of which was missing. I need to go and talk to the cook.'

———————

Martin hadn't thought that he'd be able to sleep, but exhaustion overtook him, and he was surprised to wake and find it already becoming light. He was thoughtful during the squires' morning duties, but as he was often quiet nobody noticed. Once the earl was ready he sent Robert off to find Walter de Courteville, as he wanted to speak with him – Martin could only imagine the contents of *that* conversation, but was fervently glad that he wasn't Walter – and told the other two that they should go and find Edwin. Martin sent Simon off, for he had a task of his own which he needed to see to before he spoke to anyone else.

He eventually found Joanna in the guest quarters, and watched her for a moment. She was singing softly to herself as she shook down the heavy palliasse from her mistress's bed. He stepped into the room to help her with it, looking around warily first in case the Lady Isabelle should also be there. Joanna saw him and smiled.

'She's not here. My lady said that she wanted some time to herself this morning, so she's gone for a walk out in the grounds. She wanted me to turn this – it's straw and not nearly as comfortable as the feather one in the great chamber which she's used to. She's having trouble sleeping.'

That was an obvious opening for Martin to broach his subject, but he couldn't find the words. Instead he held his tongue while he hefted the palliasse back into place, and stood silently by while Joanna arranged the covers to her satisfaction. Then she stepped back and smiled once more.

'Now, what brings you here this morning? Were you looking for my lady?'

Damn it, she was so pleased to see him! On a normal day nothing could have given him more pleasure, but today wasn't a normal day. What was he going to say? How could he ask her what was on his mind?

She noticed his consternation.

'What is it, Martin?' She paused, unsure. 'Has something else happened? Have you found who killed the earl?'

He could hold it in no longer. The words burst out.

'Why didn't you tell me?'

She looked puzzled. 'Tell you what?'

'About the night the earl died. You came over to us, you said you wanted to help us with our task, and then you lied to us. How could you do that?' He was surprised by how hurt he felt. 'I thought you wanted to be with m– … with us, but when we asked you the question, you said you knew of nobody who might have been abroad that night. And yet now we find that the Lady Isabelle was wandering round the castle throughout the night, as well as others. You're her companion, you must have known, and yet you didn't tell us!' He was becoming more agitated, not sure if he wanted to hear her answer. His voice rose. 'What are you hiding?'

She looked at him and burst into tears.

Immediately he was ashamed, feeling like the worst kind of bully. He helped her to sit down on the bed and awkwardly patted her shoulder. He had no experience of this sort of thing – it was not the same as when Simon had cried sometimes when he was little. What was he to do? He sat in silence.

Eventually she looked up, sniffing. 'I don't know what to say, how to begin.'

He spoke more gently. 'Just begin at the beginning.'

She shrugged, helplessly. 'Where is the beginning? But to answer your question, I was sorry for her.' He made as if to reply but she forestalled him with a wave. 'Yes, I know, it's foolish. How could I feel sorry for her? But she was so unhappy. She desperately wants to be married again, but my lord won't arrange anything. And then she seemed so glad when Walter de Courteville came to stay, I thought that they might be lovers. She slipped out the other night, and I'm sure she went to meet him somewhere, although I don't know – I stayed here in the chamber. I'm her companion – how could I possibly tell a group of men and boys that my mistress had been abroad in the night to meet a lover? It would be unthinkable. I had to be loyal. And yet ... I was so keen to be a part of your group, to help you. I've never felt part of anything before and it felt good – I was happy. But now I've ruined everything, and I'm so lonely!' She started crying again.

Martin looked at her helplessly, wondering if there was something he should be doing. Tentatively he held out his hand, and she grasped it. She held it tightly as she continued speaking, breathing in great gulps. 'You see, I've always been lonely. I'm only the unwanted cousin in my family. Nobody knew what to do with me, so they gave me to my lady as a companion when she married into our family. It was supposed to be something to be proud of, serving the sister of an earl, but I was so young, I didn't know what to do sometimes, and she was always so impatient with me. I felt so alone.'

'Don't you have family of your own?'

'No. My parents both died when I was young. I did have one brother, Giles, who loved me and looked after me. He said he would never let anything happen to me, that he would take care of everything.'

Martin didn't want to ask the question, but the words were out of his mouth before he could stop them. 'What happened to him?'

'He went off to be a squire to another lord, of course. He used to come back and visit me when he could. Then one day he told me that he would have to go on a campaign with his lord, that he would be away for a while, but would try and write to me, and would come back to see me as soon as he could. Before he went, he gave me this.' She pulled at the necklet which she wore. Hanging from it was a small coin, polished to brightness, which had a hole bored in it for the thong. 'He said it was a good luck charm, that it would keep me safe until he returned. I chided him, saying that he sounded as though he was embracing the supernatural, but he said that God had given him the penny – he'd found it one day in a field – so God would watch over it. So I took it, and we said goodbye.'

There was another silence. This time Martin didn't ask.

'He never came back. I knew that something had befallen him, but I didn't know what it was for a long while. Then I received a message from his lord. And do you know what it was?' Martin shook his head. 'Giles had survived the battles and sieges of the campaign, and then he'd died taking part in a tournament in France. A *tournament!*' Her voice became bitter. 'Why do men do such things? I know of course that they must fight wars, for that's why they're on God's earth, but why don't they ever think about those left behind? Why must they then risk their lives in the pursuit of leisure? It's so selfish. Although I loved him, and love him still, I find it hard to forgive him. An instant's carelessness and he broke his neck as he fell from his horse in the melee, leaving me all alone, to be parcelled up and sold off by my relatives. So now I have nobody. Nobody wants me.' She began to cry again, not the heaving sobs of her earlier emotion, but with a steady helpless rhythm of utter misery.

Feeling powerless, Martin did the only thing he could think of, which was to regale her with the whole story he'd heard from the priest the previous evening. She listened to him in growing astonishment, her tears drying. When he'd finished, she stared at him in total disbelief, unwilling at first to give credence to something so outrageous. But why should he lie? And it certainly explained her mistress's strange behaviour over the past few days. Amazing that such a thing could happen. The more she thought about it, though, the more she was convinced of one thing. She began to laugh quietly.

'What is it?'

'I was just thinking that I certainly wouldn't want to be in Walter's shoes when he's confronted by either the earl or his sister this morning!'

———❦———

Robert stood flattened against the wall as the full force of the earl's wrath raged before him. In some ways it was gratifying to see Walter de Courteville cowering, realising that he'd gone too far and raised the ire of a man who was not only one of the most powerful lords in the kingdom, but who was also a Plantagenet, a family legendary for their rage and said to descend from the devil. At this point he could well believe it. It was also truly awe-inspiring to watch. In all his years of service he didn't think he'd ever seen his lord so angry, and a small part of him wondered how he would survive if such fury were ever to be directed at him.

He'd summoned Walter from his bed, as ordered, as soon as it was light enough to see his way across the ward, and had given him no time to put on his finest clothes or prepare himself for the encounter, saying only that the earl wished to see him on a matter of the gravest import. Walter had at first seemed nervous, but had become more confident as they neared the keep, and he was almost jaunty by the time they reached the council chamber.

However, it had been comical to watch him collapse as he realised how the earl had thwarted his little plan; he had simply deflated like one of the pig's bladders the boys about the castle sometimes played ball with. Walter became smaller as the earl seemed to grow, the ferocity of his wrath making him tower. Nobody in future would seek to impugn his family honour.

And yet, as soon as there was a break in the tirade, Walter tried to bluster his way out of it. How could he even think that would be possible? But there he was, claiming that the earl must be lying. Lying! To accuse his lord of such a thing to his face! He should be struck down at once, but Robert dared not move to intercept. Besides, the earl could easily take care of such a man. Walter was now demanding that the priest be fetched, goading the earl by suggesting that he would conveniently be in some unreachable location and unable to corroborate such a wild tale. Robert honestly didn't know how the earl refrained from striking him down there and then.

What he did know was that Father Ignatius was standing ready outside, having been summoned earlier by Sir Geoffrey. Robert opened the door and pretended to tell a guard to bring the good Father, and then returned to wait in silence. He watched as the two men stood square with each other. At first Walter tried to meet the earl's gaze, but those flint-grey eyes had stared down better men than he, and eventually he dropped his gaze and shuffled awkwardly. He began to look less sure of himself as he looked around him, arms folded, scuffing the toe of his shoe on the ground.

After some while, the earl gave Robert an imperceptible nod, and with a loud 'I think I hear the priest now, my lord,' he opened the door to admit Father Ignatius. With a look of grim satisfaction, the earl bade him tell his tale.

The priest began in an uncertain tone of voice, but with the support of his lord behind him he grew in confidence. Robert listened and watched Walter growing hot and uncomfortable as he heard the words detailing the unsanctified oil with which he had supposedly been blessed, the crucial parts of the service which had been omitted. Robert was willing to wager that Walter was no scholar, and that he wouldn't have realised that some of the Latin had been missing. No doubt his previous experience of weddings had been to let his mind wander while all that sort of thing was going on, and then to get to the ensuing feast as quickly as possible. By the time Father Ignatius ended by saying that he would be prepared to swear on any holy relic, before the Pope himself if necessary, that his words were true, Walter had crumbled completely.

It was at that point that the earl *really* let loose his temper. Robert had thought that the previous burst was something to be reckoned with, but this was even worse. However, it was a fairly safe conjecture that none of it would now be directed at him, no matter what he did, so he settled back to enjoy the spectacle. In fact his lord seemed to be enjoying himself as well, gaining some satisfaction from unleashing his rage at the man before him. By the time he'd finished bellowing and cursing, Walter was reduced to cowering in the corner. The earl paused to catch his breath and then drew to a close by saying that Walter could stay within his walls exactly as long as it took to get his brother into a coffin and onto a cart, and if he was not out of the gate within the hour, he could expect to be driven out by main force. If he ever fouled the earl's lands again with his presence, his liberty would be forfeit and his very life in danger. The regent would have no qualms in supporting him against the man who had tried to trick him – it didn't matter how important the de Courtevilles might be to the present cause, William Marshal valued honesty above all other qualities.

At this juncture the earl flung wide the door with a dramatic gesture to show that the interview was at an end, only to find his sister waiting outside. Robert had no idea whether her presence was coincidental or planned, but if the latter then it was a masterstroke, as Walter had to scurry out past her while she looked on in triumph. Once he'd fled down the stairs, she entered the room with a joyous smile, and brother and sister embraced.

Walter was mortified. How had this been allowed to happen? God had abandoned him. His face was red with shame as he stumbled down the keep's stairs. He sensed that all those he encountered were smirking at him – how many of them were in the know? He slowed as he neared the bottom of the stairs. He must compose himself before leaving the keep. It was one thing to be shamed and thrown out of the earl's private apartments, where there were only the earl's close associates to see, but it would be another matter entirely to be seen fleeing across the yard. If the general population were to see him, they might start to have suspicions about yesterday. He stopped and took some deep breaths. He needed to think.

He was calmer as he went out of the door and made his way down the wooden staircase. He would take a walk in the morning air, on the pretext of going to the stable or something, so that he could consider his position. He was to blame in this for not having thought the matter through. It had been a somewhat spur-of-the-moment plan, to wed the earl's sister. Next time he tried something he would have to consider it more carefully. His current position was weakened, but it wasn't desperate. Warenne wouldn't tell too many people about the incident, for fear of making his sister look foolish. He wouldn't want to damage her marriage prospects in the eyes of the world, for fear that people might think that she'd done more than visit a chapel. If any thought that he'd bedded her, she would be ruined.

There. That was his next line of defence. He wouldn't tell anyone about the incident – he didn't want to look foolish, either – but if the earl should ever bring it up against him, he would retaliate by claiming to have consummated the union. He began to feel happier as he crossed the courtyard. As he went out of the inner gate, he knew where he would go – he would pay a visit to the carpenter who had been entrusted with making the ornate sealed coffin. He cheered himself at the thought. It looked as though he was going to get away with everything. His brother was dead, and he was only one step away from an earldom in his own right. A lot could happen to little Stephen before he reached manhood. Walter thought again of his departed brother lying in a coffin. By the time he got to the carpenter's workshop against the outer curtain wall, he was positively cheerful.

***

Edwin had only rarely been in the castle's kitchen, for it wasn't often he had business there. The heat was intense; it was probably quite a pleasant place to work on a cold winter's day, but now in the warmth of May it was uncomfortably hot, and it must be stifling during the summer months. Everywhere he looked there were figures scurrying, carrying huge dishes, chopping vegetables on the massive table which was the room's only furniture, and moving things around on the vast fires. He certainly didn't envy the scullion boys who were nearest the fire – surely they were as close to it as the meat they were roasting? How did they manage not to get burnt? His curiosity overtook him as he stopped to watch.

A figure standing still amid the bustle was sure to be noticed, and Edwin was disturbed in his thoughts by a large hand on his shoulder. Richard Cook didn't stand for idlers in his domain.

He put his large, red face next to Edwin's and bellowed in order to be heard above the din. 'What are you doing here? We're busy with the dinner, so you can get out if you've no business here.'

Edwin had to shout back in order to make himself heard, and after he'd explained his purpose the cook drew him to one side, into a relatively quiet corner where they could at least speak at a normal volume.

Richard looked perplexed. 'I don't understand. You're searching for my missing knife?'

'Yes. I think there is a possibility that it might have been used to kill the visiting earl and Berold, so I wanted you to tell me what it looks like, so I can search for it.'

'Well, I'll have no trouble showing you what it looks like – it's here.'

'What?'

'Murder weapon or no, it was taken from here a few days ago, but somebody returned it yesterday.' He called to one of his minions, who returned in a few moments with a large knife which he handed to Edwin.

Edwin looked at it. After all this fuss, it couldn't possibly be the weapon he was looking for. The dead earl had a very thin, neat scar around his neck, and, although this knife was sharp – Richard would permit nothing else in his kitchen – it was very large, with a wide blade. There was no way that this had caused the injury he had seen, to say nothing of the difficulty of anyone hiding it on his person. Anyone who had had his throat cut with this would have bled like a slaughtered pig. However, it could still have been the weapon which killed Berold … but wait.

'When did you say it was returned?'

'Yesterday morning, before dinner.'

Before dinner. Before Berold had been killed. So it couldn't have been used to stab him either. Damn it.

The cook was still looking at him quizzically. 'Is that all you wanted? I'm grateful, to be sure, that you've taken all that trouble over my knife, but I must get back to the dinner, or it won't be ready in time. Do you need to look at it some more?'

Richard was looking at him as though he were simple-minded, and Edwin felt hot and foolish. 'No, no, I don't need it. I'm sorry, I've made a mistake.' He nodded to the cook and exited the kitchen as quickly as he could while still retaining some dignity.

Once outside he felt both stupid and overwhelmed. All that precious time spent looking for the knife, and now he was right back where he'd started. No murder weapon, no suspects, no idea. And he had only until sundown to present the culprit to the earl. How on earth was he going to tell him that he'd failed? How would he face up to the shame? How would he look after his mother? There would be no question of the earl employing him for anything else if he failed in this, the first task he'd been set. The problems he faced whirled around in his head as his steps directed him without thinking.

As he reached his parents' house he looked up, surprised, having no idea how he'd got there. Well, either he was losing his mind altogether or God had guided his footsteps. The sense of dread was still there, but perhaps it was lessening: he felt only a slight reluctance to cross the threshold and had little trouble in quelling the feeling. He stepped inside.

———⋙◆⋘———

Peter was in heaven. At least, he couldn't imagine that heaven could be any better than this. He was warm, dry and had a full belly, and even the unaccustomed sensation of being clean didn't worry him overly.

When the knight had first come into the stall, he'd been terrified, burrowing as far under the straw as he could in a futile attempt to make himself invisible. But he'd been dragged out, and was cowering, preparing himself to be struck and thrown out into the cold, when he realised that nobody was trying to hit him. This was so unusual that he risked looking up. The face looking down at him was full of compassion and kindness – the face which he'd seen the day before, when it had heralded something to eat. He began to feel more hopeful.

Sir Roger had looked at the pathetic creature before him and felt nothing but pity. The boy was a peasant, was supposed to be beneath contempt, unnoticed as he lived out his life solely in order to serve those above him, but Roger had ever been cursed with the ability to see the peasants as people, and their hardships struck him anew every time he was faced with them. It was very complicated. How was he supposed to reconcile God's law with the way the world worked? The bible told him to give freely to the poor, which was something that most nobles did, with greater or lesser degrees of generosity, but had not Jesus said that it was easier for a poor man to reach heaven than a rich one? Had He not encouraged His true disciples to give away all that they owned, and even to serve the poor? How was this to be, in a world where only a small number of the people even existed in their own right? He was no theologian, but he felt the fundamental contradictions of it all in a way that his fellow knights and nobles didn't seem to. The ability to think was a definite disadvantage.

But anyway, what all of the fine thoughts and philosophical debates boiled down to was the dirty, hungry, frightened child before him. The Lord's word was clear on this – he must be helped, given charity. But what was charity? A meal now, to be forgotten by evening? Even a new cloak wouldn't keep him warm forever. No, Roger needed to do something more permanent, and he had an idea.

Thus it was that Peter sat in the luxury of the knight's tent, having first been washed thoroughly and somewhat roughly by some soldiers outside. Roger watched as the boy looked around him, marvelling at the wooden bed with its mattress and covers, the stitched hanging which divided the tent, the chest containing what must be to him all sorts of strange items, and the stool on which he sat. While he marvelled, he ate. He crammed the food into his mouth so fast that eventually Roger had to stop him lest he make himself sick. Roger had watched the boy's eyes open wide, and felt ashamed that surroundings which seemed plain to him should be seen as such luxury. Once the child had finished eating and had had the chance to draw breath, Roger told him of the plan he had. There was no way, of course, that he could take the boy on as page, for it was not his place and the rules absolutely forbade it, and the Lord knew how many people he would offend if he tried. No, each must keep to his allotted station in life, but within that there were … possibilities. Why should he not take on a servant? Normally he lived plainly, but it would not be out of place to take on a body servant, given that he couldn't afford a squire. The boy would be cheap to keep – he could work for food and lodging for now, no need to worry about wages until he was older. Of course, there was the matter of releasing him from his servitude on the earl's estate, but even with his meagre funds, Roger felt that he could offer the earl enough of a fee to release one homeless child. If he himself should have to go hungry a night or two to afford the cost then it would do him no harm – in fact it would be good for his soul.

He explained all this gently to the boy, unsure of the reaction he would get. Would the call of his birthplace be too much? He'd surely never travelled outside of the village or its surrounding fields, and mayhap the thought of travelling far away would be too much. But he had underestimated the nature of hunger. The boy was looking at him with disbelief at his good fortune – regular food and a roof over his head. How sad and yet how comforting to know that a person could want so little. No cares about wealth or status, just a simple need to stay alive. Roger decided that they might as well start the boy's employment now – he could speak to the earl later, there would perhaps be the chance to catch him after dinner – and issued his first order. It wasn't difficult, merely an instruction to take out the plate and cup which he'd just used and wash them, but it was heart-warming to see the alacrity with which Peter jumped up, ready and eager to serve. Roger felt as though he had made the world a little happier, and perhaps put a smile on the face of the Lord.

Edwin's eyes adjusted to the semi-darkness inside the cottage as he stepped in. His mother was making the most of the weather and had the door and shutters open, but it still seemed dark after the brightness of the day outside. As he stepped over the threshold he felt something catch his shoulder, and cursed inwardly as the loose nail by the door made another tear in his tunic. He really must get that fixed – his mother, much shorter than he, might hurt her face on it. In fact there were many things he must do, if only he could find the time. The cottage might be one of the best in the village, but it still needed regular maintenance, and again he realised that he hadn't kept up with it. The cottage was certainly not about to fall down, but the signs of unkemptness which he had noticed before were still there – a couple of patches of daub fallen off, a thinning of the thatch on one part of the roof and, of course, that loose nail. He didn't want his mother to end up living in squalor just because he couldn't find the time to carry out the duties of the man of the house.

His mother came to greet him warmly, exclaiming at his haggard look. She fussed about him, insisting that he sit down and partake of the meal she was about to serve to father. Edwin realised with a start that it was late in the morning – he'd been speaking with William and with the cook much longer than he thought. He sat down on a stool by the warmth of the cooking fire and sank into his own misery, but the hot meal started to bring him back to himself, and he was able to think once more.

'How is he?'

His mother shook her head in silence. She now looked resigned rather than upset, and Edwin knew that the end must be near. And yet the fear was not so overwhelming. He sensed that it had started to be replaced with a deep feeling of sadness, and didn't know whether this was better or worse.

'Can I go and see him?'

'Yes, of course.'

Edwin rose to go through to the bedchamber, but turned back to his mother. 'Why don't you come too?'

She demurred. 'I have things to see to … you might want to see him alone … '

Edwin stopped and took her hand. 'Mother. We might not have much time left together, so let's take the opportunity now. Come with me and we'll all sit together for a while.'

It was difficult to know who needed the comfort most as they sat on either side of the bed. The dying man, living his last days in pain; the widow-to-be, soon to lose her husband and means of support; or the young man worried about the task he'd been set, worried about his mother's fate, his father's soul, his own future. He reached out to take both their hands and they sat in silence.

As the quiet washed over him, thoughts came unbidden to his mind. Later he would attend Berold's burial and the Mass for his soul, and he was still disturbed by the thought that the death might have been prevented if only he'd been more alert. He cast his mind back to the last time he'd seen him alive. Berold had hailed him and had wanted to talk. But then he'd stopped, and stopped suddenly. Something had caught his eye and he'd changed his mind about speaking. What had he seen? Or more to the point, whom had he seen?

Edwin closed his eyes and tried to recall the scene in greater detail. He and Martin had been standing in the inner ward. They had been facing the gatehouse, and so Berold must have been looking at the keep …

Suddenly he stood and disentangled his hands, to leave his parents alone with each other in their sorrow. He ached to be able to support them, but he couldn't. He needed to see Sir Geoffrey, for he knew who had killed Berold.

Chapter Eleven

Sir Geoffrey was leaving the keep with Robert when he was surprised to be confronted by a panting Edwin, who reached out and grasped his arm.

The boy sucked in a deep breath – really, he would have to do some training if he was going to serve the earl properly in future – and managed to push out some words. 'Sir Geoffrey, I think I know who killed Berold.'

The knight felt his heart leap. 'The same person who killed de Courteville?'

Edwin stopped halfway through another breath. 'I'm not sure about that, for I can't put the two things together just now. But I'm sure that Berold was killed by Walter de Courteville.'

Had the day just got a little brighter? 'Well then, we must apprehend him immediately, for he's probably guilty of the other killing as well.' That would wrap it all up very simply and satisfactorily. He started to move off.

But Edwin had not yet relinquished his arm. 'Please, Sir Geoffrey, don't. Or at least not yet. Listen, I'm sure that he was the one who killed Berold. Yesterday I was in the ward when Berold came up to me, excited, saying that he had something that he needed to tell me. But then he saw someone over my shoulder, said that he'd changed his mind, and then ran off. I am certain that the person he saw coming out of the keep must have been Walter.'

Sir Geoffrey thought back. Yes, de Courteville had been in the keep yesterday morning, as he himself had stopped him attacking Edwin, and had then accompanied him to see the earl. But he didn't grasp the significance of why this was important.

Edwin explained. 'I think that Berold had seen something, something which may be related to the first murder. He was going to tell me, but then on seeing Walter, he didn't. I think that it must have been Walter whom he saw doing something, and then instead of telling me about it, he went to speak to Walter directly. Perhaps he hoped to gain something – some payment for keeping quiet. But then Walter killed him.'

Sir Geoffrey wished his mind could keep up with the young man's. 'So, Berold must have seen Walter killing his brother, and then threatened him with the knowledge? This still leads us back to him being the murderer. I'll find him now.' Again he turned.

The hand was still on his arm. 'Please, Sir Geoffrey, I need some time to think it through, as that still doesn't seem right.'

Sir Geoffrey hesitated. It would make things extremely convenient if he were simply to arrest Walter, but he himself had asked for Edwin to be the one to investigate as he knew he was clever, so he supposed he'd better listen to him now. 'Explain.'

The younger man's face assumed a pained expression. 'I still don't know who killed the visiting earl, but the more I think about it, the more I believe it isn't Walter. If he wanted to kill his brother, why wait until he was here, in a strange and hostile place? Surely it would have been easier to arrange some kind of accident nearer home. And Martin and I have already been through the times and places and we can't find that Walter would have had a chance to go up to the top of the keep and then down again. And then, why marry the earl's sister? What has that got to do with anything? If he'd come here to kill his brother, surely he wouldn't get involved in something else so complicated?'

This was all very confusing. Sir Geoffrey tried to work his way through it. 'So Berold's death was nothing to do with de Courteville's? Or was it? I thought you thought that the same person had killed both of them.'

'Originally I did, but now I'm not so sure. And Walter is a powerful man, I can't just accuse him with no justification.'

Edwin looked downcast, but Sir Geoffrey knew what he was going to do, something he was more suited to than trying to keep all these things in his head at once. Powerful in name he might be, but he was sure that Walter de Courteville was a physical coward, and that was something which could be exploited. But Edwin didn't need to know what he had in mind. 'They are burying Berold this afternoon, are they not?'

Edwin nodded.

'Then you get down to the church and attend. I'm sure you'll want to be there. I'll consult with the earl over what is best to be done, and I'll speak with you later.'

Edwin looked as though he was about to say something, but evidently he didn't dare disobey a direct order. He departed.

Sir Geoffrey turned to Robert, who had been standing silently by all the while. Here was a kindred spirit. Robert would help him take action.

'Good, that will keep him out of the way for a while. Come with me.'

Robert looked at him enquiringly, but Sir Geoffrey didn't want to say too much. 'What I mean is, it may be better that he doesn't know of this. He's a very clever lad, but I feel that he has a few things to learn about the way the world works, and the evil of which men are capable.'

The squire still said nothing. Sir Geoffrey sighed. Evidently he was going to have to be more direct.

'Do you not agree that our friend Walter has been acting very suspiciously, regardless of what Edwin says about him not killing his brother?'

Robert nodded. 'Yes, Sir Geoffrey.'

'Good, I'm glad you agree, as I think that you and I ought to go and have some words with him.'

Robert's eyes registered surprise and he opened his mouth to speak, but Sir Geoffrey held up his hand.

'Oh, never fear – I don't intend to hold him captive for torture, or even to beat him. But I do think that we need some more answers from him on exactly what happened the nighht before last, and in particular, where he was at the moment when his brother was killed. He has just been given a tongue-lashing by our lord, so hopefully we can catch him before he's recovered properly and get truthful answers to some questions. Come.'

Walter looked closely at the coffin. It was large and ornate, but not so much so that he would have to pay a premium price for it. Ralph had never been a particularly generous brother, so Walter didn't see why he should spend good coin on anything lavish for him now that he was dead. He needed something solid enough, he supposed, for it wouldn't look good to arrive back at the estate with the body in a plain box. Apart from anything else, the stink would be unbearable, so for his own comfort and convenience as much as anything else, he'd ordered it lined in lead. Once Ralph's body was inside it would then be sealed up to keep the stench of decay locked away inside as they travelled.

He nodded to the carpenter and turned to leave, colliding as he did so with Ralph's squire, who had been following him everywhere for the last few hours.

He was irritated. 'What do you want?'

The boy — what was his name again? — was ingratiating. 'Only to see if there was anything you required, my lord.'

'I don't require anything, and I'm not your lord.'

The boy said nothing, but looked at him with a smirk. Walter realised that, actually, it was rather pleasant to be addressed as 'lord' and to have someone fawning over him. He looked at the boy again.

'You'll be looking for another master now that Ralph is dead.'

'Yes, my lord. I was a good squire to him, saw to his every need. I would be very happy to do so for you, my lord.'

'Oh you would, would you? Well, I don't think I'm looking for a squire just at the moment, and certainly not one who's been Ralph's lackey for the last few years.' He started to move away.

David – yes, that was it – followed him. His voice became desperate. 'But my lord … '

Walter was enjoying the power. It was nice to be able to ruin somebody else's life for a change. 'Be off with you. I don't need you, and you may starve in a ditch for all I care.' He was gratified by the look of fear which passed over the boy's face, and turned away. He didn't, therefore, see the cunning expression which followed it. The voice came from behind him as he sought to walk away.

'But I know things, my lord.'

Walter stopped and turned.

'What do you know?'

David clearly sensed that he had his fish on the hook. 'I know things about you, my lord, things which your brother let slip while he was talking sometimes.'

Walter shrugged. He could probably ignore this. But David had one more arrow in reserve.

'And I saw what you did, my lord.'

Walter stopped dead, feeling panic rise. What had the boy seen? He had to deal with this right now.

He strode up to the squire, oblivious of the fact that they were having this conversation outside the carpenter's booth in the busy outer ward. He put his hand on the boy's shoulder and dug his fingers in, watching him wince.

'You know things, do you? You saw me, did you? Well, what makes you think that I wouldn't be better served by having you removed altogether? What makes you think I should take you on as squire?'

David now looked as though he realised that he'd gone too far. Walter felt powerful and dangerous. The squire tried a different approach and looked at him with a wheedling expression. 'Please, my lord, I hadn't finished. Not only do I know things about you, but I also know much about your brother. Have I not been his body squire for the past five years? I know where he's been, what he's done, and who he's spoken to.' He was pale and sweating.

Walter's mind mulled over the implications of that. How interesting it would be to know exactly what Ralph had been getting up to. How useful. Besides, there was nothing he could do about the squire here in this crowded ward, and it wasn't worth taking the risk. He made his decision and spoke magnanimously. 'Very well, I will take you on.' He could always change his mind later when he was in a less public place.

David was effusive with relief. 'Oh thank you, my lord, I'm so grateful, I'll never let you down … '

Walter cut him off with a gesture.

'Yes, yes, that will do. Now, you may begin your duties immediately. The carpenter will want some money for the coffin in there, and as I have no doubt that you have managed to steal whatever you could find from Ralph's possessions, you can start by going in there and paying him whatever he requires out of your own pocket.'

David's face fell. Walter felt satisfied.

'And don't think you can get away with whatever sort of tricks you used to play on my brother. You will do exactly as I say at all times – you've made your bargain with me and you must keep to it. Otherwise you may remember what I said about having you removed.' He spoke in what he hoped was a chilling voice and was rewarded by another momentary flicker of fear. 'Now go.'

The boy sulked back to the carpenter's booth, and Walter was starting to walk through the outer ward in a satisfied frame of mind when two figures suddenly appeared beside him, one on either side. They closed in, jostling him. But before he could open his mouth he realised who they were: Warenne's eldest squire, and the old castellan. Both faces held determined expressions as they gripped him by the arms. Walter suddenly felt a sinking sensation in his stomach and looked around for help. But his new squire had disappeared and there were none of Ralph's men – his men – close at hand. He felt himself being steered up the path towards the inner ward.

'What do you want?' He tried hard to keep his voice from shaking. He tried to free his arms, but was taken aback again by the strength of the old man on his left, who held him in an iron grip. Neither could he move his other arm, as the squire was also surprisingly powerful. He started to panic. What was it with these men who trained with weapons all the time? Clever men like himself who preferred to think with their heads ought to be able to outwit them at every turn, but again and again it all came down to physical strength. Walter had never shown much interest in combat – he was above such things – but occasionally it would have come in useful.

The knight leaned towards him and spoke in a low tone. 'Have no fear, we won't hurt you. We're all going to find a nice quiet room where you can answer some questions for us. Don't try to make a scene in public, for there is nobody here who will take your part.'

He was right. Looking around, Walter could see that people were starting to look at them, for surely the sight seemed odd, but his captors seemed to engender respect from others. Not only would nobody step in to help him, they would almost certainly obey any command from the knight to restrain him. He stopped his struggles. He would be better employed using his energy to think his way out of this. He should have no problems outwitting these louts. He walked calmly with them through the gate to the inner ward, round to the household quarters, up some stairs and into a spartan chamber of the wooden building.

Finally they let go of him, the squire turning to shut the door, and Walter rubbed his arms as he looked around. He had lost his bearings, but as the room had one stone wall, he supposed it was one which backed directly on to the curtain wall around the ward. There was very little furniture: a wooden bed, neatly made; a stool; a kist in the corner, and next to it a pole on which was hung a mail hauberk, slightly old fashioned in style but in immaculate condition.

He turned to face his captors, trying at first to bluster his way out.

'You have no right to hold me here, none at all! I demand that you release me … '

He was stopped short by an explosion of pain as the knight's fist cracked into his face, knocking him backwards so that he fell over the stool. God, but that had hurt! The old man had the strength of a battering ram. He held his jaw and cowered as the knight stepped nearer. The squire hovered in the background, looking worried. 'Sir Geoffrey … ' he moved as if to intercept.

Walter started to duck, but the knight merely grabbed a fistful of his tunic, heaved him to his feet, turned the stool the right way up, and pushed him down on to it.

He spoke. 'That was for the insult to my lord and his family. For daring to think you could be wed to his sister, never mind for tricking her so cruelly. I won't hit you again, but bear in mind that I could if I wanted to.'

Walter nodded, dazed. How was he supposed to think with his head ringing like this? He'd never felt such pain.

The questions started.

'Now, we know that you were in the keep the night before last, as you've already confessed to that.'

Walter didn't like the use of the word 'confess'. What were they trying to accuse him of? If they thought that he'd bedded the woman … but as the knight continued it seemed that this wasn't what they were about.

'Did you arrive first in the chapel? Did you see your brother at all?'

So that was it. They thought he might be a witness. Or … ice entered his blood as he realised that they might try to accuse him of the murder of his brother. The two men loomed over him as he sat nursing his face, and he was afraid. His stomach twisted.

'We're not accusing you of anything – yet. But we must have some details from you. Tell us, or things will go badly for you.'

Walter gulped and started to speak, screwing up his face as he tried to remember the details. 'I wasn't first in the chapel. Isabelle –' the knight raised his fist again – 'Ah, that is to say, the *Lady* Isabelle, was already there, but not the priest.' He tried to recall more, the memory of that night returning to him.

He had tapped his foot impatiently as he waited in the chapel. Isabelle was sitting expectantly in the corner: he'd already had to fend off her effusive greetings as he arrived, but luckily he had the excuse that they were only one floor below her brother's bedchamber, and the last thing they needed at this point in time was an angry earl descending upon them. Finally he'd heard footsteps on the stairs, so he'd put his head out of the door ready to remonstrate with the priest. His shock upon seeing his brother round the corner had been immense, and he'd only just ducked back into the chapel in time to avoid being seen; he'd pressed his back against the wall as his heart pounded. Surely he'd been heard? But no, fortunately Ralph had been wrapped in his own thoughts, and without pausing he'd continued through the passageway and up the stairs which led to the upper floor and the staircase to the roof. What on earth could he have been doing there at that time of night? Walter could think of no plausible answer, but he'd been saved from further conjecture by the arrival of Father Ignatius, who was huffing and puffing with the effort of climbing the stairs. He'd taken his place at the small altar, and Walter and Isabelle had come to kneel before him.

'So,' the knight continued, 'you weren't alone – or you say you weren't alone – when you arrived at the chapel. And your brother arrived before Father Ignatius did. He – Father Ignatius, I mean – came straight into the chapel? He didn't go further up the stairs?'

Walter shook his head. He was still afraid that the knight might hit him again, so he struggled to recall anything else which might be useful. Was he in real danger of being accused of the murder? What would happen to him if so? Would he be put in some cell, beaten, even hanged? He could feel the noose tightening around his neck …

He started swaying on his stool. The squire stepped forward and shook him, which didn't help. He fended the fellow off.

The knight spoke again. 'All right, so that was before the wedding – the so-called wedding. What about afterwards? What happened then?'

Walter thought hard again, and placed himself back in the chapel in the darkness of the night …

The second part of the plan had not proceeded as well as the first.

He'd thought that arranging the wedding would be the tricky part, but it had proved surprisingly simple, thanks in large part to the gullibility of the priest, who had accepted his explanation without a murmur. The clergy – or at least the real men of God, as opposed to those who joined the Church for political reasons – were always easy to fool. No, the problem was trying to persuade his new bride to keep their wedding a secret. Once the ceremony had been completed she'd wanted to announce their marriage in public, but Walter, with his superior intellect, could see that this would be a disaster. Why on earth should they risk the wrath of both of their brothers when they didn't have to? Besides, he'd had his own particular reasons for not revealing the alliance, as he wanted to be certain of winning either way. If Warenne died childless he would make it known that he was married to the heiress, but if the earl should father a son and disinherit Isabelle it wouldn't be in his best interests to have lumbered himself with such a wife, so he would simply not tell anyone about the match and start looking elsewhere. As an added security, of course, there was always the possibility that something would happen to his dear brother before little Stephen reached the age of majority, and who would be a better guardian for the fatherless boy than his own affectionate uncle?

Yes, Walter had been very pleased with himself, but his fortune would only be made if he could persuade the silly woman not to go blabbering about the secret wedding. The priest wouldn't talk: the promise of an annual donation to church funds as long as he remained silent had seen to that. He'd left the chapel, and Walter had been left alone with his new wife. Disentangling her amorous arms from around his neck, he'd braced himself and given her a kiss before insisting that she shouldn't betray their secret – and reminded her that as his wife she was now bound to obey him. She'd agreed – one of the few joys of marriage, at least – and he'd sent her out to return to her bedchamber. He would follow on in a few moments: it was better that they should leave separately just in case either of them should be seen. He watched her go out of the door and turn to go down the stairs. Life was good.

Sir Geoffrey pounced.

'So, you were left alone in the chapel?'

Walter realised the import of what he'd just said. But it was too late to take it back now.

'I was, but all I did was sit there for a few moments before going down the stairs again and back to my chamber.' He looked at them; they were both sceptical. He started to panic. 'I swear it!'

The knight was remorseless, looming over him. 'But why should we believe you? You've already shown yourself capable of lying and deceiving. How do we know that you didn't creep up the stairs, murder your brother, and then come back down? Who's to tell?'

Walter was terrified, his voice rising to a squeak. 'But I didn't! I just went down the stairs and back to my chamber, I swear it! I went back to bed and slept until it was full light. I didn't kill Ralph, I didn't!' They were going to accuse him of murdering his brother. Dear God, he would lose his head. He panicked.

'You don't understand! I wanted to inherit an earldom, but it was to be Warenne's earldom! His sister is his heir, so I had to marry her, but all I was thinking about was keeping it a secret so he didn't find out! By the time the ceremony was finished I'd completely forgotten that Ralph was even in the keep – all I was concerned with was getting the woman, the priest and myself out of the chapel without anyone noticing. It was so important it took everything else out of my mind, so when that blasted man-at-arms said he'd seen me … '

As soon as the words had left his mouth he knew he had made a terrible mistake. But it was too late.

There was a huge silence.

It was broken by the squire. 'It was you!'

Walter tried to shake his head, to renege on what he had just said, but the squire wouldn't let him. 'It was you! Edwin knew you had something to do with it and he was right! He's been feeling guilty, as Berold came to him to say he knew something, and he didn't find out what it was! God's blood, but I'll teach you a lesson … ' He strode forward.

Walter flinched, convinced he was about to die, but he was saved by the intervention of the old knight, who grabbed the squire and pinioned his arms. He was saying something but Walter didn't hear what it was. He was in a world of his own, remembering the horror of what he had done.

He'd been leaving the keep after his interview with the earl, having been told about his brother's death. The news had come as a shock, and the possibilities in his mind hadn't yet had the chance to become more definite plans. So he was unprepared when he'd been accosted by the fellow, and had very little time to react. The man said he'd been on guard on the curtain wall during the night and had seen Walter making his way into the keep. No doubt he wanted to make something out of his knowledge. But the one thing which had been uppermost in Walter's confused mind was that it was now more important than ever that the marriage be kept a secret – Ralph's earldom was now a better wager than Warenne's, so the wedding needed to be quietly forgotten.

He'd told the man that they needed to find somewhere to talk and had led him to the stables. He didn't know what he was going to do: as they spoke privately he agreed all sorts of things just to shut the man up – he would pay him, would give him anything he wanted. Then the man had turned to go, and in that instant Walter had perceived that they were alone, had taken the knife from his belt and had stabbed him in the back. He would never forget it, the feeling of the knife entering the body, the ghastly gurgling sound made by the man, the blood pouring out of the wound. He couldn't believe what he'd done. Somebody would come in, and here he was standing over a dying man with a bloodied knife in his hand.

Quickly he'd shoved it inside his tunic and wiped his hands on the straw as best he could, before walking – calmly, he hoped – out of the stable and back towards the guest chambers. Everyone had seemed to be looking at him. But miraculously there was no hue and cry, and he resisted the impulse to keep looking behind him. Once he'd reached his chamber he'd barred the door, torn off his tunic and shirt and hidden them in his baggage. When the fire was lit in the evening he would burn them. The knife was more of a challenge, but there was water in the room and he washed all the blood off the blade and off his hands before it could dry.

He had no idea how he managed to sit through the dinner in the hall. He had almost no recollection of it at all: the only thing he could remember was that he'd thought he must be there in order to keep up appearances. He'd encouraged his neighbour to talk so that he wouldn't have to. By this time the body had been discovered, but it was easy to feign indifference. After dinner he'd gone back to his chamber and barred the door, before being sick and sick again.

He lay on the bed most of the afternoon, awaiting the knock at the door which would seal his fate, but none came.

As the time went by he became aware of the possibility that he was going to get away with it all, and he started to contemplate a rich future. It was just his luck that as he left his quarters he should be waylaid by Isabelle and pulled into her chamber. The absolute last thing he needed at that moment was for her to make public their marriage. He'd wanted to encourage her again to keep it a secret, but his nerves and the effect of the long afternoon had got the better of him, and he'd let slip his true feelings. No doubt that was what had sent her running to the earl.

But he'd been so close to getting away with it! And now here he was in this little room with two strong men who had no sympathy for him at all. He broke down and sobbed.

Sir Geoffrey was having trouble pinning Robert's arms. A few years ago it would have been easy, but now he was getting old and the squire was a grown man. He managed at last to wrestle him away from the wretch on the stool, and held him until they both stood panting and still.

'For God's sake, Robert, how do you think it will look for the earl if you beat or kill de Courteville's brother. Think!'

He needed to do some thinking himself. Walter had killed Berold, there was no doubt about that. But much as Sir Geoffrey would like to punish him for that, in terms of the political situation nobody would be interested in taking action against a nobleman who'd killed a common soldier. It would be unheard of, and the earl wouldn't want to risk any credit he still had with the regent by doing such a thing. De Courteville murdered under the earl's own roof, and then his brother put on trial for a crime which most would see as trivial? There was no possibility of bringing Walter to account for the killing, although to look at him now you wouldn't think so.

But the main question still needed answering – who had killed Ralph de Courteville? The sobbing wretch was repeating over and over that he hadn't killed his brother, but how was Sir Geoffrey to know that this was the truth? He didn't know what to do. The man was such a snivelling coward that he couldn't bring himself to strike him again. If he was going to fight he wanted it to be against a real man, one worthy to be his opponent. The wreck before him was beneath his attention. And yet, how did he know whether the man was lying or not? He looked to be telling the truth, but what if he were merely acting a part? As he had done many times in his life, he cursed his own straightforwardness. Give him a horse and a sword, and he would deal with any enemy, but this … he wished Godric were here. Godric, with his intelligence and his years of experience in this sort of thing, would be able to tell him at once whether Walter was telling the truth or not. He sighed. Never again would his friend stride up to him with a smile, a quip, a light-hearted gesture. He looked again at Walter, still sunk in his own misery, and at Robert, waiting for him to act. If even Edwin were here, he would be able to come up with some clever question which would trap Walter into telling the truth. He was sure of it. The boy was so like his father it was almost frightening. But there was no point in continuing this – they would all just end up repeating themselves until somebody gave in, but that still might not lead them to the correct answer.

Suddenly he knew what he would do next, and spoke quickly to Walter. 'Get out.'

Walter looked up at him, a glimmer of hope on his face.

Sir Geoffrey spoke again. 'Get out, you're free to go from this room. For now. But do not attempt to leave the castle, or I will come after you and I will hunt you down.'

Walter, wide-eyed and pale, stood up shakily and then fled the room. Sir Geoffrey turned to Robert.

'I'm going to find Edwin and then talk to Godric. You find Martin, see if he's discovered anything else, and bring him down to Godric's cottage. You and I may be men of action, but we need to lay all this before the clever ones to see if they can make any sense of it.'

Robert nodded wordlessly and left. Sir Geoffrey sat down heavily on his bed for a moment to consider the import of what Walter had said, but he could make little sense of it, so he rose again in order to find someone who could. Besides, he wanted to have a final chance to converse about distant memories, before the last companion of his youth was gone.

He felt old.

Chapter Twelve

The burial had been awful. It wasn't as if any burial was particularly enjoyable, but Edwin had felt that everyone was looking at him, blaming him in some way, although of course that was only right as he carried a terrible responsibility for the death. He couldn't meet the eye of Berold's father, now condemned to grow old with no son to support him in his dotage.

It was as Edwin was trudging back up to the castle that he encountered Sir Geoffrey, who had clearly been watching for him. The knight looked grim, and steered Edwin into the steward's office before saying anything, indicating with a movement of his head that William, who was puzzling over a list of something, should leave them alone. William took one look at the bleak expression on Sir Geoffrey's face and departed in silence.

They sat and Sir Geoffrey came straight to the point. 'There is news, but you're not going to like it.'

Edwin readied himself and listened first with satisfaction, and then with growing horror followed by outrage as he heard the tale of the knight's encounter with Walter.

He could barely keep his seat. 'But he is a murderer! How could you let him go?' This was just too much, on top of everything else, and he felt himself growing livid as the shards of rage pierced him. His voice rose. 'How could you!'

Sir Geoffrey repeated himself, about the threat to the earl and his estates, and the paramount importance of keeping in the regent's good graces, but Edwin was too far gone in indignation and fury to care.

'And so Berold's life counts for nothing? He was an innocent who was cut down in cold blood, and you're telling me that the man who has confessed to killing him is to walk free simply because he's a noble? And Berold's death doesn't matter?' Edwin boiled with rage, jumping fully out of his seat this time.

'Sit down!'

The voice cracked like a whip, and belatedly Edwin realised to whom he was talking. His knees folded.

Sir Geoffrey continued, harshly. 'You're right, his death doesn't matter.'

Edwin was so taken aback that he could say nothing.

'It might sound harsh, and indeed it is, for he was a decent man, no worse than any other. But the earl, and I, and you for that matter, have to think of the situation outside of this village.' He loomed over Edwin. 'While it is regrettable that Berold is dead, and even more deplorable that that wretch should escape justice for it, Berold's killing has no consequences outside of this village. Nobody else is going to die because of him. Nobody will lose lands. And yes, I'm sorry for his parents as I am for the families of any who lose loved ones, but that's not the point. I'm not here to feel sorrow for them, and neither are you.' He stepped back, waving his finger at Edwin. 'The reality is that it's more important to find who killed de Courteville. And that's what we must concentrate on now, unless you want to run the risk of Conisbrough in flames.'

Edwin was subdued by the rebuke. Rarely had he been on the receiving end of such a tongue-lashing from anyone, never mind the castellan, and he felt cowed. Indeed, it was only the hard experiences of the past few days and the reality of his situation which prevented him from curling up in shame on the floor. But Sir Geoffrey was right. He must try to think. There would be time to mourn and to examine his feelings once this was all over and the earl and his host had left.

Think. Concentrate. 'So Walter didn't kill his brother?' He wasn't sure whether to be pleased or not, but he'd harboured some doubts about that as it hadn't seemed logical.

'It seems not. Or at least he says so. But I can't tell whether he is lying or not. Strong I may be, but clever I'm not, and I don't have the capacity to deal with such deviousness.'

Edwin felt dejected. 'I fear that I don't either.'

'Well, you need to learn, and there is one in the village who is the master, although he has but a short time to teach us.'

Edwin gulped, but he stood in obedience and walked with the knight down to the village.

As they neared the cottage door, Edwin called out to his mother that Sir Geoffrey was accompanying him, and she appeared at the door, smoothing down her gown and apron. A moment later the two men both entered the bedchamber, and the knight came forward to sit by the bed and take his old friend's hand in both of his own.

It was a strange gesture from such a warlike man, thought Edwin, but then Sir Geoffrey had surprised him on more than one occasion during the last few days. Despite the urgency of their quest, the knight first spent some few moments speaking with his old friend. There was no sentimentality from Sir Geoffrey – he had seen too much death during his lifetime to pretend that father was anything other than hovering on the threshold of life. He didn't seek to comfort the old man with platitudes, but instead reminisced about events of their younger days. Old? thought Edwin, reflecting, why, they're the same age. Strange how the Lord can make one man seem much older than another, through illness or merely through a different way of living. He looked at them more closely as they spoke, realising that many years ago they must have been in a similar situation to himself and Robert, the one a simple village boy, albeit one who would wield some responsibility, and the other a squire destined to mix with the nobility of the kingdom.

He continued to watch them, slowly coming into the knowledge that in this conversation between the old man and the dying one, there lay echoes of his own future. He'd always assumed that he and Robert would grow apart as the years went by, as the difference in their stations grew ever greater. They might have spent their boyhoods together, but the knight would soon go off to deal with other nobles, and would forget the village boy he'd known in childhood, while the village boy would in turn stay chained to his lot in life, and spend it in bitterness and jealousy of the other. But here in front of him was real affection between two men of very different station, who had known each other nigh on fifty years, more than a lifespan for most people.

He looked again at the two lined faces, both grey-bearded but the one tanned from years in the sun, the other pale from the suffering of illness, and saw that the expressions mirrored one another. Companionship, friendship, trust. A total sense of knowing the other and his feelings. He gazed in wonder, and despite everything that was going on in his life, he felt at peace. And finally, the fear disappeared. Something moved inside of him, something fell into place, and he was able to realise without dread that his father had enjoyed a goodly span of years, but that that span was near its end. Father is content and so will I be, Edwin thought to himself.

Sir Geoffrey was halfway through some anecdote about a trick that both boys had played on some long-forgotten priest when there were more voices outside. Edwin's mother went out once more and returned with Robert, Martin and Simon. Edwin realised that people were coming to the cottage to pay their last respects to a dying man, and that the end was very near. He looked towards the bed and was heartened to see that his father actually looked better than he had done for some time. He was still emaciated and weak, propped up from his lying position by some pillows, but there seemed somehow to be more colour in his cheeks, and his voice was stronger. Edwin knew and accepted now that there was no hope of a recovery – his father would never leave the bed alive again – but it was good to see a reminder of the man he once was.

Surely this was due to the presence of his lifelong friend, who had cheered him with words and with feelings left unspoken.

Robert came to sit next to Edwin, and gripped his shoulder wordlessly. Edwin looked at him, and wondered if some of the feelings which he'd experienced about friendship would transfer themselves to Robert as well.

Martin and Simon stepped forward to the bed, Simon murmuring quietly that he could only stay for a moment as he was needed by the earl. He was wide-eyed and pale-faced in the presence of impending death, but father had a smile for him and a cheerful word. He put his hand on the boy's head and offered him a blessing, after which Simon moved back awestruck – for everyone knew that a blessing from a man so near to God was a powerful thing – to make way for his elder. Father and Martin exchanged a few quiet words, and once more Edwin was struck by just how much his father was respected. The conversation ended with a brief handshake, and Martin shepherded Simon back out of the cottage. He himself returned and stood in silence in the corner.

Father, looking more alert than he had done for many weeks, swept his gaze around at his remaining audience, and spoke.

'Now, enough of this maudlin talk. There is still a task to be done, and I would not die before it is accomplished.'

They all looked at him, surprised at the vigour in his voice. Edwin, with his newfound respect for the brevity of the time left to his father, started to say that he need not worry himself about such things, but was cut short by parental authority as his father bade him hold his tongue and obey. Edwin stopped mid-word.

He waited for his father to continue, but realised that he was looking at Martin, who had given an almighty start at the sound of his last words, and was now standing as if he was itching to say something. Father nodded to him.

'That's it!' burst Martin, excitedly. That's what was different about the body. Oh, I knew there was something!'

Edwin and Robert looked at him in surprise, as did the two older men.

Martin looked at them, stuttering in his excitement. 'The … the … the tongue! When we picked the body up from the top of the keep, the tongue was sticking right out.' He turned to Robert. 'Surely you remember?'

Robert nodded. 'Of course. It was horrible.'

Martin continued, still unusually animated. 'But when I was with Edwin later on, and we looked at it, the tongue was back in the mouth. That's why I said it looked different, only I couldn't remember why. And nobody else would have noticed, for nobody else saw the body both before and after we'd taken it to the chapel. Robert helped me down with it and then left, and Edwin didn't see it until much later on. In the meantime somebody must have come and interfered with it.' He looked around, bright-eyed at the astonished faces in the room, but then calmed down and assumed a puzzled expression. 'But why on earth would anyone want to do that? It makes no sense!'

But it obviously did make sense to Sir Geoffrey and to father, who both appeared enlightened. Sir Geoffrey spoke.

'Martin, you're young, and thank the Lord you have not yet seen many men hanged. When a man dies by having a rope or cord put around his neck, the pressure of it forces his tongue out of his mouth, where it remains. It's a sure sign that a man has died by hanging.'

Edwin had listened to all this in growing astonishment, but he was still confused. Robert voiced the question which was also in Edwin's mind. 'But how can the earl have been hanged? There is nowhere up there to do that, and we found no noose, no rope.'

Sir Geoffrey spoke again. 'I haven't finished yet, boy. It's a sure sign of being hanged, but it happens whenever a man is killed with a rope around his neck. Did you say that your dead man had a thin wound to his neck? Not much blood? Why then, he was garrotted, strangled with something fine.'

There was a moment of silence while they all took this in, then the knight continued, berating himself for his own stupidity and thumping his palm. 'Oh, why didn't I look at the body myself? As soon as I was told that the man had had his throat cut, there seemed no point – many men die in such a way. I would have been able to put you on the right scent much sooner. Edwin, I'm sorry.'

Edwin's surprise at the discovery was such that he had none to spare at the thought of a knight apologising to him. This was – well, really. All that time he'd spent looking for a knife and the man had been strangled! He himself had looked at the body, why hadn't he noticed? The answer to that was obvious, of course – mercifully, he didn't have much experience of looking at men who had been murdered or executed, so he wouldn't know the difference anyway.

He jumped up. 'I must go and look at him again, before he's sealed into his coffin.'

Martin had also moved forward, and he put his hands out to stop Edwin. 'No – I'll do it. I can easily run down there and look. What you need to do is sit and think, and you're much better at that than me.' There was no self-consciousness in his voice, only simple acknowledgement. Edwin wanted to say something, wanted to disagree, but he was given no chance as Martin bade everyone a hasty farewell and left at a run. Edwin sat down again, heavily.

It was father who spoke, his voice decisive.

'I believe that this is what we know already.' The others listened in growing amazement as he gave a succinct and summary account of all that he knew, which matched Edwin's thoughts exactly. No wonder he'd been such a good bailiff – he had the gift of hearing everything once and understanding the important issues immediately.

Once he'd got over his shock at the strength which his old friend still exhibited, Sir Geoffrey filled in the details of the encounter with Walter, including his own bafflement at being unable to tell whether the man was telling the truth or not. He turned to father for his view, but Edwin felt that he had to interrupt. He held up his hand and the other stopped.

He spoke slowly, feeling his way through the labyrinth in his mind. 'I don't think he can have had time to go up to the top of the keep and then down again. If he'd sent Lady Isabelle out of the chapel, he would have needed some time to get up to the roof, kill the earl and then come back down. Peter said that he'd seen them all, but that they'd come out one after the other. He didn't mention that Walter had been much later than the others, and he had no reason to lie.' He described his interview with the boy earlier that day, and wondered again where he might have got to.

Father took all this in and spoke again.

'I agree with Edwin – Peter had no reason to lie, and if he is telling the truth then the man would not have had time to murder his brother. There is also the fact that he appeared to you to be in much distress – when a man is in *extremis* he normally resorts to telling the truth simply because it is easier, and he does not have the courage to lie. There is always the chance that he is just a very fine dissembler, but from what I have heard I do not think that is the case. So, we have ruled out one of the main suspects. Now, what is the best way forward from here? You have only a short time, Edwin, and although you have others to help you – ' he looked around at the others, 'including you, my old friend, and you, the friend of my son – it is *your* task, Edwin, to find the culprit. What are your thoughts?'

Edwin did not know if he had any opinions at all, so confused was his mind and so impressed was he with his father, but he tried to gather his wits. Eventually, one thought struck him above all others.

'Every time I have spoken to anyone about the dead earl, they've told me that he was an evil man and that he did many foul deeds, but nobody has actually said what any of these deeds were. I'm more convinced than ever that the key to this mystery lies in the *past*, not in the present. He came here but a few days ago – nobody knew him, or at least nobody knew him well, and it's very difficult to think that he might have offended someone so badly in such a short space of time that they would want to kill him. No,' he said, realising that he was speaking his thoughts exactly as they fell out of his head, but also that they were starting to make some kind of sense, 'the answer lies somewhere in the past. Somewhere at some time he did somebody a great wrong, and someone has decided to avenge it.'

Everyone was looking at him. He dropped his head. 'Well, that's what I think, anyway,' he mumbled.

'You mistake us, Edwin.' It was Sir Geoffrey who spoke. 'We are looking at you in pride, for you've hit upon something which nobody else has considered. I've been trying to think of anyone he might have offended since he's been here, but this seems implausible. Your theory about the past fits much better. You're right – he did commit some foul deeds, and I at least know some of them. And so does your father, for I told him of them long ago.' He looked at father, who indicated that he should continue.

Sir Geoffrey cleared his throat. 'The worst, the very worst of these deeds, happened fifteen years ago in France. It was when we were on campaign with the old earl, during the war which decided the succession.'

He looked around at the bemused faces of the young men, and realised he would have to start from the beginning. He sighed.

'Pay attention, boys – I don't want to say all this twice.'

Automatically they both straightened.

'When King Richard died – may God rest his soul – there were two claimants to the throne. The king had no children, but he had one surviving brother, John, and one nephew, who was the son of their dead brother Geoffrey. If the law of succession were to be interpreted strictly, it would have been this nephew, Arthur, the Duke of Brittany, who inherited the throne, as his father had been John's elder. However, he was only a boy of twelve who had never even visited England, so it would have been risky to put him on the throne. John and his supporters were in a much better position to seize power, and they invoked the old custom that the younger son of a king was nearer to the throne than a grandson whose father had never ruled. So John became king. However, Arthur decided to make a bid for the throne, or at least the barons who were supporting him did. Why did they do it? It's possible that they truly thought that Arthur might make a better king than his uncle, for John was unpopular even then. But it's more likely that they simply saw an opportunity to cause trouble and to profit by it. And so the realm endured civil war.'

He stopped to draw breath before continuing.

'Most of the fighting took place over in France, in the Angevin domains. The war went on for three years, three disastrous years during which time many good men were killed. During that time Arthur grew from a small boy to a slightly older and more effective one, and there was some talk that his cause might succeed. However, he was captured at the siege of Mirebeau. John had him taken to his stronghold of Falaise; after that he was moved to Rouen, and nobody ever saw him again.'

Edwin had never thought to hear of so many evil deeds in just a few short days, but he was already becoming accustomed to it. 'Murdered?'

Sir Geoffrey nodded grimly. 'Aye. The rumours that floated around said that the boy had been blinded, then stabbed and his body thrown in the river. And one of the men at Rouen was Ralph de Courteville, then just a relatively minor lord. But shortly after Arthur's disappearance, de Courteville was named earl, and nobody knew why, other than that he had performed some "great service" for the king.'

Robert exhaled. 'You mean – you think that de Courteville murdered the boy himself?'

Sir Geoffrey looked tired. 'Yes. The supposed method of the killing bore his mark. He always swore that he had some grudge against Arthur, for the boy had been arrogant to him and made him lose face in public at one time. So he built up this slight into a need for revenge. He was always particularly harsh on those he captured – and what man in his right mind would put out a boy's eyes before killing him? Why do it? There is no reason other than vindictiveness.' He gave a shudder. 'Clearly the prince needed to be kept under tight rein, in case his cause surfaced again, but even the strongest-willed among the king's party were squeamish at the thought of the cold-blooded murder of a boy.'

Edwin could hardly take it in. But even so, his mind was working on his own problem. How could this relate to de Courteville's murder here in Conisbrough? Surely none of Arthur's supporters could have borne a grudge for so long? Or was revenge a fire which could be kept alive and stoked during many years?

Sir Geoffrey seemed to see into his mind. 'I don't know how much help this is in our present situation, but it shows that de Courteville was responsible for an atrocity, and where there is one, there might be more.' He was struck by a thought. 'There were some who said that the deaths of two other knights at around that time might have been connected to de Courteville as well. Recall, Edwin – the arms you were looking at on the roll. Those two men supposedly died in accidents, but de Courteville was in the area, and shortly after their deaths their names were struck from the lists of knights and arms, as though they'd never existed. They must have done something that greatly displeased the king, although I can't think what it might have been.'

Robert's mind was evidently working faster than Edwin's, for he spoke, a little shakily. 'What if those two men had done something which the king wanted them to, but he'd decided afterwards that he didn't want anyone to know about it?'

Everybody looked at him.

Edwin had already taken the next logical step and he grasped it first. 'You mean, maybe they killed the prince, and then the king had them murdered?'

'Yes. Or perhaps all three of them, de Courteville as well, murdered the boy, and then de Courteville killed the other two to keep them quiet.' Robert's eyes grew large. 'Monstrous!'

Sir Geoffrey spoke slowly. 'Robert, I think you might have stumbled upon something which has kept the rest of us guessing this past fifteen years.' He thought carefully. 'It all seems plausible now that you explain it that way. The times and places are all right.' He looked thoughtful.

The expression on the knight's face reminded Edwin of something. 'That's strange. Simon looked exactly as you do when I spoke to him about times and places yesterday.' The others turned to him, so he explained further. 'Martin and I were talking about the time at which the earl must have been killed – we were working out whether Father Ignatius might have seen someone going up the stairs – and Simon suddenly went very quiet and said he was thinking about something, but it couldn't be right.' He stopped.

Robert spoke. 'So what was it?'

'What was what?'

'What was Simon thinking about?'

'Oh. I don't know – he wouldn't say.'

That was probably not much help. The room fell silent.

Edwin had something else on his mind. 'But I still can't understand how a man would murder his own nephew, or at least have someone else do it. And if this prince Arthur knew about the danger, why did he continue in his bid for the throne? Surely he was well off as a duke and had no need to be king as well, if it was that dangerous.'

It was father who replied, snorting. 'In that, my boy, you have revealed your innocence and naivety. Noblemen will always seek power – they are drawn to it irresistibly. Once King Richard died, there were only ever two choices for Arthur – take the throne or die. It was his right, his duty to fight, for the crown was his through his father. It was not the boy's fault that his father happened to be John's elder brother, and not the younger. He had to do it.'

His energy seemed to waver, and after a look at his old friend, Sir Geoffrey continued the theme. 'For are all our places in the world not governed by our fathers? King, noble, knight, peasant – all have their station due to their fathers, and their fathers' fathers.' He reflected. 'But it was also not his fault that he was only a boy of twelve who had not come to his full strength, and therefore never had a chance. It was not his fault that he died only three years later, alone in some dungeon.'

There was silence for a few moments, before Robert was the first to break it by rising, saying that he must get back to the castle lest the earl miss his presence. He took his leave of Sir Geoffrey and lingered a long moment by father's bedside.

'Master Godric, I must bid you farewell. By morning we shall be gone, and I don't know how long it will be before I return … '

He left the rest unsaid, but father understood. He raised one lined hand and laid it on Robert's arm, looking into the eyes of the younger man.

'God be with you always, my boy, for I have watched you grow, and you have ever been the friend of my son. May the Lord bless us both, whether our lives be short or long.'

Robert looked at him quizzically for a moment, then put his strong young hand over the frail old one, oddly gentle, before turning and leaving the room, trying not to let the others see his face. He was already at the door of the cottage when he remembered his manners and stopped to take his leave of Edwin's mother, leaning on the doorframe as he did so. Then he left the cottage to make his way back up to the castle in the waning sun.

The three men remaining looked at each other.

Edwin was starting to panic again. 'But how does all this help? I still don't know who killed the earl, and I only have a few hours left.'

Father took charge again. 'Well, we now know more than we did before. Let us go over everything once more, leaving nothing out, and see if we may start to trace some patterns which were not visible to us up until now.'

Wearily, they started again.

It was some time later when Edwin heard a gentle throat-clearing noise from the door, and turned to see his mother hovering there. The smell of milk posset came from the other room, and he realised that she probably needed to give father some food. But it seemed this was not why she had disturbed them.

'What's this? Does it belong to Robert? I found it over by the door, so perhaps he dropped it on his way out.' She held something up in the slanting rays of the setting sun, and they all peered at it.

She passed the item to Edwin, who was nearest, and he turned it over in his hand. It was the thong from around Robert's neck, the one he never took off, but the leather was new and hadn't been properly knotted. Clearly it had slipped open and fallen to the ground. The thong was passed through a heavy ring, and Edwin examined it closely, holding it up to catch the last of the sunlight. It was a signet ring, fashioned into the shape of a snarling lion's head. The design was strangely familiar – where had he seen it before? He stared at the object as he tried to let memories wash over him. *A lion's head …*

A moment later he was running towards the castle, breathlessly, running so fast he thought his heart would burst.

Chapter Thirteen

Simon was puzzled. As he wandered slowly down the stairs in the gloom of the keep, he tried to make some sense of it. *Someone must have gone past the bedchamber to get to the roof.* They were all sound sleepers, or at least they were normally. But Simon had awoken in the darkness of the night, not knowing why he had done so. And when he woke, he'd seen …

He was so engrossed in his own thoughts that he never felt the hands that reached out towards him. He was barely aware of being propelled forwards, was conscious of falling only for a fraction of a moment. Fortunately he had no time to register what was happening before his head crashed down on to the cold stone step and he knew no more.

———

Sir Geoffrey looked at his friend.

'What happened?' He was confused.

Godric, however, was looking out the door after his son and speaking into the distance. 'My pride and joy. My boy, but a boy no longer.' Suddenly he fell back on the pillows, weak with exhaustion. His voice became hoarse. 'Well do I remember that spark of sudden knowledge which Edwin has just experienced. Aye, and the danger too, although the lad does not know it yet. If I am not mistaken, he has just put all the facts together in his mind, and run off to confront a murderer.'

Sir Geoffrey stared at him. 'What?'

Godric managed a laugh, though it made him choke. 'You knights! You are men of action, but perhaps your minds have been affected by all those blows.'

Sir Geoffrey was too confused even to appreciate one of his friend's oldest taunts. He still didn't understand.

Godric used one of his failing breaths to spell it out to him. 'He has gone to find a killer.' He inhaled again, his breath rasping. 'He is not used to such things. You are the man of action – he will probably need you.'

Finally he succeeded, and Sir Geoffrey stood. The years fell off him as he prepared to fight for justice, as was his calling. He strode towards the door, but paused before leaving. His friend, his friend for nearly fifty years, was drawing his last breaths on God's earth. But he must leave, must save the son so that the father might die easy. He bade his friend farewell.

By the time Edwin reached the keep he was gasping. He rushed up the outside steps, past the bemused guard who stood aside for him, and tore up the first flight of stairs. At the first landing, outside the earl's council chamber, he stopped, aghast.

Simon's crumpled body lay on the stone flags, his neck and limbs at grotesque angles which destroyed immediately any hope that he might still be alive. His head was smashed, and the blood was pooling slowly on the floor. Over him knelt a figure, shoulders shaking in grief.

Slowly, Robert turned his tear-streaked face to Edwin.

Edwin could say nothing. His heart seemed to stop, as did the world around him. It couldn't be true. He waited, waited for Robert to say something that would prove his suspicions wrong, but the words, when they came, were not the ones he wanted, the ones he would have given his heart to hear.

'It was an accident. I swear to you on all that is holy, it was an accident!'

Edwin said nothing, and Robert became more insistent, moving towards his friend, still on his knees.

'Edwin, please! Please say you believe me.' His voice cracked. 'I never meant to hurt him. I couldn't hurt him. I only meant to stop him, to ask him what he knew. But he overbalanced, I couldn't stop him.' He repeated himself in disbelief. 'I couldn't stop him. I saw him fall … '

Edwin was in an unreal world. He couldn't possibly be standing here over the body of a nine-year-old child, listening to his best friend describe how he caused the death. But surely, surely Robert couldn't have wanted to harm the boy. Simon adored him. Robert couldn't be capable of …

'It was an accident.' He said it more to try and convince himself, his eyes boring into his friend's face. There he found the answer he was seeking. Robert hadn't meant to kill Simon. So perhaps he was wrong in his other suspicions. He had to ask. But how could he ask? How could he ask the companion of his childhood, the man who knelt in front of him, whether he was guilty of such a crime? He screwed his eyes up against the tears, forced the words out over the heaving of his chest.

'And de Courteville? Was that an accident too?'

And then he knew that he was right.

———⊙———

The sun was setting in a beautiful golden burst as Sir Geoffrey strode up to the castle, but he didn't notice. As he passed the inner gate, the porter stepped out to say something to him, but retreated hastily after one look. Sir Geoffrey entered the keep and mounted the inside stairs steadily, knowing that he wasn't going to like whatever he was about to see. Despite his worst suspicions, though, he was unprepared to round the corner and see the small figure on the ground, the blond hair matted with red. Robert was on the floor cradling the head and crying, and the knight felt for him. Children died all the time, at birth or from illnesses or accidents, but it was still a shock to see the body which had been full of such life and joy.

'Robert, what happened here?'

The squire didn't answer; he was deep in grief. Sir Geoffrey spoke more gently.

'Robert, you must tell me what happened. Edwin has discovered who killed de Courteville, and has run off to find him. He may be in grave danger – it looks as though the killer has struck again.' More urgently now, afraid for the young bailiff. 'You must tell me – do you know where Edwin is?'

Still Robert didn't answer. He rocked backwards and forwards, bent over the small body, tears running down his face, incapable of speech. But another voice issued from the shadows of the stairwell. Edwin's voice.

'I have found him.'

Still the knight didn't understand.

The voice continued, strangely expressionless. 'I have found the killer, and you can take him away. He isn't dangerous.'

And finally Sir Geoffrey understood.

———

It was later. Edwin didn't know how much time had passed, but it was nearly dark and he was standing in a cell opposite his best friend. His friend, the killer. What were the emotions going through his mind? He couldn't even put words to it. He supposed that betrayal was one of them, but the word just didn't seem to cover the way he was feeling. The horror, the sickness, the sheer unreality of it all and the hope that he would soon wake up to discover that it hadn't happened, coupled with the realisation that it wasn't just a bad dream, and that this moment would have an impact which would last all his life.

'Say something.'

Edwin was jolted out of his trance by Robert's voice. 'What do you want me to say?'

The tone was desperate. 'I don't know. Say you understand, say you don't understand. Say he deserved it; say he didn't.

Only for the love of God say something and don't just stand there staring at me! If there is one person in the world I need to talk to, it's you.'

Edwin looked at him curiously, trying to get past the incomprehension that he felt. 'All right. Tell me why you did it. And tell me why this,' he held up the ring, 'is so important, although I think I know already.'

Robert reached out one shaking hand and took the ring. His eyes refocused, looking through the wall and out into the distance.

'I was five years old. Five years of love and happiness, and then *he* came.'

He paused, but Edwin didn't interrupt. Robert was in a different time and place.

'We heard his men outside, heard him come in. My father didn't think he would hurt us, but then we heard the screams. He knew they were going to die, and he gave me his ring. He told me always to remember who I was. Then he put me inside a chest and told me not to look. It was the only thing he could do for me.'

He stopped again, staring in fascination at the ring.

'But I did look. I saw my mother dead, and I saw my father killed. By him.'

He looked at Edwin, angry, more angry than Edwin had ever seen him, his voice hissing with fury as the violence of his emotions built up and overtook him. 'Now do you understand? *Now* do you know why I killed him? From that moment I never saw him again until a few days ago, but I knew who he was. He was the man who murdered my parents, who burnt my home and who left me with nothing. All I did was to fulfil my father's last wish: to remember who I was. And in doing so I have avenged him.'

There were many things that Edwin longed to say, the least of which was that he'd now created another young orphan who would probably grow up with vengeance in his heart, but he didn't speak his thoughts, couldn't utter them while he was faced with the rage in front of him. He would find something else to ask.

'But how did you escape? And how did you get here?'

The anger subsided almost as quickly as it had arisen. Robert rubbed his hands over his face and spoke in a more subdued way. 'I don't really know. The men never found me. Either he didn't know about me, or he assumed that I was already dead – there were other children downstairs with the servants.'

Edwin's heart went out to them – innocents whose lives had been cut short because of events of which they knew nothing. But such was the lot of the common people, as he had recently learned to his bitter cost.

Robert continued. 'They set the house aflame and then left. There was smoke and heat – I must have managed to climb out of the chest and escape, although to this day I don't know how. All I remember is flames and darkness – I thought I must be in hell – and then after that, daybreak and the ashes of my home. I was there when another man arrived. I knew nothing of him except that he had a kind face and he rode a horse. He took me away and said I could stay with him.'

'Who was he?'

'It was the old earl Hamelin. He was a great man – the brother of a king, although base-born. He brought me here and said I could be his page, although I was full young for the post then. I learnt to serve him, and aye, to love him too, but he died soon after our return here. Everybody I loved was gone, and nobody knew who I was – they knew the earl had brought me back from France and that my father was dead, but I suppose they thought me the son of a knight who had died in battle. The old earl said that I shouldn't use the name d'Eyncourt, lest anyone discover me and kill me, so he renamed me Fitzhugh, as a remembrance of my father. It's a common enough name.'

He continued, his voice dead. 'So, no name, no family and no master – but I was lucky that the earl's son, our present lord, took me on, for he had need of a page himself. From that day to this I have served him faithfully and never thought of my own life. Not until *he* came, and awakened the vengeance inside me.'

Edwin was silent. Odd how you could know somebody your whole life, or nearly the whole of it, but still not know them at all. He examined his own feelings. Had he ever wondered where Robert came from? Probably, but it was not for him to judge the nobility's practice of sending their sons away from them at an early age, something which seemed repellent to him. Robert was just Robert – it mattered not from whence he came, only that he was here and that he served the earl. He'd never thought of Robert having an identity of his own – even when Martin and Roger had occasionally visited their families and Robert hadn't – so he supposed he had failed his friend in some way.

Robert was continuing, the words spilling out now. 'As soon as I saw him, saw that *smile*, I knew who he was and what I had to do. It was easy, really – he was already searching for some hint that my lord wasn't loyal, so I wrote him a note saying that I had information which I would give him if he would meet me on top of the keep at midnight. It was easy to deliver: as you found out from the porter, when people see you every day they never notice you, so who would remark upon the earl's squire moving in and out of the great chamber? I guessed that he wouldn't be able to resist, so as midnight approached I left the earl's bedchamber to go to the roof. I chose my location well: all I had to do was go out the chamber door and up the stairs, there was no one to pass, no one to see.'

'Except Simon.'

The silence was vast, swallowing the room. Robert sat down on the stool which was the cell's only furnishing and put his head in his hands. When he eventually looked up his voice had changed.

'Simon. Yes. I was sure they were all asleep, but he must have woken and seen that I wasn't there, and that was what was puzzling him. You asked us if anyone had gone past the bedchamber, but he must have realised that someone could leave the chamber just as well.'

His voice was near to cracking again. 'But you must believe me, it was an accident. I could never have harmed him. I meant only to stop him, to ask him what was bothering him: if he'd said openly that he knew I wasn't in the chamber I could have said something, given him a reason that he would have believed. But he wasn't paying attention, wasn't looking where he was going, and he fell so quickly that I couldn't catch him. Please, Edwin, please, you must believe me.'

This was the one reassurance that Edwin was able to provide. 'I do believe you.'

Robert heaved a deep sigh. 'Thank you,' he said, simply, as though a weight had been lifted off him. 'But,' he stood up again, 'deliberate or not, I caused his death, and for that alone I deserve to die. For that, not for what I did to de Courteville.'

Grimly, Edwin realised that he must ask for details which he did not want to hear. 'What *did* you do to him?'

Robert began pacing up and down, casting his mind back to the darkness on top of the keep. 'I waited for him. I knew I would only have one chance, for he was strong and an experienced warrior. I'd already made my plan – I couldn't stab him, or I'd get covered in blood, and then everyone would know it was me. In some ways I wouldn't have minded, for I would have made public what he did to my father and mother, and that I'd only taken revenge. But I knew this would lead to my death, and I found that I had a strange desire to live. It was as though my life could start once he was dead. So I had to find another way. Besides, he didn't deserve to die by the blade. That's a knight's death, it's the way men die in battle, and it was the way my father died. So I came up with something altogether more fitting.'

Edwin watched mutely as Robert held up the ring, the leather thong new and pale.

'I used this. Or rather, I used the old one: the leather was thin and strong. As he walked around the roof, all I had to do was step out, throw it around his neck and pull.' As he spoke, he matched his gestures to his words, and Edwin looked on, horrified but unable to drag his eyes away.

'It's easier than you think. He didn't have time to get his hands in the way, so it went right around his neck. I put my knee into his back and pulled with both hands, watching him struggle. I pulled as hard as I could; it didn't just strangle him, it cut right into his neck, and I was glad to see it. As I was doing it I told him who I was and why I was killing him – I wanted him to know what was happening, to know who was being avenged. I sincerely hope that he understood.'

There was silence for a few moments.

'Once it was done, I went back down to the chamber, thinking that no one had seen me. The next day I realised that my necklet was covered in blood so I got rid of it, and I was also able to dispose of the letter. I hadn't realised Adam knew about it, but I managed to convince him that it wasn't important, and while we were supposedly looking for it I took it and hid it. I had to tell you of its existence, though, even if it meant I might be damning myself: if I hadn't, and Adam had mentioned it, you might have wondered why you'd been left to find out from a stranger and not your best friend.'

There was silence while they both considered the import of Robert's last two words. Robert spoke again, more quickly, as if to fill in the gap.

'So there you have it. One thing which I didn't imagine, though, was being sent up to fetch the body – although I suppose I should have expected it. I hadn't seen him properly the night before, as it was dark, but in the light of day he looked grotesque. Martin took one look at him and lost his stomach. I just stared at him, trying to see if I felt anything, but all I could think was that I was glad he was dead, and that he'd suffered, and that I could now put the past behind me and embark on a new life. Then I realised that if anyone saw that tongue sticking out, they would know he'd been strangled. Not that that would have led anyone to me, particularly, but I wanted to make things as difficult as possible. I didn't know that my lord would set you to find out what had happened. If I had, I would … ' he trailed off, unable to finish.

'What would you have done? Left him alive?'

Robert considered his answer. 'No, I couldn't have done that. I don't know what I would have done, but I'm sorry that you should have got mixed up in it. I didn't think – I had nothing else on my mind except revenge, and I didn't consider the consequences, other than that I might die.'

So now Edwin knew everything. Or not quite everything, for how could he now say that he knew what was going on in Robert's mind? There was still one very large aspect which he couldn't understand.

'But how could you kill? How could you take a human life like that, in cold blood?'

Robert gave a rueful laugh.

'Oh, Edwin, my friend, there is the gulf between us. All my life I've been trained to be a knight, and that's what we do: we take lives. We rule over manors and sentence people to death, we ravage the lands of others and kill their commoners, we fight in battle to kill others, and when we're not fighting wars we take part in tournaments which maim and destroy others. We kill; it's our purpose in life. Had I faced de Courteville on a battlefield I would be praised for killing him, would be rewarded by my leader for my deed, but as it is … as it is, I shall die for it.'

The starkness of the words shook Edwin to his very core. And yet there was no other way. A life – two lives – had been taken, and a life must be forfeit in return. Robert was right: this was the difference between them. For Edwin could never hold human life as cheaply as did the nobility. For all that he sometimes associated with them, he was much closer to the ordinary people, the people who lived and worked and died on the estate, who lived in fear of the bad harvest or an outbreak of disease. Children who died in the winter, mothers who died in childbirth, men who died in accidents. And through all of this the people struggled and fought with every sinew to hold on to their lives, and to make them worth living. He could never disregard that.

Robert was continuing, unaware of his friend's thoughts. He had only a very short time left to live and there was so much he wanted to say. How could he express it? How could he put his overwhelming feelings into speech?

'Edwin, I … '

There were no words.

He tried again.

'Edwin, I can't say that I'm sorry de Courteville is dead, for I'm not. If I could live the past few days over, I would still kill him. But I'm sorry at what has happened, sorry about Berold, sorry that you've been brought into it. If you'd failed to find out that it was me, failed in the first task that the earl set you, your future wouldn't have been certain, and that's something I regret deeply. I've had my revenge, my father's revenge, but I've pulled in those around me. I'm sorry that you were involved, and Martin, and Simon,' his voice shook, 'and most of all the earl. I've served him all my life, and it's my regret that I couldn't keep him out of this.'

'But you didn't keep him out of it.'

Edwin and Robert both turned to the door, which had opened without them noticing. There stood the earl, his face showing nothing. Edwin moved to allow him to enter, and Robert backed away against the wall, ashen, needing the support it offered.

The earl stepped into the room and moved first to Edwin, who felt afraid. The face, the authority … *not just the lord of the manor, but one of the most powerful men in the kingdom.*

The earl saw his fear and spoke. 'You have done well. You have fulfilled your promise to me, even though you may wish that you had not. This I value, and you shall not go unrewarded. But for now, leave us.'

His word was law. Edwin escaped, grateful but ashamed of his fear, out into the coolness of the night.

Martin was standing outside. He caught hold of Edwin's arm and gripped it tightly, painfully. His eyes pleaded, wanting Edwin to tell him that it couldn't be true, that there had been some terrible mistake. Edwin couldn't give the reassurance that was needed; he merely looked up into the other's face, eyes huge and dark with suffering, and shook his head. Martin slackened his grip, and each turned away to be private with his own grief.

The earl turned to Robert, who fell to his knees.

'Get up.'

Robert couldn't respond; he was paralysed.

'Get up and face me.'

The power was overwhelming. Robert had never disobeyed an order from that voice, and he couldn't do so now. He stood, and slowly raised his face to gaze into the steel-grey eyes.

'You have betrayed me.' The voice was like the judgement of the Almighty.

'My lord … I didn't do it to betray you. It was personal – to suddenly see, after all these years, the man who killed my parents … I couldn't help myself!'

'Yet you had no thought for those who have sheltered you since that time. Who have fed and clothed you, and brought you up as one of their own.' The voice was implacable.

'But my lord … '

The earl continued, speaking over him and forcing him to silence. 'You could have caused civil war! Or at least more of a civil war than there already is. The barons were in revolt against John, me included, and through this we allowed that

French whoreson to come into the country and attempt to take it. He may be an able man, but he's not our king, and never will be. Our king is a boy, a boy who needs our support against the invader. We're rallying behind him and you've jeopardised all this – you've put into peril the alliance of lords at a time when we need to fight together. The king may be a boy, but he's our king, and he should not be made to suffer for the deeds of his father.'

The sense of having nothing left to lose made Robert react rashly, and he lost his temper. 'Not suffer for the deeds of his father? What do you think I've been doing for the whole of my life?' His voice rose with emotion. 'Have I not suffered for the deeds of my father? He did what he thought to be right for the good of the kingdom, and he was murdered and ground into dust, his arms erased as though he'd never existed. How is that fair? How have I not suffered for what he did?'

In his anger he stepped forward and laid his hands on the earl, who exploded into fury. He grabbed Robert by the shoulders and shook him, incandescent with rage. 'You stupid boy! Of course you've suffered, but does this give you the right to make others suffer in their turn? Do you have any *conception* of the consequences of your actions? You kill a man here, in my home, a man who is on his way to support the regent, the most powerful lord in the kingdom. If he takes against me, do you know what could happen? My lands invaded, war raging here. Your friend Edwin dead, and his mother and father too. The villages burned, the castle besieged, the people starving … is this what you wanted? Because, by God, we will be lucky to avoid it!' He shook Robert harder and slammed him back against the wall.

At long last the consequences of his action sank in on Robert. He slumped, covered his face with his hands and began to weep, his shoulders shaking.

But the earl hadn't finished. He stepped back and composed himself before speaking in a more level tone, his voice relenting.

'But all this I could forgive. I could forgive the murder, I could forgive the consequences, and I could even forgive the betrayal of the man who has been close to me these many years, as close to me as my own son.' Robert's shoulders shook more, and he couldn't look up. 'But Simon.' The earl's voice dropped to a whisper. 'I could never forgive you for Simon.'

Robert collapsed utterly, falling back against the wall and sliding down it until he was in a weeping heap on the floor.

The earl looked down upon him, about to pronounce words he could never have imagined saying to his faithful squire. 'You will hang at first light.'

This jolted Robert from his state. As the earl turned to leave, he reached out and clutched his boot. 'My lord,' he whispered.

The earl turned. Surely, surely Robert wasn't about to make this worse than it already was by pleading for his life, a request that could never be granted. He couldn't be that far sunk in self-pity. But this was not what Robert wanted to say.

'My lord, please … not the rope. Please, not that.' Hoarse, he cleared his throat. 'My father died in secret, with nobody to mourn him and his line. For his only son to die in shame would further blacken his name, and he doesn't deserve that. For the love of God, my lord, let me die by the sword. I deserve to die, but in avenging my father, have I not earned death by the blade?' He looked up, surprised to see that the earl was listening. 'Please, my lord, please, kill me now. If I have ever been your faithful servant all these years, grant me death by the sword.'

The earl looked down at the young man who had been by his side for many years, and remembered the cheeky page, the spirited squire, the growing responsibility of the man, and above all, the loyalty. His heart melted with pity, but what could he do? The only way to avoid certain destruction was to conduct a very public denouncement and execution. One more murder in a dark cell would do no good, would not stave off the wrath of the regent. The murderer of de Courteville needed to be named and seen to die. Besides, there was no possible way he could bring himself to run Robert through in cold blood. Many things he had done in the name of justice, but this would not be one of them. He looked again at the man before him, and was about to utter the fateful words that would condemn him to a shameful end when an idea came to him. He shouted to the guard outside to fetch the priest.

'You intend to *what*?'

Sir Geoffrey was outside the cell with Edwin and Martin. He was so shocked that he'd spoken rashly, and he hastened to apologise. 'Forgive me, my lord, for speaking so, but is that not an unusual proposition in this sort of case?'

Edwin couldn't believe what the earl had just said. Trial by combat? He'd heard of it, of course, knew that it was something the nobility did – one more example of using their sword arms instead of their heads, his father had once said – but he'd never seen it happen. There was a question which he longed to ask, but he dared not address the earl, so he stayed silent. Luckily Sir Geoffrey asked it for him.

'But surely, my lord, he has confessed? Normally combat is only used when both sides disagree on something.'

The earl replied. 'We know that, but nobody else does. As long as we say nothing,' his glance swept all three of them, 'nobody will know any better. I can explain it to the regent in confidence when I see him. Robert,' he jerked his head back at the door, 'is confessing to the priest as we speak, so that he may be shriven before he dies, but that confession is between himself, Father Ignatius and God. The good Father is not permitted to divulge anything told to him during the sacrament of confession. So I will accuse him, he will challenge me, we will fight, and he will die.' The finality of the words were chilling.

Edwin had spotted a potential flaw, and again his thoughts were voiced by Sir Geoffrey. 'But my lord … erm … ', he pulled at the neck of his tunic, 'what if he kills *you*?'

The earl seemed taken aback, and paused for a moment before speaking with finality. 'He won't. Firstly, God will support me, and secondly, he knows he's guilty.' A less spiritual and more practical thought struck him, thinking of the wreck of a man he had left inside, gasping his final agonised confession to the priest. 'And thirdly, he is in no fit state to fight.'

Sir Geoffrey tried again, hoping to spare his lord the indignity of the public combat. 'My lord – in such cases as these, when a man is challenged by one so far below him in rank, he may choose a champion to fight on his behalf.' He drew himself up. 'My lord, I would … '

The earl cut him off, speaking grimly. 'No. It is my task, and I will do it. You will need to organise the field of battle.' He turned to Martin. 'Fetch my armour and come with me.'

Edwin was gradually stepping back, assuming he had been dismissed, when the earl spoke to him directly. 'You will have to help Robert. He can't arm himself – ' he spoke even more bleakly, ' – and I have but one squire.'

———⟶●⟵———

There was nothing Edwin wanted to do less than to step through that door. He'd waited outside while a servant fetched armour and weapons, serviceable but plain items from the castle's stores – had I counted that set? thought Edwin to himself, in a rare moment of down-to-earth reality – and left them with him. He'd continued to wait until Father Ignatius came out, shaking his head in sorrow but saying nothing. Then there was nothing left to wait for, but still he hesitated. Then he opened the door.

Robert was sitting on the stool, calmer now. Edwin stood in the doorway, framed in torchlight.

'You can come in. I've made my peace with the Lord and am ready to die.' The hollow voice was not Robert's, couldn't be Robert's, and yet it was. Edwin advanced, bringing some of the equipment in with him, and then went back outside in silence to fetch the rest. Still without speaking, he faced his friend. His friend, whose life was about to end.

He had very little idea of how the armour went on, and his hands were clumsy, but Robert guided him through the procedure, having been used to it since childhood. Eventually he stood there, an alien figure to Edwin's eyes, enclosed in metal. Even in his grief Edwin had been surprised by just how heavy all the items were, could hardly stand up himself while he was carrying everything, but Robert stood unbowed with the weight draped around him, chausses on his legs, gambeson and hauberk on his body, mittens on his hands, coif on his head, sword belted around his waist. All that remained on the floor were the large shield and the helmet which would cover his face, separating him from his friend for the last time. Mutely Edwin picked it up and held it out to him. Robert paused a moment, finding the courage to speak.

He shook off his mittens, leaving them dangling from the hauberk's sleeves, and awkwardly removed the ring from around his neck, hauling it out from under his gambeson and holding it out to Edwin.

'I want you to have it.'

Edwin backed away. 'I can't – it's your father's ring, your family keepsake.'

'And much good it will do me when I'm dead and in the ground. I'm the last of my line, there's nobody to wear it.'

'But still … your father's ring … '

'Edwin.' Robert held it out to him again. 'Don't argue with me, now of all times. You are the brother I never had, the closest thing I have to a family, and I want you to have it. Keep it safe for me, and … remember me when I'm gone.'

How could he argue further? He held his hand out and Robert gave him the ring. Edwin held it up by the leather, watching the ring turn. A thought struck him. 'Do you know, I've often seen this around your neck, but for some reason I always assumed it was some kind of gift from Mistress Joanna.'

Robert was taken aback. Then he laughed, and for a moment a final flash of his old self shone through the darkness. 'Joanna? Oh no, my friend. Not me. You must look elsewhere for the man who has taken her heart.'

Edwin was about to reply when he heard the sound of tramping footsteps outside. Robert looked at him once more, serious again. 'And now, my friend, my brother, the time has come. Help me on with this so that I might go out and meet my fate.'

He put the mittens back on as Edwin raised the helmet, his hands shaking. They were trembling so much that he could barely fit it on to Robert's head, and his friend had to guide him, his own hands as steady as a rock. Then his face was gone, and, anonymous, he manoeuvred the shield onto his arm and turned to face the door as it opened.

———————

Outside it was dark, but as Edwin walked he could see a mass of torches down on the tilting ground. A space had been cleared behind the encampment, and it was surrounded by the knights who had mustered and by their men, each carrying a flickering flame. At the four corners of the space stood braziers, casting further light and dancing shadows. The earl stood at one end of the battleground, resplendent in his armour. Facing him across the ground was Robert, and if he was afraid he did not show it.

Edwin knew that he couldn't watch what was about to happen, and he tried to back away quietly, to find somewhere, anywhere, that was away from this nightmare. But he was stopped by an iron grip on his shoulder, and he turned to look into the face of Sir Geoffrey. The knight looked at him in understanding, but his voice was firm. 'No, you will stay. If you are to be the earl's man, you must witness his justice.'

Edwin didn't understand his meaning, but he was so tired and emotionally bruised that he felt this wasn't surprising. Once more he tried to calm his breathing, and stood erect between Sir Geoffrey, who schooled his face to show no emotion, and Martin, who looked so sick he was barely able to stand.

Father Ignatius had finished absolving the two combatants, and it was time for the trial to start. The earl stepped forward and proclaimed his challenge, his powerful voice ringing out across the silent space as every man stood unmoving.

'I, William de Warenne, Earl of Surrey, do hereby accuse the squire Robert Fitzhugh of the murder of Ralph de Courteville, and I stand ready to prove it with my body. The Lord will see justice done.'

His voice echoed away, to be replaced by Robert's. Less powerful, less confident, but steady.

He enunciated his words carefully, so that there should be no misunderstanding. 'I, Robert fitz Hugh d'Eyncourt, do hereby state that I am innocent of this crime.' At last, he could be his father's son. At the mention of the name, gasps could be heard from the older knights around the field, who knew the import of it. A murmur arose as those who didn't know were told. The earl was on the verge of stepping forward to begin the combat, but Robert hadn't finished. Taking a deep breath and perhaps realising that he had nothing left to lose, he bellowed once more. 'Furthermore, I declare that the deceased Ralph de Courteville murdered my father, the knight Hugh d'Eyncourt, fifteen years ago.'

More surprise was evident, as knights and men turned to each other, but there was no time for conversation. Edwin forced himself to stay upright and face forward. The flickering torches made everything seem strange and unreal as the two men moved close to one another and began circling. Beside him, he heard Martin give a stifled sob.

It didn't last long. Robert didn't give up straight away, fought long enough to do himself credit, but he had known before he started that there could be but one outcome. Edwin watched it all happen as though very slowly, Robert's parries becoming weaker as the earl's blows became stronger, and then a manoeuvre forcing Robert to move his shield and leave himself open to the final blow. The earl's sword, which Robert himself had lovingly sharpened, moved forward in a practised movement and ran him through. Edwin would never forget the noise it made as it entered his friend's body, splitting and crushing the links of the hauberk and forcing and cracking its way through flesh and bone. The earl had chosen his spot well and struck accurately, and Robert had barely time to look up at his executioner before his eyes glazed over and he fell. The earl caught him in his arms and lowered him gently to the ground, before grasping his sword again, ripping it back and stepping away. In a hoarse voice he declared, 'Justice has been done, and you are all witnesses before the Lord.'

Edwin stood as still as a stone as Sir Geoffrey moved away from him towards the earl. Martin had fled. All around him men were moving, were talking of what they had just seen, but all the voices became one rushing, echoing sound that washed over him as he stood. Still he stood as the earl took one last glance at his dead squire before moving away with his faithful castellan. Still he stood as the field emptied, leaving the body in the middle, to be tended by the priest. Still he stood as the soldiers placed the body on a stretcher and bore it away. Still he stood, unhearing, as somebody spoke to him.

It was the pain, more than the voice, that eventually brought him back to himself. The pain was in his hand, and he unclenched it slowly from around the ring, which he had been holding so tightly that it had imprinted the lion's head on his skin. He looked at it in wonder, watching the face snarling on his palm.

The voice was still talking. He turned and looked at the speaker, taking a few moments to realise that it was William Steward. William tried to reach him once more, repeating his name over and over. Finally he was heard.

'Edwin, I'm sorry.'

Edwin nodded and looked again at the field, now dark and empty. 'He was my friend,' he said, softly.

William spoke once more.

'No … you don't understand.'

He received a blank look.

'Edwin, I'm very sorry, but your father has just died.'

Slowly, Edwin crumpled to the ground, and wept.

Epilogue

Edwin looked around him as the sun began its slow rise over the horizon. All around men were scurrying, packing and mounting, ready for when the earl should order them forward out of the gate. He looked around him, but could take in none of it.

The events of last night and this morning played through his mind. The logic of it still escaped him. He couldn't think straight, could only arrange his thoughts in the most simplistic terms: a good man is killed by a bad man, who goes free; a bad man is killed by a good man, who gives his life in payment. It seemed a mockery of justice. The earl had overheard him expressing these sentiments to Sir Geoffrey, and had told him in a voice like stone that there was no justice, only politics. There had been a further conversation with the earl, in which the earl had said that Edwin was a valuable man to have around, and that he wished him to come to the muster at Newark, for who knew when he might need a quick mind about him. There had been the promise of being the earl's man, the wages for which would be enough to keep his mother in comfort in her widowhood. His mother, who had been weeping over the body of her dead husband.

He tried to shake the image from his eyes, and to clear his mind he looked about him again. At Martin, who was bidding farewell to Mistress Joanna, and being given something by her which he stowed in the purse at his belt. At the boy mounted behind one of Sir Roger's men, who on closer inspection turned out to be Peter, well and warmly dressed in what Edwin recognised sadly as one of Simon's tunics. At Adam, who was proudly leading the earl's warhorse to the rear of the baggage train, and being given some last-moment advice by Sir Geoffrey. And at the three coffins which were about to start a journey of their own. The largest and most ornate was accompanied by the squire David – subdued at last – who waited upon his master Walter, prior to beginning their trek home. The other two were plainer, one of medium size and one heart-rendingly small; they were loaded on to a cart ready to be taken down to the church in the village. Edwin reached unthinkingly under his tunic for the ring which was there, and grasped it tightly. The scenes washed over him in much the same way as the rays of the rising sun which touched his face.

At last the earl was there, accepting tearful adieus from his sister, mounting his courser and ready to lead the procession on its long journey. Sir Geoffrey was bidding him farewell. Edwin had already said his goodbyes – the final one to the cold figure of his father, looking younger in death now that the pain had gone out of his face, and the hopefully short-lived one from his mother, who wept all the more without knowing whether it was from sadness or pride. He had left her at the door of the cottage with her sister and with William Steward, before the first light of day broke the horizon.

The earl was signalling for the long line of horsemen and carts to move forward, and at last Edwin came to himself, ready to control his mount. He'd ridden short journeys before, mounted on a hack to accompany his father to outlying villages, but this long journey on a finer horse would be something of a challenge. He hoped he wouldn't fall off and disgrace himself. He hoped he would be of some service to the earl. He hoped he would return to see his mother again.

He hoped the pain would go away.

What was it he'd thought to himself only a few short days ago, in his childish envy? *Honour and glory and a chance to see the world.* How strange that he would now gladly exchange it, exchange everything he owned or was ever likely to possess, for the quiet life he had then feared.

As his turn came, he put his heels to his mount and followed the earl out of the gate.

ḥistorical ḍote

The early thirteenth century is a fascinating period of English history, full of action and intrigue. The events depicted here are set against the background of those which took place over the course of the twenty years or so just before and at the beginning of the new century.

Richard the Lionheart achieved many things during his reign, but in one of the most important aspects of medieval kingship, he failed: he did not father a son to succeed him. Thus when he died in 1199, there was no accord on who should rule next. Richard had been the second of four brothers to survive infancy: the youngest, John, was still alive; the eldest, Henry, had died childless; and the third, Geoffrey, had been killed in a tournament twelve years before. However, Geoffrey had left a son − Arthur, the Duke of Brittany − and, if the laws of primogeniture had been interpreted strictly, this son should have become the king. However, there were three main problems with this: firstly, these laws were not yet as fixed as they became later, and tradition held that the younger son of a king was nearer to the throne than a grandson whose father had never ruled; secondly, Arthur had never been to England and had no experience of life there or of how to rule such a difficult realm; and thirdly, he was twelve years old.

This set the scene for several years of civil war, with some lords − mainly those who hailed from Arthur's lands of Anjou, Maine and Touraine − supporting him, and the rest of the barons − predominantly those of England and Normandy − backing John. The war continued in a savage vein for three years, until Arthur, by now fifteen years of age and becoming a more dangerous opponent, was captured at the castle of

Mirebeau in July 1202. He was later transported to Falaise Castle and then on to Rouen, where he disappeared in April 1203, never to be seen again.

Even at the time, credible rumours circulated that Arthur had been murdered, that he had been blinded and his body thrown into the River Seine. Tellingly, John never denied these rumours, but instead got on with the business of being a king, undisturbed by further claimants to the throne. Trouble returned to haunt him later in his reign, though, in the shape of rebellious barons such as William de Braose. During de Braose's rebellion against the king his wife and eldest son were captured; Matilda de Braose was told to hand over her other children into John's custody, but she stated publicly that she would never place her children in the hands of a man who had murdered his own nephew. This shows either that rumours were still circulating, or that the truth was widely known but not commented upon, but it did little for Matilda herself: she and her son were kept captive in Windsor Castle, where they starved to death.

Towards the end of John's reign, the barons lost patience with him still further, and he was forced to sign the Magna Carta in 1215. Still dissatisfied with his conduct, they then sought to overthrow him, and invited Prince Louis, the son of the king of France (later Louis VIII) to invade and take the crown. The very idea of the lords extending an invitation to a Frenchman, a hereditary enemy, shows the lengths to which they were prepared to go to relieve themselves of John's rule. However, during this invasion John died unexpectedly, leaving as his heir his nine-year-old son, Henry III. This caused many of the barons to undergo a change of heart – ostensibly because they could not justify levelling accusations of misrule against a new young king, but also in part because a child monarch would be much easier to control than a French prince who was a seasoned veteran.

Early in 1217, many of the lords had defected back to the royalist party, led by William Marshal, the regent, and by the Earl of Chester. However, Louis still had the support of a number of nobles, and was in control of most of eastern England. One of the most important strongholds was Lincoln, where the French and rebel English forces had taken the town, but not the castle. They were besieging it when William Marshal summoned 'all loyal men' to muster at Newark and then march to the relief of Lincoln.

One can only imagine the mixed feelings this summons may have caused to those who were wavering in their allegiance. One such noble was William de Warenne, the Earl of Surrey. When the civil war first broke out, he had sided with John, and was one of the royalists who were present at the signing of the Magna Carta. He later served as a royalist commander in Sussex (where he also held lands), and was appointed to take charge of the Cinque Ports in May 1216. However, just one month later the rebel army led by Louis was allowed to enter his castle at Reigate unopposed; later in the month Warenne came to Louis and offered him his support. Why did he change sides? His motives are not clear – perhaps he was hoping that Louis might restore his lands in Normandy, lost in John's war there fifteen years before; or perhaps he had simply come to the conclusion that the royalist cause was doomed. A number of other lords such as the earls of Salisbury and Arundel defected at the same time, so his opinions were clearly shared.

Whatever his reason, his rebellion was short-lived, and, following John's death in October 1216, he wavered again. In April 1217, he entered into a truce with the royalists; and then in May, the regent's summons was sent out.

This sets the scene for our action, but the other events which occur and the characters who appear, with the exception of Warenne's sister Isabelle, are entirely fictitious. There was no Earl of Sheffield, but it is plausible both that there were noblemen around who knew what had happened to Arthur, and that there were those who sought to cause trouble by proving that one earl or other was switching sides again.

Many of the aspects of life depicted in this book are based on real evidence. Noble families did send their children away at early ages to be raised and trained by someone else. For boys this meant working as a page and then as a squire, but the fear and nervousness felt by a seven-year-old packed off to a strange place far from home is not something which is normally read about. Girls, too, were sent away, either as child brides to be brought up by their husband's family, or as companions to noblewomen of higher rank. Every child was a commodity to be used by the head of a family as he saw fit, and the experiences of the child and the treatment he or she received depended entirely on chance.

The lives of nobles and commoners at this time were almost completely separate. Life was hard for everyone, but for the common people it was particularly brutal. Agriculture was the main source of employment, and there had been very little technological advance for centuries: the process of growing enough food for communities to survive was dependent upon back-breaking manual labour, with almost everyone at the mercy of the weather. One bad harvest could spell disaster for many a community. Illness and death were rife: fewer than half of all children lived to see their fifth birthday; women frequently died in childbirth or after it; and both sexes and all ages were at risk of accident, sickness or infection. In times of war, the common people counted for very little: opposing armies saw them only as a wealth-producing resource, and it was considered well within the bounds of civilised behaviour to start an attack on a rival's lands by killing his peasants and burning their villages.

However, the commoners were not – or at least not always – mere serfs to be slaughtered or bought and sold at will. A national system of justice was replacing long-standing local custom, and well-organised village communities knew their rights: any lord who sought to impose his whims upon his people might find himself involved in a long legal dispute. The process of trial by ordeal (whereby an accused person had to undergo a test such as plunging their hand into boiling water or picking up a red-hot bar) was starting to fall out of practice, to be replaced by trial by jury. Trial by combat, on the other hand, was still very much alive amongst the upper classes in 1217, so the earl's battle is a plausible event. Indeed, the practice continued for well over another hundred years – in one famous incident in 1355 no less a personage than Robert Wyville, the Bishop of Salisbury, was challenged to a duel; he elected to have a champion fight for him, an incident which is depicted on the bishop's memorial brass which can still be seen in Salisbury Cathedral.

I have indulged in one or two incidences of poetic licence. I have moved the death of Earl Hamelin de Warenne forward by exactly one year, from May 1202 to May 1203, in order to give him enough time to rescue and bring home one forlorn child. A lesser alteration is the cadency marks which Sir Geoffrey explains to Simon during his heraldry lesson: heraldic devices were in use in 1217, and it would certainly have been useful for a page to be able to recognise the arms of friends and foes, but heraldry had not yet evolved into the complex science of later centuries, and cadency marks representing the order of sons in a family did not become common until the fifteenth century. Still, Simon was having so much fun with his lesson that it seemed a shame to deprive him.

Finally, those familiar with Conisbrough Castle will notice that I have taken a couple of liberties with its layout. The chapel in the keep is actually on the upper floor which contains the bedroom, rather than the one below next to the council chamber; however, this did not suit the nefarious goings-on which are depicted in this story, so I hope that the moving of the chapel might be excused. Equally, the current layout of the keep means that visitors actually have to walk through each room in order to reach the next flight of stairs, but I was sure that the earl would not want people traipsing through his bedchamber in order to reach the roof, so I have invented passageways going round the rooms in the thickness of the walls. In this case I may only be reflecting an earlier plan: those who look closely at the architecture of each of the keep's rooms will see the ghosts of other archways in the walls, suggesting that such passageways may actually have existed.

The castle at Conisbrough is well worth a visit: it is one of the most striking designs of any twelfth- or thirteenth-century castle, and is still surrounded by most of its curtain wall, and by the foundations of the stone buildings in the inner ward. Earl Hamelin's spectacular white keep is still intact, a landmark which has dominated its setting for over eight hundred years.

Acknowledgements

My thanks are due to a number of people who helped in many different ways while this book was being written.

First of all, my love and appreciation go to my husband, James, and our children, for putting up with me during all the time I've been glued to my computer; James also spent a lot of time making a beautiful electronic map of Conisbrough based on my rather sketchy, hand-drawn effort.

Then there are those whom I approached for criticism, who gave me a great deal of feedback on early drafts which was, at times, so eye-wateringly honest that I could only look at it through my interlaced fingers: Rob Hemus, Stephanie Tickle, Roberta Wooldridge Smith, Richard Skinner and China Miéville.

I'd also like to acknowledge the contribution of those who encouraged me to keep writing even when it wasn't going so well, and who have listened to my endless moaning on the subject. There are many of these, but I'd like to thank Susan Brock, Andrew Bunbury, Adam Cartwright, Julian Moss and Martin Smalley in particular. Matilda Richards, Commissioning Editor at The History Press, has been an absolute delight to work with, and I would like to thank her for answering all my emails promptly, fully and with good cheer, even the picky ones!

Finally, my thanks go to the academic who, many years ago when I first thought of writing mediaeval murder mysteries, told me (in a nice way) that all historical fiction was necessarily rubbish, but that I should at least try to write plausible rubbish. I hope that readers of *The Sins of the Father* find it not only plausible but enjoyable as well.

About the Author

C.B. Hanley has a PhD in mediaeval studies from the University of Sheffield and is the author of *War and Combat 1150-1270: The Evidence from Old French Literature*, and a number of scholarly articles on the period. She currently teaches on writing for academic publication, and also works as a copy-editor and proofreader.